I0819943

BORDER WAR STORIES

By the same author:

THE ATOM BOMB
THE U-BOAT FILLED WITH GOLD
SHELL SHOCK
FIVE WARS, FIVE NAMES
THE PROPHECIES OF REVELATION
PASTORAL CARE AND COUNSELLING
HOW TO MANAGE A FLOURISHING CHURCH
EFFECTIVE COMMUNICATION IN THE CHURCH

This book is dedicated to the memory of all the men who fell during the Namibian Border War

ADELBERT SCHOLTZ

BORDER WAR STORIES

STORIES AND SKETCHES WITH THE NAMIBIAN BORDER WAR AS BACKGROUND

RESOURCE *Publications* • Eugene, Oregon

BORDER WAR STORIES
Stories and Sketches with the Namibian Border War as Background

Resource Publications
An Imprint of Wipf and Stock Publishers
199 W. 8th Ave., Suite 3
Eugene, OR 97401

www.wipfandstock.com

PAPERBACK ISBN: 978-1-6667-8140-3
HARDCOVER ISBN: 978-1-6667-8141-0
EBOOK ISBN: 978-1-6667-8142-7

CONTENTS

READ THIS FIRST:

This collection of successive war strories is simply just that – a number of stories, fictitious tales, entertaining narratives, with the Border War of 1966–1989 in northern Namibia – previously South West Africa – and southern Angola as background. There are various references to historical events, but the role players in these stories are, with a few exceptions, the creations of the author's imagination.

Although most chapters are meant to be complete stories on their own, this collection can also be seen as a single story with various episodes because all the different stories are told from the perspective of the main character. It can almost be classified as a novel consisting of a number of chapters.

The reader will encounter the names of certain historical personages from those times; the deeds and words ascribed to them are, though, the products of the author's fantasy. Certain liberties were taken with the description of a few historical events, although it was endeavored to make these stories as credible and true to life as possible. All the places where these stories unfold are real places and photographs of some of them appear in the text. Four maps appear at the end of the Introduction to help the reader to lcate those places.

The present author took part in this war on five shorter occasions as a part-time military chaplain and he participated in an operation inside southern Angola during 1983. He was forced by circumstances on two occasions to assume leadership of a company of infantry while taking part in operations within South West Africa. He also led a squadron of armored vehicles on a navigation exercise in the bush when the commander requested him to do so, because this commander wanted to spend time with his wife before departing for a course for battalion commanders – which was, of course, somewhat irregular. The present book is, therefore, partly based on the author's personal experiences.

Apart from that, the author was also the part-time senior chaplain of an infantry brigade of the Citizen Force – consisting of nine battalion-sized territorial units, manned by reservists and volunteers – and that brought him into contact with military personnel on a weekly basis. He, therefore, knew the South African Army with its characteristic culture intimately.

This book is a sequel to the author's previous war novels, especially THE ATOM BOMB. Characters from those publications appear in some of these stories.

Explanations of medical, psychological, and neurological conditions are reliable. The author, who practices as a professional psychlogist after his retirmement from the ministry, has attende courses in neuropsychology.

Unfamiliar expressions, often in Afrikaans and part of Army slang of those times, are explained in footnotes.

At the end of the book, the rank structure of the South African Defence Force during the times covered by these stories is explained for the benefit of the reader.

Gratitude must be expressed towards all members of the old South African Defence Force with whom the author had contact through the years – too many to mention. Their experiences were, in certain cases, the inspiration for more than one story in this book.

INTRODUCTION

It is neceaary to provide a very brief historical background to the stories contained in this book for readers who are not familiar with the events and places mentioned in this book.

South West Africa – nowadays Namibia – became a colony of the German Empire during the 1880's. During the First W0rld War, in 1915, the Defence Force of the neighboring Union of South Africa conquered the territory on behalf of Great Britain and administered it after 1920 in accordance with a mandate given by the League of Nations.

The South West African People's Organizatin (SWAPO), a political organization that drew its members mainly from the biggest tribe of the territory, the Ovambo's in the northern parts of the country, agitated for independence since the 1940's. An armed wing, the People's Liberation Army of Namibia (PLAN), was created in 1962, mainly with the backing of the Soviet Union.

PLAN operated from bases in Angola and could never establish its own bases within South West Africa or conquor parts of the country. The first clashes with Police patrols occurred during August 1966. Groups of insurgents crossed the border from Angola to recruit support in the northern parts of the territory, to spread the doctrines of communism, to assasinate people who were suspected of cooperating with the South African government and thereby terrorize the population, and to attack Police stations and other government installations (and later, also military bases).

Since the Police force could not deal with the situation on its own, it was decided in 1975 to deploy the South African Defence Force (SADF). A number of Army bases were established along the northern border and air fields were constructed for use by the Air Force. To strengthen the SADF, conscripton was introduced and all young white men had to perform national service of 24 months. After completion of their initial national service, these men became reservists and members of units of the Citizen Force and could be called up for shorter periods of service, called camps.

A number of Army units consisted of volunteers from black and other indigenous communities were formed. The Bushmen, for instance, served in 31 Battalion and were mostly employed as trackers with their suberb knowledge of the environment, gained over many generations. Perhaps the most feared Army unit was 32 Battalion, consisting mainly of Portuguese-speaking men from Angola. This unit had the Portuguese nickname of "Os Terríveis" (The Terrible Ones).

The main task of the Army was to patrol the areas bordering on Angola, either by means of foot or motorized patrols of sction or platoon strength with the goal of picking up the footprints of insurgents and to pursue them.

A civil war raged simultaneously in South West Africa's northern neighbor, Angola, after Portugal had decided to grant independence to this colony in November 1975. One of the fighting groups, the People's Movement for the Liberation of Angola (MPLA), managed to take control of the largest part of the country with the aid of the Soviet Union and Cuba. The MPLA's military wing was known as the People's Armed Forces of Liberation of Angola (FAPLA). SWAPO and PLAN were given protection and bases in the parts controlled by the MPLA.

The main opponent of the MPLA in the civil war was the National Union for the Total Independence for Angola (UNITA), which controlled the south eastern parts of the country. UNITA found an ally in South Africa since SWAPO insirgents were not tolerated in the areas under UNITA domination. The result was that the PLAN fighters had to limit their efforts mainly to Ovamboland, further to the west.

Another opponent of the MPLA was the Frente Nacional de Libertação de Angola (National Liberation Front of Angola, or FNLA). Some of the fighters of this group were recruited by the South African Army and they became 32 Battalion, mentioned above and based at Buffalo in the far north eastern parts of South West Africa.

The SADF often attacked SWAPO bases in Angola and in the process often also clashed with the forces of FAPLA and their Cuban allies. It also happened that offenses of FAPLA against UNITA had to be repulsed by the South Africans – often with catastrophic losses for FAPLA.

The result was that the war consisted for most of the time of low-intensity skirmishes – called "contacts" by the Army – and occasional flare-ups when Swapo bases inside Angola were raided and even conventional battles with infantry, artillery, and armor, when Angolan and Cuban forces were confronted.

Initially, South Africa had the backing of America in its war against PLAN and FAPLA as a result of the aid given by the Soviet Union to these movements by providing them with copious amounts of weaponry and the training of their fighters by Russian and Cuban advisors or instructors. This support from the USA was later retracted because of South Africa's policy of apartheid or the segregation of racial groups, which was condemned by the international community.

The Border War ended in a stalemate in 1988 and South West Afrca became the independent Republic of Namibia during April 1989. During peace talks, it was agreed that South African forces would leave Angola and later retreat from an independent Namibia, while Cuban and Soviet forces and advisors would leave Angola.

By this time, the Soviet Union was on the brink of collapse and had no appetite anymore for adventures on other continents. A democratic constitution for Namibia was drawn up and the possibility of a communist state – which would have amounted to an ally of Soviet Russia – on the border of South Africa was averted. During the first elections, SWAPO received 57% of the vote.

Since Namibia was saved from the catastrophe of becoming a failed communist state, the South African authorities of the time felt that the Border War was worthwhile and that independence for this country was justified. This collection of stories, therefore, reflects something of the Cold War that ended with the collapse of the Soviet Union at the end of 1991.

The SADF divided South West Africa into seven sectors, each with a regional command. The largest were Sector 10 with its headquarters at Oshakati in Ovamboland and Sector 20 in Kavangoland with its headquarters at Rundu (see maps below). Both bordered onto Angola from where the PLAN isurgents mostly operated. The border between Ovamboland and Angola is mostly and imaginary east-west line through the countryside. The SADF cleared this line of vegetatin to enable its patrols to spot the footprints of PLAN gangs coming from Angola and to pursue them.

The SADF was engaged in another struggle against the African National Congress (ANC) and its armed wing, Umkhonto we Sizwe (MK) – formed in 1961 – since the 1970's. The ANC, founded in 1912, was initially a peaceful organization with the aim of gaining political rights for the black people of South Africa.

MK, operating from bases in Zambia and Tanzania, started a campaign of terror and sabotage, but never posed a military threat to the SADF. Due to international and internal pressure from churches and other organizations, the governing National Party decided to abolish all apartheid laws. The ANC was unbanned in

1990 and negotiations for a new democratic constitution were started.

Nelson Mandela, who was released from prison after having been found guilty of high treason, became the leader of the ANC in 1991.

This all meant that the SADF was embroiled in two wars at the same time – the Border War in northern Namiba and Angola on the one hand and the war against terrorism inside South Africa on the other hand.

The stories in this book must be read while keeping these military and political circumstances in mind. Some stories contain political comments on events of those times.

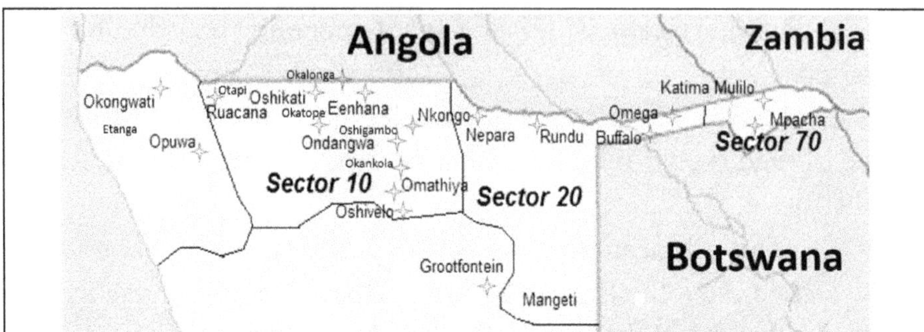

Map of the so-called Operational Area in northern South West Africa. Most of the action took place in Sector 10, which covered Ovamboland. The following towns play a rol in this book: Oshakati, Ondangwa, Eenhana, Ruacana, and Grootfontein.

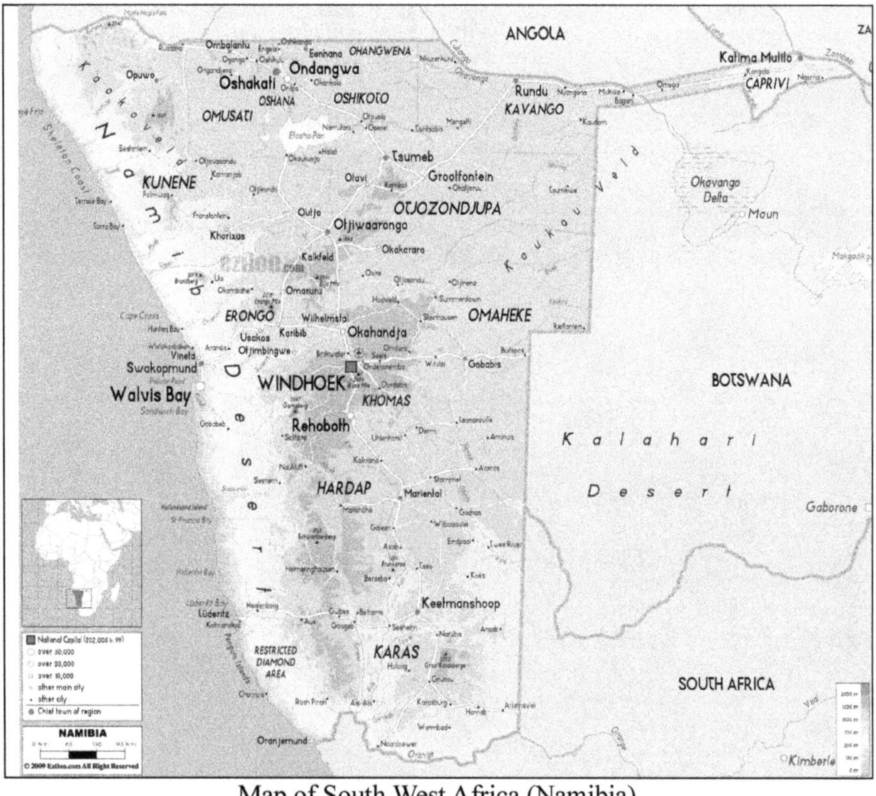

Map of South West Africa (Namibia)

Map of the Cape Peninsula and adjacent areas in South Africa. The following places are mentioned in these narratives: Cape Town, Wynberg, Simon' s Town, Stellenbosch, and Gordon's Bay.

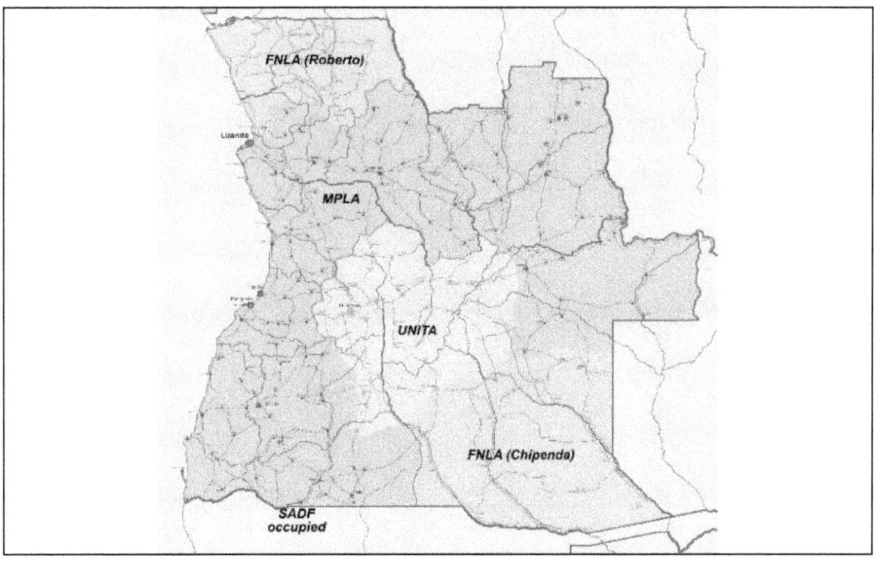

Angola during the civil war in the 1980's, showing the areas controlled by the MPLA (supported by the Soviet Union and Cuba), Unita (backed by South Africa) and the FNLA (also backed by South Africa)

1. OPERATION RADIATOR

Southern South West Africa, Wednesday, 10 December 1975

"Dammit! Blasted! Shit!"

Hannelore, standing next to me, declares: "You had better swear in German. Remember, you are now in South West."

"All right. What the hell must I say in German?"

"Scheisse! Donnerwetter! Kreuzitürken!"

"What the fuck does that mean?"

"'Shit', 'thunder' and 'crucify the Turks'."

"OK. Scheisse! Donnerwetter! Kreuzitürken!" I roar it with abandon.

"Did it help?"

"Of course, it helped fuck-all. But it helped me somewhat to blow off some steam, just as the damn radiator of this bloody red Ford Cortina is blowing out some steam, right now."

Two minutes ago, I heard a bang under the bonnet of my car. Steam started to blow through the grill and I immediately stopped.

Fortunately, I keep a torch in the cubbyhole and with that I went to investigate. When I lifted the bonnet, with Hannelore next to me, I immediately saw that the radiator had it. It exploded and steam was blowing through a hole.

Hannelore places her hand on my right shoulder: "Herr Doktor David Scholtz (she pronounces it in German), you and I will have to spend this December night here on this road. Do you see that crescent moon? It will disappear behind the horizon in an hour's time and then it will be totally dark. 'Pechschwarz' (pitch black). It won't help if we try to walk to the farm because we won't be able to see where we are going."

"Do you want to tell me that we will have to spend the night in this damned deserted desert, on this dirt road?"

“Not in the open air. We can settle ourselves in your automobile. That will prevent us from getting wet from the dew.”

“How far is your dad’s farm from here?”

“Anything between twelve and fifteen kilometters. It will take us hours to get there on foot. That is something we will have to start tomorrow morning at first light.”

“OK, you know this part of the world. It seems as if we don’t have any choice.”

“Nein, we don’t have a choice. You may be dead sure that not a single Auto will come this way on this road before next week-end.”

I close the bonnet of the car and we get into the Cortina again. Fortunately, it is a mild December night and we open the windows somewhat to get fresh air.

In the last bit of moonlight, I take another look at the beautiful German girl whom I have been dating for the past six months. I can never get enough of her perfect profile. My dad, Doctor David Scholtz, is very satisfied with my good taste. He studied medicine in Berlin before the Second World War. The outbreak of the war prevented him from leaving the country and he had no choice but to work as a military physician and surgeon in a unit of the infamous “Waffen-SS”[1] – otherwise, a concentration camp was his fate. His first German wife was killed during an American bombing raid on Berlin.

It was dangerous to return to South Africa after the war because he would have been charged with high treason for aiding

[1] “Waffen-SS” – German for “Armed SS”. The SS or Schutzstaffel (Protection n Squadron) was initially Hitler’s bodyguard but developed into the political police of the Nazi Party. A number of SS divisions fought alongside the regular Army divisions and these were known as the Waffen-SS.

the enemy. He worked in a German colony in Argentina for three years as a medical practitioner before he was granted amnesty. With his military background, he was appointed as a military medical practitioner in the Union Defence Force of South Africa and he rose to the rank of brigadier in the meantime and he was, amongst other, in command of a military hospital.

After we have been sitting siltently for a quarter of an hour during which I held Hannelore's hand, I start to speak: "I have a world of knowledge and training and I don't know how to get this damn car to go again! It's horrible.The stress hormones are pumping rapidly through my arteries."

"Relax. It's only a hole in the radiator. It can be fixed again. And in the meantime, we can sit here and enjoy the night air. Perhaps we may even hear a jackall or an owl."

"You know, I may regard myself as a highly trained and learned person. Only the day before yesterday, the degree of M.B.,Ch.B. was awarded *cum laude* to me and I may call myself a doctor now – the same as my dad. I know almost everything about the human anatomy, although I would like to know more about the brain. I know the name of every tiny muscle. I know the functions of every organ. I can identify every little bone in the skeleton. I have a name for every little artery and nerve. I know about bacteria, virusses and parasites. I can diagnose hundreds of diseases and illnesses and disorders. I know about aneurysms, beri-beri, chronic ear infections, dental corruption, eating disorders, frontal lobe degenration, gastro-enteritis… and everything further down to infections with the Zika virus. I know which medication to prescribe for every illness. I know how the blood circulation system works. I have a good idea how the immune system runs. I understand how digestion takes place. There isn't a single hormone or enzyme or neurotransmitter of which I am not aware. I can catch babies and remove an asshead of an appendix or toxic tonsils and burn waspish warts. I can fix bloody broken legs..."

"Hmm."

I hit the steering wheel in front of me with my open hand while I hiss with emphasis: "And I cannot get this crammy car to move any further!"

"Hmm."

"And I'm a trained parabat. Directly after I have finished school, I had to present myself for a year's national service and military training. I was super fit and then I volunteered for the Parachute Battalion. After weeks of terrible tests only ten percent of the volunteers remained. And I was one of that ten percent. I can work with whole range of weapons – rifles, pistols, machine guns, mortars, bazookas, bayonettes, everything you may care to mention. I may wear a sharp shooter's badge on my 'step-outs'. I can throw hand grenates and can shoot rifle grenades. I can plant land mines. I can blow up bridges, buildings, and barricades with explosives. I have jumped thirty times from the door of a Dakota and landed a few minutes later on Mother Earth without getting injured."

"Hmm."

"Yea, I know you know about all these things. And you know how my head works because you already have four years of medical studies on your record. But what does all this education help us? We are sitting here between nothing and nowhere. Helpless, hopeless and homeless with our hands under our bottoms."

"Dave, this is not the end of the world. My folks will assume that we encountered some ill luck on our way from Stellenbosch and they won't be worried when we don't arrive tonight."

"Tell me more about your folks. I know that I must address your father as 'Onkel Heini' and that your mother must be called 'Tante Heidi."

"Right. My dad is Heinrich Hahnefeld and my mother was born as Heidemarie Hennig. My two brothers are Helmut and Horst."

"You seem to be the H team. All of you have names that starts with H – yours as well."

"Our neighbours and friends always called us the 'H-Mannschaft'[2]. The H also points to hell-out crazy and hell-out bedevilled. We Germans don't allow anybody to mess with us. My grandpa, also Helmut, was an Oberleutnant[3] in the Schutstruppe[4] and after completing his time he bought himself a farm here in the mountains, northwest of Seeheim and next to the Fish River. My dad inherited the farm and my elder brother, Helmut, will probably inherit it from him some or other time. And, yes, in addition, my father's brother is Onkel Herbert and he is married to Tante Hildegard. Their sons are Helmut and Holger."

"Well, well. You really are the H Team. Fortunately, I took German at school and I will probably be able to understand your folks when they speak German. My dad insisted that I take German at school because he speaks German fluently after having lived and worked between the Germans for many years."

"Just as all South West Germans, my people, can speak Afrikaans well. But it will be good if you can impress them with your German – even if it is somewhat crooked and skewed."

My mood has improved a lot by this time and Hannelore and I prepare ourselves to spend the night in my car. We decide to improve our knowledge of the human anatomy.

---

[2] "Mannschaft" – German for "Team".

[3] "Oberleutnant" – the German rank of lieutenant.

[4] "Schutztruppe" – German for Protection Troops, the German Forces protecting South West Africa before the First World War.

Southern Sout West Africa, Thursday, 11 December 1975

Directly after the first glimmer of dawn became visible in the east we started walking – before it gets too hot. Fortunately, I always keep a full water bottle in the car and I put that that into my rucksack before we started walking. There is, unfortunately, nothing for breakfast.

While we were walking along I asked Hannelore to tell me how the Germans celebrate Christmas because it was our intention that I spend Christmas on the farm to get acquainted with her family. It all sounds familiar, because that's also how my parents celebrated Christmas. After all, my father has absorbed many German customs. Hannelore has already met my parents and she and my dad conversed a lot in German.

It's almost eleven o' clock when we arrive at the farm – tired, hungry, and thirsty. The December sun in this desert almost grilled us.

Tante Heidi lets us sit down in the kitchen, pours some cold water for us and starts to prepare breakfast. Onkel Heini enters a little later and tells us that he is grateful that we arrived safely: "Fortunately, we are far to the south in these parts. Those terrorists of Swapo haven't been able to reach these parts from up north untill now."

After we have rested our weary legs, Hannelore and I drive with Onkel Heini in his truck back to the spot where my car is stranded, to tow her to the farm.

"David, you told me that it's the radiator that got bust?"

"Yes, Onkel Heini."

"Fortunately, I brought a cannister with water. We must go and see what we can do."

"Vielen, vielen Dank!"

We arrive at my car where she is parked next to the road. I unlock her and pull the lever to open the bonnet.

Onkel Heini asks: “Does one of you perhaps have a bar of soap in your luggage?”

“Ja, Vati. I’ll fetch it,” Hannelore answers her dad.

“Why do you want to use it?” I enquire.

“That hole in your radiator is big enough to cause trouble, but it’s small enough that we can seal it with soap as an emergency measure. You would have been able to reach us last night if you have done it that way.”

I feel the urge to say “blasted” and “dammit” but I keep myself in check in the presence of the father of my girlfriend.

Hannelore hisses: “Scheisse…

2. OPERATION TOAST

Seeheim, Saturday, 17 December 1977

My mom clutches my arm with a worried expression on her face: “Dave, how are we going to prevent your father from making a fool of himself?”

“Relax, Ma. Please remember, Pa is a retired brigadier. He was an officer for the biggest part of his life and he will always behave himself like a gentleman. You may trust him.”

I look in the direction of my dad and I’m not so sure that he won’t mak a fool of himself. He stands between his new daughter-in-law in her bridal gown and his new brother-in-law, the father of the bride. Each one of them holds a big mug of German beer while they merrily sing along in German with the brass band accompanying them. They rock to and fro on the beat of the music.

“Ma, you musn’t go and quarrel with Pa at this moment. He’s back in his days during the war with his Waffen-SS unit where he was their medical officer. We will never get that little bit of Germany out of his system, although he has buried it very deeply, most of the time. Remember, he lived and worked for fifteen years with the Germans and the Nazis! He even wears his Iron Cross, First Class, which he has received from a German general in 1944. He never dared to wear it together with his South African medals on his South African Army uniform. He dug it up, especially for Hannelore’s and my German wedding.”

My mother: “I’m afraid that he will burst out in tears while longing back to his first German wife who was killed by an American bomb in Berlin. Please understand me, I’m not jealous that he sometimes has a longing for her.”

“Ma, he is very, very much in love with you. You may be sure of that. You became part of his life, there in Argentina, when he had a rough time. Thank you that you allow him to, sometimes, long after his first wife. According to the photos that I've seen, she was a beautiful girl – the same as you. I would also have fallen madly in love with her. It was a bad shock when he got the news of her death while he was fighting the Russians on the far northern front."

Secretly, I think that my bride, Hannelore, looks remarkably much like my dad's first wife. Her name was Josephine. I wonder: what it does to my dad to have the splitting image of his first wife here next to him? I also have a strong suspicion that he also has some remaining shell-shock after the war.

My father-in-law, Heini Hahnefeld, organised a swanky military wedding for his only daughter. For this purpose, he rented the whole Hotel Seeheim for the long week-end so that all the guests from far away – such as my parents, my brothers Pieter and Johannes, as well as my father's twin brother, Uncle Willie and his family – had a place to stay. The wedding ceremony took place in the big dining hall and the reception is also taking place in the same space.

Fräulein[5] Ärtztin[6] Hannelore Hahnefeld and Herr[7] Artzt[8] David Johannes Philippus Scholtz were marrid by two clergymen – my brother Johannes, a minister in the north of of South West and who serves as the part-time chaplain of the local commando[9], and

---

[5] "Fräulein" – German for "Miss".

[6] "Ärtztin" – a female medical practitioner.

[7] "Herr" – German for "Mister".

[8] "Artzt" – medical practitioner.

[9] South African servicemen who have completed their initial national service in the Defence Force, were organized as reservists in commando's, battalion-sized units. Afrikaans-speaking people formed "commando's" since the early eighteenth century in the Durch Cape Colony to defend themselves against native tribes and they were commanded by an officer called a "commandant" – more or less the equivalent of a lieutenant colonel.

Herr Pastor Albert Arendt, the missionary of the Rhenish Mission Congregation in Keetmanshoop. Hannelore received her medical degree last week and she is now, the same as me, a medical practitioner. Because she had received a bursary from rhe South West African Administration, she has to work six years for them and she has to do her house doctor's year next year in Swakopmund, a town on the Atlantic coast.

My father, who retired four years ago as a senior staff officer: personnel in the office of the Surgeon General and who even, for a few weeks, officiated as the Surgeon General's deputy, could pull a few strings so that I was transferred to the sick-bay at the nearby military base at Walvis Bay. I was trained as a military medical officer the year before last year and performed my house doctor's year last year at 2 Military Hospital in Wynberg, Cape Town, usually called Two Mil. That made it possible for me to be near Hannelore while she was doing her final year of medical studies at the Stellenbosch University.

Father-in-law Heini, who is a captain in the Keetmanshoop Commando, got permission from his commandant[10] to organize a military wedding for his daughter. With that in mind, he wears his step-out uniform today with three stars on his shoulders. He invited a section of men from his company – all of them German-speaking – to act as a guard of honor. They are under the command of my brother-in-law, Helmut, a sergeant.

Johannes, the chaplain, is also in his step-out uniform.

Because my father is retired, he attends the wedding in civilian clothes. He fastened his South African medals to his jacket, but the Iron Cross, First Class, also hangs conspicuously on his chest.

---

[10] See the rank sructure of the South African Defence Force at the end of this book.

As bridegroom, I'm also in uniform. On my shoulders are two stars in accordance with my rank of lieutenant. On my left chest are my wings as a qualified parachute soldier and on my right chest is a name tag and a badge as sharp-shooter. There is also a badge consisting of two snakes curling around a staff because I'm a medical officer. I haven't served long enough in the military to have been awarded any medals.

After Hannelore, my father and my father-in-law have finished their song, I join them to hear what they are talking about. My father-in-law asks: "My brother, please tell me, how did it happen that you got that beautiful Iron Cross?"

My dad is usually reluctant to talk about his war experiences, but the German beer, the assembled uniforms and the German atmosphere loosen his tongue: "I fought the Russians for three years. As medical officer in the best division that took part in the whole war – the Sixth Mountain Division of the Waffen-SS, also known as the Division Nord. We were special troops, moun-tain troops. I was also, at the same time, a trained artillery officer.

"While we retreated from Finland, after the Finns and the Russians made peace with each other, our Division had to form the rear-guard for all the other German divisions. I was the temporary commander of the division's artillery regiment because all the other senior officers were either killed or wounded. We gave the Ivans hell. And that's why Generaloberst Rendulic gave me this Iron Cross and promoted me to major. In the SS, the rank was actually 'Sturmbannführer'."

Father-in-law Heini: "When was that?"

"The end of forty-four."

"What did you do after that?"

"Our division fougfht against the Yanks a few weeks during the beginning of forty-five. And then the remnants of our division were transferred to Austria where we shot the shit out the Russians in the mountains. We prevented them from progressing any further into Austria till the end of the war when we surrendered to the Americans in Steiermark."

"Were you again a military medical doctor in that time?"

"In that time, I actually had two jobs – doctor and commander of an infantry battalion."

"Where were you after the war?"

"I was hiding in Argentina – at a German colony in a town with the name of Bariloche."

"Aaah! We are aware of the fact that Hitler survived the war and took refuge in those parts. Did you ever see him. Was he, perhaps, your patient?"

I observe how my dad jerks as if he gets a shock, but he recovers rapidly and declares firmly: "Hitler died in April forty-five! Suicide! Everybody knows that!"

My father-in-law laughs heartily, turns away, silences the brass band and calls to the guests in the hall: "Hi, everybody! Achtung! Listen here! We have the honor to have a German war hero in our midst: Herr Sturmbannführer Doktor David Scholtz! Let's drink a toast on his Iron Cross, First Class!"

All those present stand up, grab their beer mugs and lift those high up.

My dad stands at attention. He glances at Hannelore, lifts his right arm and calls out: "Heil!"

The tears roll over his cheeks.

My mom takes a seat on the nearest chair and covers her face with both hands.

3. OPERATION CANE

Swakopmund, Friday, 27 January 1978

Hannelore strolls with me after work to the beach at Swakopmund and we sit down at a spot where we can watch the jetty. It's a pleasant summer evening and we contemplate the setting sun over the Atlantic Ocean. On our way here, we passed the oldest German "Kneipe"[11] in town and heard that a jolly party in there was in progress.

My new wife is doing her house doctor's year as medical practitioner here in Swakopmund's state hospital. We live in a rented apartment and I, as a military medical practoitioner, drive the forty-three kilometres to Walvis Bay with my red Ford Cortina each day to work at the sick-bay at the military base there. Walvis Bay, which is actually a South African enclave and part of the Cape Province of South Africa, houses a lot of Defence Force personnel. There is

[11] "Kneipe" – saloon,

Number Two South African Infantry Battalion – popularly known as Two SAI – an Army unit that has taken part in an operation deep inside Angola – other Army units, an Air Force base, and a Naval Station at the harbor.

As we sit down, I ask: "Do you know why there was all those celebrations over there? It sounded like a bunch of inebriated Germans. They sang old battle songs, or that is how it sounded."

"Today is a non-official holiday here in Swakopmund. The birthday of the late Kaiser Wilhelm the Second. The gang of old Germans still celebrate it every year. It is actually only a good excuse to drink as much beer as possible."

"Oh, thanks. And how was your day at the hospital?"

"So-so. Caught two babies, dispensed medicine and did dormitory rounds. But we also had an important visitor."

"Who was that?"

"The new mayor of Swakopmund. It's a woman and she wanted to see what we're doing."

"Did she come with her chain?"

"No. She wasn't chained to anything. She was free to move all over the place, just as she wanted."

"I didn't mean that sort of chain."

Hannelore giggles mischievously: "She did have a very beautiful fancy necklace around her neck to show that she's the mayor. And how was your day?"

"Quite OK. Actually, jolly interesting."

"Yes?"

"Frans van den Berg, the commandant of Two SAI, called me this afternoon with the request that I inspect a certain troop thoroughly – but only from the outside. I wasn't allowed to ask him any questions, only inspect him. I made the troop stand at attention with his Paradise uniform without any fig leaves in my consulting room and I inspected him from top to bottom and from the front and from behind. On his bare bums I found a number of lashes, which must have been administered by a cane. Ugly red stripes."

"Did somebody assault the troop?"

"Yes. Rather badly."

"Who?"

"You won't believe me. The commandant himself. He gave the troop a horrible hiding,

Yes? Why?"

"That's a long story. I went back to the commandant to report to him – before I knew where the red warts on the troop's bottom side came from. I reported that somebody must be in big trouble because the troop was badly assaulted and beaten. The commandant gets a fright because he confesses that he is the guilty party. He was compelled to punish the troop in this manner."

"What did the poor troop do?"

"A number of naughty things. Last week, Monday morning, the commandant arrives at his office after the week-end and his adjutant, Major van Aswegen, stops him and announces that he has very bad news for him. The commandant wants to know more, but van Aswegen tells him that they must get into a truck because he wants to show him something. They drive to the bird sanctuary at the wetlands between the base and town, next to the main road. There was a scene that would have taken anybody's breath away and would make his blood pressure rise with fifty points. There were three Army vehicles stuck in the mud of the wetlands."

"How did that happen?"

"It appears that this chap, whom I had to inspect today, stole a truck from the base on a Saturday night, a fortnight ago. He could have done it easiily because he is a trained driver. He knows where the keys are being kept. He then goes to town to pick up his girlfriend and takes her to the bird sanctuary – to show her the birds in the dark, or perhaps also to show her to the birds. After they have watched the birds, or whatever, he wants to drive back, but the truck gets stuck in the mud. He takes the girl back to town on foot and runs back to the base. There, he steals a Samil 20 lorry and attaches a cable between the Samil and the truck stuck in the muck. Of course, the lorry also gets stuck in the mud. He again runs back to the base and swipes the break-down – a big, big vehicle. He attaches another cable onto the Samil 20 and tries to tow the lot out of the mud."

Hannelore laughs: "And the break-down also sinks away in the mud, of course?"

"Dead right, of course. All three vehicles are stuck in the muck and the more he tries to dislodge them the deeper they sink. The troop decides that it's time for him to go and visit his mother in Port Elizabeth and he starts hitch-hiking. The next morning, it appears that he is AWOL. The Military Police search for him and find him along the main road and take him back to the base.He gets a disciplinary hearing and gets two months in the Dee Bee."

"Dee Bee?"

"The Detention Barracks, somewhere in a corner of the base."

"Was that where he was assaulted?" "No, not yet. Last Monday, Frans van den Berg sits ontop of Rooikop[12], die hill next

[12] "Rooikop" – the Afrikaans name for a red volcanic ourcrop in the desert east of Walvis Bay. The military base at its foot is called after this hill.

to the base, from where he watches military exercises in the desert. Through his binoculars, he sees a truck driving where nothing was supposed to be. He sends his Military Police to intercept that truck. That was this troop who escaped from the Detention Barracks and really stole another truck. Can you believe it? The troop is, again, locked up in the DB, while an armed guard is posted to watch him around the clock."

"That guy has guts. I must say."

"Certainly. Frans van den Berg discovers that he has a problem. He has too few drivers and he sends for this troop. He gives him a choice: he can stay in the DB for the next six months or he can take the commandan'ts special treatment. The troop chooses the commandant's special treatment. The commandant makes him take off his pants and let him lie over upright part of an easychair with his stern pointng to the ceiling. He gets the worst hiding of his whole life with the commandant's cane. The troop puts his pants back on and leaves with a smile on his face – very relieved to be free from the DB."

"And then the commandant gets a fright because he has assaulted a troop?"

"Exactly. That was why he needed a medical report. After he has told me his story, I ask him whether he was afraid that the troop would lay a charge of assault against him. He was, indeed, nervous about this prospect and he asks my advice whether it would a good thing to phone the troop's mother. I agree that it would be a good thing.

"Frans van den Berg then sends for this troop again and asks him what his mother's home phone number is. No, they don't have a phone at home. Where does his mother work? At the OK Bazaars in Port Elizabeth. Frans van den Berg books a call to the manager of the OK Bazaars in Port Elizabeth and asks whether he could talk to the troop's mother. The manager says he will fetch her. After ten minutes, the manager is back on the phone and says that today is the woman's off-day. Frans van den Berg get the troop's mother's home address and he phones the Police in Port Elizabeth with the request that they fetch the troop's mother at her home so that she can phone him back from the Police station. He emphasises towards the station commander that they have to tell the troop's mother that it concerns her son in the Army. There is no reason to get a fright because he is healthy and safe, which is, of course, not totally true. He tells the station commander It is, though, very urgent to talk to this woman. An hour later the Police phone back and the troop's mother speaks to the commandant. He explains that he was forced to give the troop a decent hiding. The mother says – and I quote her words: 'Give that snot head hell, Commandant. That's the only language he understands.'"

Hannelore laughs: "Oh, the mother was satisfied that her little boy may be given corporal punishment?"

"Yes. The commandant asks her if he has her permission to administer corporal punishment to her son. She immediately gives her permission. He asks to talk to the station commander again and requests him to take down an affidavit from the mother in which she gives permission that her son may receive corporal punishment. This statement must then be sent by fax to the commandant. A quarter of an hour later the fax arrives and in it the mother appoints the commandant as her son's honourary father, as well."

"You certainly had an interesting day! Didn't they miss you in the sick-bay during this time?"

"There was nothing that the medics couldn't handle."

While we are staring at the jetty I draw my beautiful wife nearer and get her into a tight grip. I ask: "And how are we going to celebrate the late Kaiser's birthday tonight?"

4. OPERATION REINDEER

Walvis Bay, Monday, 13 March 1978

A big envelope, addressed to me in my outoppie's[13] handwriting, is being delivered at my consulting room. I am on my way to the weekly planning meeting of key personnel of the base at Walvis Bay and, therefore, I cannot pay attentionto it immediately. During the meeting, I'm unable to concentrate on the discussions and I often wonder what is hiding in the mysterious envelope.

Fortunately, the meeting braks up after fifty minutes and I rush back. I grab the envelope and open it hastily. Inside, there is another envelope with a little window. It is addressed to "68647666BT Rfn DJP Scholtz" at the address of my parents. A stamp indicates that is was sent by 2 Parachute Battalion in Bloemfontein. It is clear that this letter was sent to my father's address and that he sent it unopened to me in another envelope.

I find this rather strange because when I joined the Permanent Force as a medical officer, my rank chnaged from rifleman to candidate officer to lieutenant. I am, in addition, not a conscript anymore and the BT at the end of my force number has changed yo PE.

Another strange thing is that the Defence Force seems to be unaware of the fact that I am in Walvis Bay. According to 2 Parachute Battalion, my contact address is still in Pretoria at my parents' home.

Nevertheless, I open the envelope. It contains call-up orders and I am directed to report to 2 Parachute Battalion in Bloemfontein on Monday, 27 March, for a camp of six weeks. This is, furthermore

[13] "Outoppie" – Army slang for father or any older man.

strange, since I don't have any camp commitments because I am a full-time employee of the Defence Force since two years ago.

The sick-bay in Walvis Bay has two military medical practitioners and I show my call-up papers to my colleague, Candidate Officer (Dr) Frikkie Fourie. He is doing his house doctor year under my supervision, here at the sick-bay. He understands just as little of this as I do, but he reckons that I am looking for trouble by ignoring these call-up orders.

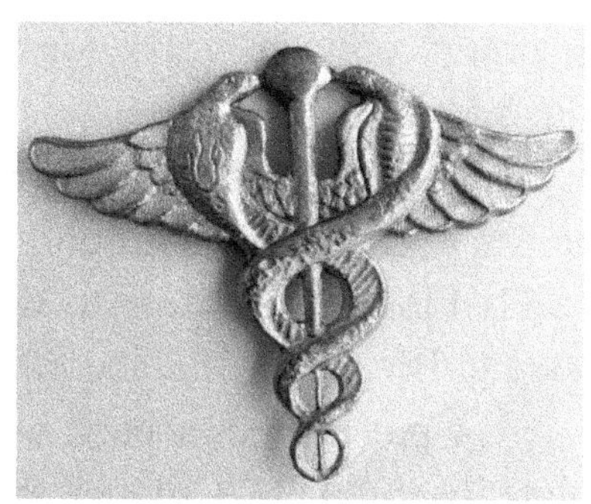
Badge of a qualified medical officer in the SADF

He thinks that perhaps I should go. It is possible that the Defence Force wants to use me as a medical officer in the newly formed 44 Parachute Brigade. He advises me to discuss the matter, in any case, with Colonel Dirk van Schalkwyk, the commander of the military base of Walvis Bay.

Fortunately, the colonel can see me immediately. After he has scrutinized my call-up papers, he declares: "There are rumors that a big exercise is to be held at Lohatla on the other side of Kimberley. The parabats are supposed to be part of this exercise. Perhaps to prepare for some or other operation in Angola, or something of the sort. Doc, I don't think you will be able to wriggle yourself out of this thing. When you arrive at 2 Parachute Battalion, you appear in your uniform with two pips on your shoulders. I will give you a letter in which I confirm that you are a Permanent Force medical officer who is employed at Walvis Bay. I will attach a copy of the signal of the Personnel Section at the office of the Surgeon General in which we were informed that you were detached to us here. I will immediately make an entry into my diary so that I won't forget."

I ask: "Colonel, how will I get to Bloemfontein? This call-up orders only provides for free transport between Pretoria and Bloemfontein."

"No problem. I will arrange with Commandant Williams of the Air Force, here next door, that a seat be booked for you on the weekly Flossie[14] that flies to Waterkloof[15]. From there, you can then move to Bloemfontein, according to your travel voucher."

I put my beret back onto my head, stand at attention, and salute the colonel: "Colonel, thank you, very much!"

That evening, I show my call-up papers to Hannelore. She sighs: "Both of us are civil servants. I suppose we must do as our bosses tell us to do. The Germans use to say: 'Befehl ist Befehl!' If you refuse to travel to Bloemfontein it may amount to mutiny. I don't want the Military Police to drag you out of here. I will probably be able to survive six weeks without you."

Bloemfontein, Monday, 27 March 1978

At the headquarters of 2 Parachute Battalion in Tempe, Bloemfontein, the home unit of Citizen Force members who have done their national service at 1 Parachute Battalion, I stand in a long queue of men to clear in. I am dressed in my "browns"[16] with two stars on my shoulders and I have my documentation in my hand.

It takes almost an hour before I reach the front the of the row. An angry staff sergeant sits behind a table and he barks: "Call-up papers!"

---

[14] "Flossie" – Army slang for the Hercules C-130 transport plane.

[15] "Waterkloof" – the Air Force base north of Pretoria.

[16] "Browns" – Army slang for battle dress.

After he has studied my call-up orders and looked at me from top to bottom, he adopts an expression as if he smells something bad or finds my appearance to be odious. He sneers: "Troop, do ye realize that it's an 'orrible offense to pretend that you're an officer? Remove those pips from y'r shoulders. Immediately!"

With a smug smile I hand him the letter of Colonel van Schalkwyk, together with the signal from the office of the Surgeon General.

The staff serhgeant's attitude changes immediately: "Sorry, Lootenant. Or must I rither call ye 'Doctor'?"

"Both are Okay."

"What the hell are we goin' te do with ye? Ye're not supposed to be 'ere. Some or other arsehole never noticed that ye're now a Papa Foxie[17]. We can't call ye up for a camp. I purpose ye go and chat with the adjutant, Captain Willemse, immediately. Here's y'r papers."

"Thanks, Staff."

The staff sergeant really salutes me when I take my papers and I reciprocate.

I find the adjutant's office easily and I ask his clerk, a girl corporal, whether I may speak to the captain. She wants to know who I am. I reply that I am Doctor Scholtz – in spite of the fact that my family name is stitched onto my shirt, together with the badge that I am a medical officer, namely two snakes curled around a staff.

The captain is a jovial round little man. Although he sports the wings of a parachute soldier on his shirt, I doubt whether he has jumped from a plane during the last five years. For that, he clearly likes eating too much.

"Yes, Doc, what can I do for you?"

---

[17] "Papa Foxie" – Army slang for "Papa Foxtrot", the radio alphabet for "P F", the abbreciation for "Permanent Force".

I hand him my call-up papers and the letter from Colonel van Schalkwyk. He laughs: "Doc, you should have phoned or sent a signal to explain that you are a Permanent Force member now. You must certainly know that Permanent Force members don't do camps – they do get detached somewhere else, at most, for temporary jobs. But, here you are now. Do you want to go back home? Or do you prefer a nice action-filled holiday with all expense paid? By the government."

"Do I have a choice?"

"These call-up orders are a miserable mistake. A fucking fatal flaw. Some or other stupid simple sot never read the signal that you are no longer a member of this unit, but that you fall under the Surgeon General. (On my own I think that this stupid simple sot must be this adjutant because the personnel matters of this unit are his job.) But we can use you if you choose to stay. You seem to be an active type of chap. Perhaps it will be a good thing to sweat together with the troops and become fit."

"I'm already fit. Trotted off the Dune Marathon between Swakopmund and Walvis Bay only last week and came sixth. That was done to be ready for this camp after having been called up."

He grins: "Then you don't need our softening-up processes. The question is: do you stay or do you go home? Which one of these will you enjoy most?"

"I think I'll stay. I am already here, after all. I will only make a fool of myself if I suddenly reappear in Walvis Bay the day after tomorrow."

"All right, I'll place you on our strength. Welcome."

"I've been caled up with the rank of rifleman. Will I receive my pay as a rifleman, and not my PF salary for the duration of this camp? Or perhaps both at the same time?"

"You're not greedy, but you do like a lot. I must say. Okay, let's do it. And, should it happen that you are sent somewhere into the operational area, you will receive danger pay, as well. How'z that?"

"Double danger pay on my PF salary and my pay as a common footslogger?"

"Well, yes, that becomes rather complicated. But, on the ther hand, you are actually two people – Doctor Scholtz and Rifleman Scholtz. Do you have two bank accounts?"

"I'll ask my only wife to organize that. Am I supposed to pay tax on both remunerations? Won't the tax man become suspicious?"

"Tou're correct. Tax evasion and tax fraud are criminal acts. And of course, somebody at the Paymaster General will pick it up that two payments go to the same force number. Okay, you go simply as Doctor Scholtz and you draw danger pay if you land beyond the Red Line[18]. Well, then you have to go and report immediately at our sick-bay. Our medical officer is Captain Thorny Thomson. He will surely be glad if you could take over most of his work."

At the sivk bay I find a long row of troops who have to be undergo a medical check-up. I proceed to the front of the row and salute the captain who is listening to a troops heart with his stetoscope. He growls: "Dammit, don't jump the queue. Await your bloody turn."

When I stay standing, he looks better at me and see my rank insignia and the curled snakes on my shirt: "Sorry colleague. I thought you were an arrogant troop who wanted to push his luck. Get a table and a chair somewhere. My medic will help you with

---

[18] "Red Line" – the southern border of the so-called operational area consisting of Sectors One Zero, Two Zero, and Seven Zero in the war against Swapo insurgents (see map on page 6).

that. And then you make sure that every troop who passes you is a G1K1[19]. We can't afford to have invalids and wheel chair cases here! Make sure that everyone still has his own teeth. Disqualify anybody with a glass eye. Count their fingers and toes."

Grootfontein, Wednesday, 3 May 1978

Now I am back in South West, but at a place where I haven't been before, the Air Force Base Grootfontein, directly south of the Operational Area. We were downloaded shortly after dark by a number of Flossies and we must make ourselves at home in a big hangar. Everything happens under the greatest secrecy because Swapo must not know that we are going to hammer them with heavy blows tomorrow morning early, even before they have swallowed their morning coffee.

During the past four weeks were were rigorously retrained. The troops are all members of the Citizeb Force and they have forgotten much of their previous initial training in the meantime. We had to practice a few jumps from a Flossie, practice fire-in-movement, make sure that we are familiar with our shooting irons and make sure that we are very fit. Although we were initially informed that we would participate in a big exercise at Lohatla, we were taken to De Brug, a military area west of Bloemfontein, for retraining. There was no opportunity of making contact with the outside world and we all realized that we were being prepared for a secret operation. Although I am an officer, I did everything together

---

[19] "G1K1" – the military classification for healthy and fit troops – perfect cannon fodder. The classification of G2K1 was used for men who wore spectacles, but wereotherwise healthy and fit. Somebody with a G2K2 classification or lower had some ailments or other disabilities. G5/GP: The SADF considered these men as ready for the graveyard and of no use and they were discharged on medical grounds..

with the troops – just as Thorny Thomson, as well as the other officers.

We were divided into six relatively small companies. Thorny and his medics are supposed to accompany Alpha and Bravo companies, consisting of five platoons with four sixty millimeter mortars. My taak will be to go with Delta Company, consisting of two platoons under the command of Captain Tommy Smit, as well as two anti-tank platoons under Lieutenant Pierre Peters, together with my medic. Echo Company serves as reserve force. The medical personnel, together with a few sappers and intelligence guys and signallers, form part of HQ Company.

We were throughly informed about the attack plan of Operation Reindeer so that everybody knew where he fitted into the bigger picture. It was planned that the bombers of the Air Froce would start bombing the Swapo base at Cassinga, deep inside Angola, at 08:00. That was supposed to coincide with the morning parade of the Swaps[20] when all the fighters would be assembled in a group.

Directly after that, a smallish battalion consisting of about 370 men under command of Colonel Jan Breytenbach, would be dropped with parachutes from the Flossies onto Cassinga. Alpha and Bravo Companies had to attack from the west, Charlie Company and an independent platoon had to attack from the east an the north, while Delta Company had to approach from the south. The anti-tank platoons, armed with RPG-7 rockets and mortars, had to cover the road to the south, because it was possible that the Angolans and the Cubans at a base about 15 kilometers to the south, could get it into their heads to aid the fighters of Swapo with their armored vehicles. They had to be destroyed before they could interfere.

---

[20] "Swaps" – Army slang for members of Swapo's armed wing.

The Swapo base at Chetequera, not too far north of the border with South West, would be attacked simultaneously by a conventional force on vehicles. It was, though, supposed to be a separate action, although it was also deemed to be part of Ops Reindeer.

Thorny was but too glad to have a second medical officer on this operation because he would have been the only doctor otherwise. He made sure that I took enough fitst aid equipment along in my back pack. That meant that I carried a little less ammo than the troops – just enough for self-Defence.

After supper and a short service led by a chaplain, we sat around in the hangar until it became bed-time. Some of the men read story books, others read in the Bibles, some more men write letters. Most of us make sure for the last time that our R-1 rifles are clean, that the magazines are loaded and that our hand grenades are packed in such amanner that they can be reached easily. A long row of men await their turns at the limited bathroom facilities. Everybody saw to it that their water bottles are filled and their bladders empty.

Cassinga, Angola, Thursday, 4 May 1978

It's Ascension Day tday. Many Swaps are destined to reach heaven – or somewhere else – today before the sun sets at the end of the day. A few of us may perhaps also be redeployed to heaven.

We are woken at 04:00 and we stand ready for our last orders at 06:00 before we board the Flossies. The flight northwards is rather bumpy because we were warned beforehand that we would fly "treetops' – just above the trees to prevent enemy radar from picking us up. We approach Cassinga from the east and just before we reach the target, the Flossies shoot up into the air to give us enough height so that our parachutes can open before we hit Mother Eart.

During the few seconds while I am hanging on my parachute before striking the earth to the south of the base, I see that the place is already on fire. There are explosions – probably the enemy's ammo stores that were hit by the Air Force. The last Mirages fly away just as I land on my feet and roll over.

Due to some or other unknown reason, we land a few hundred meters south of the spot where we were supposed to land, but we rush as fast as possible to the point where we have to attack. My services are needed immediately because a few men of Delta Company get hurt from shards being hurled all over the place due to the explosions. While I patch a few of them up, the rest start to attack the base.

Some shots are directed in our direction from the base but that ceases when our men move nearer. It seems as if the defenders have fled. We don't have any casualties. The men of Delta Company hide behind trees and in trenches to stop any Swaps who would try to flee in our direction. The anti-tank platoons spread out behind us to await any dangerous movements from the south.

It takes a rather long time before the other companies get into action. They apparently jumped too late from the Flossies and landed too far away. It takes a good half-an-hour before they are ready to start their attack – and then all hell breaks loose. There's a deafening racket as rifles, machine guns and mortars sow death and destruction and decimation onto the defenders of Cassinga. The defenders shoot back with rifles, machine guns and rapid-action light artillery. I believe that a few men get wounded and that Thorny and his medics will have their hands full.

Colonel Breytembach orders Delta Company to attack the light artillery from behind and silence them. I move along with them. It shocks me to see a number of women and children together with the Swapo fighters in the trenches – and quite a few of them are dead on account of our attack. It seems as if the fighters used the women and children as human shields.

In the meantime, our bombers came flying back and they help to shoot Swapo's artillery positions to bits.

The shooting stops more or less at mid-day when the resistance of Swapo is finally broken and the remaining men surrender. A few snipers still shoot at us from some trees, but they are taken out rapidly.

We have quite a number of wounded men and I and Thorny attend to them. It appears that three of our men fell. A fourth man is missing and it is assumed that he also fell. There are dozens and dozens corpses of Swapo fighters littering the place. Our men took a number of POW's – prisoners of war – and I take care of the wounds of a few of them.

From a southerly direction we hear some vehicles approaching at about 13:00 – certainly the Cubans and Angolans who came to help Swapo , although it's already too late. Colonel Breytenbach gets onto his radio and hears from the anti-tank men that they will probably not be able to destroy the five tanks approaching them. He calls the Air Force and our bombers appear once more. We hear how they throw some bombs onto the approaching column and then disappear again. There is, though, one last Buccaneer that sweeps to and fro over the Cubans and Angolans, but it seems as if it's ammo is spent. His mock attacks become too much for the enemy – those of them who are still left – and we hear frm our men that the the rest started looking for hiding places in the bush.

One half of us get the order to run to the helicopters that have landed east of the base to extract us. In the meantime, the rest of us must hold the base, while we are wary that the Cubans and Angolans may attack again.

The choppers return after half-an-hour and the rest of us are able to depart. We are compelled to free our POW's because there just isn't space in the choppers for all of us and them. A few women and children beg us to take them with us. They tell us that they were abducted by Swapo and that they want to return home, but it's impssible to accommodate them.

Just as our helicopters start to take to the air, the last Angolese tank appears and starts shooting in our direction. Fortunately, his aim is bad and his shots all miss and we leave a scene of destruction, killing, spilt blood, wreckage, and chaos behind. I swallow the last bit of water in my water bottle and wipe the sweat from my face.

Walvis Bay, Monday, 8 May 1978

Colonel van Schalkwyk looks at me with a wide grin in his office, directly after our weekly planning meeting.

"Welcome back, Doc. And how was your camp with the parabats?"

"Colonel, thanks. We got some refresher training most of the time at De Brug. And I survived that, though."

"And afterwards you went to Angola, didn't you

"What makes you think that, Colonel?"

"The whole world knows that our parabats were blasting the Swapo base at Cassinga. Doc, of course, you were there."

"Okay. I was there. I admit it, although it was sipposed to be a secret ops. Colonel, you may perhaps know about it, I believe."

"The whole world knows about, except for the people of Suth Africa. How many terrs did you help to bite the dust?"

"Perhaps a few. My job was actually to check up on our boys who were bleeding."

"I read in our weekly intelligence report that Swapo calls all the hell's condemnations and curses upon your heads. They are screaming bloody murder, awful arson, hellish homicide. They are spitting burning embers, cobra venom, and glowing gasoline. You are being accused of being abhorent assasins, vicious vandals, and rotten rapists. Cassinga was supposed to have been a refugee camp with hundreds of Defenceless women and children. And then you went to kill these poor people and burned the place down! Shame on you!"

"Defenceless fugitives who shot at us with machine guns and light rapid-firing artillery?"

"Were there women and children?"

"Yes. And some of them are dead. But there are always women in every Swapo camp – the women and sex slaves of the fighters. I haven't counted the number of corpses of fighters and civilians, but there were hundreds of them."

"It's as clear as clean water: you have achieved a great victory, but Swapo has gained the sympathy of the world. And the bad news is – there are thousands of young men who are going to replace those fallen fighters. The Russians will only donate thousands upon thousands of tons of equipment to compensate for everything that you have destroyed or ruined."

I sigh: "I believe that we have injured Swapo so much that they won't recover easily."

“But they will recover. With the help of Russia and Cuba. Watch out…”

5. OPERATION HONEYMOON

Walvis Bay, Monday, 15 May 1978

Directly after lunch, somebody knocks on the door of my consulting room, I call out: “It’s óóóh-pen!”

An attractive female corporal enters and salutes me.

“Doc, I’m your new admin assistant.”

“Corporal, welcome. I’m grateful that you are here because I have struggled for the past week without an admin assistant. Come, get a little nearer so that I can read your name on your name tag on your blouse.”

She steps forward and pushes her beautiful boobs out so that I can see her name on her name tag on the right hand side of her blouse. Her family name appears to be ‘Jordaan’.

“All right, Corporal Jordaan, what is your full name? I don’t want to address you the whole time on your rank.”

“It’s Jacqueline Jordaan, Doc. Or simply just Jackie.”

“Right, Jackie. Have you found a place to sleep in the female dormintories?”

“Doc, I only arrived today with the airplane and my fiance met me and helped me with my luggage. He took me to the HQ and from there we wemt to the quarters for female members.”

“And who is your fiance, if I may ask?”

“He is Lieutenant Kobus Kotze of Bravo Company, here at Two SAI.”

“Oh, so you already know somebody at this base?”

“That’s why I applied for a transfer here. To be near to him.”

“Fantastic. Before you can take your place at your desk over there, I will have to show you around. Fortunately, today is rather quiet here in the sick-bay and I have the time to take you everywhere. First of all, I must introduce you to Colonel van

Schalkwyk. He is the commander of the whole military area. He's also my direct boss."

The colonel can see us immediately and I introduce my new administrative assistant to him. I explain that she came here to be near to her fiance.

The colonel: "Ah! So you are already engaged, Corporal? And your fiance is also based her, as the Doc has said?"

Jackie stands at attention and her blouse get stretched over her bewitching bosom: "That's right, Colonel."

The colonel: "And who is the lucky mann, if I may ask?"

Jackie: "Lieutenant Kobus Kotze of Bravo Company at Two SAI."

"Right. It's Monday today. The two of you are getting married on Friday afternoon, at five o' clock. Doc, will you please organize with the chaplain?"

Me: "Will do, Colonel." I also stand at attention.

The colonel: "And then you have your reception in the officers' mess at six. And then you see to it that you get into bed at eight!"

I and the girl corporal mumble very surprised: "Right so, Colonel."

The colonel: "I wish you well with everything. Good-bye."

As soon as we get into the passage outside the colonel's office, Jackied asks: "Doc, I suppose there is no way for us to disregard the order of the colonel?"

Me: "The colonel has the last say in this base. I will have to help you that you acquire an apartment in the married quarters immediately. But, first of all, we must find the chaplain."

Jackie: "It was actually our plan to get married only in December."

"It's clear to me that the colonel does not wish an attractive girl like you to move amongst all these men as a single woman. If you are married you are safe and everybody will know to keep their paws away from you.You are then ‘off-limits’. As an engaged girl you are still a fair target for any young man whose hormones give him problems.”

“Doc, it won’t be possible for my parents to come to my wedding at such a short notice. Will you please give me away as a stand-in father?”

“With great pleasure. There is certainly no time for you to get a wedding gown ready before Friday. Make sure that your step-outs are clean and tidy. It is, after all, a military wedding.”

Walvis Bay, Monday, 22 May 1978

It is Monday morning again as I march into the sick-bay and find Jackie already behind her desk.

“Had a nice week-end? A good beginning to the honeymoon?”

“Doc, it was horrible. Terrible, actually.”

“Yes?”

“We only got into bed on Friday night long after eleven – not at eight as the colonel had ordered. The party in the mess just lasted far too long.”

“And?”

“And then bugger-all happened. Both of us were far too tired. And also somewhat tipsy. Actually, more than tipsy.”

“But you had the rest of the week-end, haven’t you?”

“Doc, you won’t believe this. I am still a virgin in spite of the fact that I was married three days ago.”

“How the hell did you manage that?”

“Something that that colonel failed to tell us the other ay, was that he knew that Kobus and his company were due to leave for the bush early on Saturday morning for a secret operation on their Buffels. That’s why he was so eager to get me out of circulation and get me married. And now I will see Kobus again only after three months! And, Doc, can you guess what the name of this bloody operation is?"

"No. What is it?"

"It's Operation Honeymoon, of all things. Damn it!"

A Buffel armored troop carrierm built upon a MercedesBenz Unimog chasis

6. EXERCISE CRICKET BALL

Walvis Bay, Wedensday, 1 November 1978

It's almost dark when we both reach our home. Hannelore wants to know: "Were you very busy? Lots of work?"

Me: "Yea. And how!"

"Tell me!"

"Please, give me a chance to wind down. I'm going to get a shower and jump into more comfortable clothes."

Half-an-hour later, I and my lovely wife get seated at the table for the delicious supper she has prepared.

Me: "Okay. You wanted to know whether I was very busy?"

"You looked dead tired when you came home. You're supposed to have had a sports parade on a Wednesday afternoon. What kept you so busy? Sprinting after a soccer ball?"

"No. It was surely the shortest cricket match in the history of the South African Defence Force. Only three balls were played and then the game was stopped and abandoned."

"That couldn't have exhausted you so much? How come?"

"No. It's what happened before the game and then afterwards."

"I'm all ears!"

"It wasn't so bad before the game, actually, except that I had to laugh about it. Everything that happened after the cricket wasn't so pleasant."

"Yes? What made you laugh?"

"I had to go and visit this troop in the sick-bay this morning. The poor chap had a serious case of sunstroke. Dehidration. He lay there with a drip connected to his arm with intrevenous nutrition. He told me what happened to him and his mates. He was with his platoon on a survival exercise in the desert. And then their leader, a one-pip loot[21], lost his compass. And then they hopelessly got lost. They couldn't go back on their tracks because the wind had blown their tracks away."

"Didn't he learn how to determine directions by watching the sun and the stars?"

"The poor boy has forgotten everything that he was taught at the Infantry School. They stumbled around in the dry, desic-cated, and dusty desert. Later, they had no more food. And then the platoon sergeant, actually only a corporal, tells them: 'I have some bad news and some good news for all of us.' All of them want to know what the bad news is. He replies: 'We have no more food. Nothing is left. We will be forced to start eating sand. And here is the good news: There is more than enough for all of us!'"

Lieseltte starts laughing: "And how did these poor guys reach the base again?"

"Three search parties were sent out and they were found at last – miles awayf from the route they were supposed to walk. The worst cases of dehydration were taken to the sick-bay."

"And what happened at your cricket match?"

"Yea... I have this admin assistant and reception lady, Corporal Missus Jackie Kotze. She told me the other day that she played cricket in her high school's cricket team as an opening batsman – or batswoman. She was the only girl between all the boys in that team. Then she wanted to know why we couldn't form a team of the sick-bay personnel and challenge some of the teams on this base. The tiffies,[22] the guys from the workshop, accepted our challenge and a match was scheduled for this afternoon."

"That was when you played only three balls?"

---

[21] "One-pip loot" – a second lieutenant with one star on his shoulder (see the Rank Structure of the SADF at the end of the book).

[22] "Tiffy" – Army slang for a mechanic.

"Just so. Me and Jackie were the opening batsmen after we had won the toss and decided to bat first. The commander of the tiffies, Sergeat Major Sarel Serforntein, better known as Sarel Seemonster[23], is their first bowler. Our umpires are our RSM,[24] Sargeant Major Ertjies Esterhuizen and that English major., Freddy Ferguson-Smythe. Jackie plays the first ball that Sarel Seemonster delivers. It's clear that she knows how to hit hard and she sends that ball directly back to Sarel. He's not fast enough and messes up a catch and the ball hits him full in the face. His nose bleeds and his mouth is filled with blood."

"And then he had to receive first aid, first of all?"

"Yip. The Game is temporarily interrupted and first aid is rendered. But the sargeant major declares that he wants to play further. In the meantime, I and Jackie ran our first run and I am in front of the wickets. The second ball is wide and I and Jackie score another run. For the wide ball, we get an extra run. Our score after only two balls is already three runs. Jackie is again in front of the wickets and the sargeant major delivers yet another ball. And with that ball Jackie scores a six about which stories will be told, long after the match has ended."

"Why?"

"She hits that hard cricket ball very hard and very far. You won't believe it, but she hits the driver of a Buffel troop carrier filled with troops, far away from the cricket field. The ball hits him against the head and he's knocked out. Lights out. Unconscious. Snuffed out

---

[23] "Sarel Seemonster" (Sarel Sea Monster) was a popular character in a TV series for small children.

[24] "RSM" – regimental sergeant major – usually with the rank of a warrant officer, class I.

like a candle. The fool never wore his 'staaldak'[25] – only his soft bush hat."

"Hell! Donnerwetter!"

"And that's not all. Of course, the driver loses control over his vehicle and hits a Samil-20, also filled with troops. The Samil gets overturned and more or less the whole section of troops inside gets hurt. The driver looks worse than all the other guys because the driver's cabin is squashed. And on top of evertything, the Samil bangs against the new BMW of Colonel van Schalkwyk. Fortunately, he wasn't inside his car."

"And the the whole sick-bay team had to attend to all the injured men, of course?"

"Of course. We help the injured boys to get out of the wrecked Samil. The bloody tiffies are only interested in the three vehicle wrecks, the stupid sorry sods. The unconscious driver of the Buffel also has to be taken out, but the ttroops on the Buffel are able to help us with him – only those who didn't get hurt themselves. All of a sudden, the sick-bay is filled with bleeding men or men with broken arms or noses. One of them lost some teeth."

"And that's when you had lots of work that made you so tired? I think we don't need Swapo anymore to eliminate our troops. We do it on our own."

"Yes, you're right, dead right. Later, Major Ferguson-Smythe informs me that he and the RSM have decided to award the game to the tiffies because the team of the sick-bay abandoned the game and absconded, even if they already had nine runs after that superb six that Jackie had hit. Can you believe it!"

"Hell!"

---

[25] "Staaldak" – it can be translated as "roof of steel" – Army slang for a helmet.

"And now, the colonel is blowing fire and smoke because Jackie is such a good cricket player. But he also realizes he can't punish her because it wasn't her fault that the driver of the Buffel didn't wear his 'staaldak'."

7. EXERCISE OCTOPUS

Walvis Bay, Monday, 13 November 1978

Commandant Frans van den Berg, the commander of 2 South African Infantry Battalion (Two SAI) at Walvis Bay, calls a conference this morning at eight with all key personnel – company commanders, section chiefs and staff officers. I am also present in my capacity as chief of the sick-bay. There are also four visitors from far away and I suspect that they arrived by plane yesterday.

The commandant: "Men, we all had a nice and quiet week-end. A busy week is awaiting us, though. Please take note, it will be a jolly busy week with lots of sweat on the head, sand in the hand, and horns on your corns. Army HQ has namely ordered that we conduct a big exercise before one half of our national service-men clear out just before Christmas after two years in uniform.

"Welcome to Exercise Octopus. Don't ask me where Army HQ got this name. Perhaps it's because we aren't far from the sea.

"It's now exactly the right time to start this exercise tomorrow night because it will be full moon. Just the right time for night exercises because we will be able to see what's going on. The weather forecast tells us that we can expect a violent easterly wind. You know what an easterly wind means. Heat and dust storms. That's why I told you that we will sweat and get sand particles between the teeth.

"It also happens that we are at full strength at this moment with all our companies and other sub-units in the base. Delta Company retirned just last week from the Border and Alpha Company must travel to Ovamboland in a fortnight's time.

"I want to introduce to you our four visitors from the Combat Trainung Center at Lohatla. They will be referees or judges and they will decide which troops will be regarded as make-believe casualties

– either killed or wounded and who have to be evacuated. Every man who is declared dead or wounded, will be marked by black crosses on his cheeks so that he can be identified. Every so-called prisoner of war will be marked by a big black circle on each cheek.

On my own, I think: "It seems we're going to play naughts 'n crosses!"

The commandant: "The referees will decide which side performed the cleverest. I introduce to you Commandant Flippie Fourie, Commandant Frans Fouche, Major Bennie Boshoff and Major Bernie Bolton (and he points with his finger at each one). They will be working in two teams to monitor and judge the plans and actions of both opposing sides. They will also see to it that everybody behaves according to the rules of the game. There will be punitive marks for foul play.

"We will have an A Team and a B Team. The A Team are the attackers and the B Team are the defenders. The defenders will be mostly the men who clear our just before Christmas, the old men, in other words. That's Delta Company, Echo Company and Foxtrot Company, together with Three Four Battery of the Artillery and Delta Squadron of the Armor. The attackers will consist of Alpha Company, Bravo Company. Charlie Company and the HQ Company. Each team has, therefore, more or less the strength of a conventional battalion or combat group.

"As commander of the attackers, Major Freddy Ferguson-Smythe of Charlie Company is appointed. Are you ready, Major Freddy?"

"You bet, Commandant."

"The commander of the defenders will be Major Tinus Theron, the 2IC[26] of Two SAI. Major Tinus, can you do it?"

---

[26] "2IC" – Second in Command.

“Any time, Commandant, any time!”

“Each of these two commanders must decide how they are going to deploy their troops and which plans they will draw up. I grant you complete freedom. Let’s see what you can achieve.

“The area in which the simulated battles will be fought is the coastal strip between Walvis Bay and Swakopmund. These two towns are the only places of importance along the coast of South West and should it happen that an enemy force does attack us, it will certainly happen hereabouts. Such a force will only look for trouble by coming ashore at any other spot of the Namib desert along the whole coast of this country.

“The A Team is supposed to have landed by boat somewhere in this area, except that they won’t have any boats. They must decide on their own how they will get onto the beach and where. They may use Samil 20’s and Buffels to get there, but thereafter these vehicles don’t play any role in the exercise. We pretend that they did land with landing craft and that is why they won’t be allowed to play with the Samils and Buffels any longer. To indetify them, the A Team only wear bush hats. Their goal will be to conquor the Rooikop Base.

“The B Team must protect the interior and the base and repell the attackers by shooting them or capturing them. They wear helmets to be identified easily. They may use vehicles to move about – Samils, Buffels, Noddy Cars[27] for the Armor and Landrovers for the recoilles guns of the Artillery.

“Both teams may make use of people from the HQ – signallers, military Police, administrative personnel, storemen and so forth. That is to say, if you do need them and can use them.

“I give you the whole of today and tomorrow to work out your plans, draw supplies and to get your troops ready. The make-

---

[27] “Noddy Car” – nickname for the Eland Armored Car, an adaptation of a French Panhard armored car, usually armed with a 90 mm gun.

believe invasion then takes place tomorrow night, some or other time. The exact time I leave in the hands of Major Ferguson-Smythe. Is that OK, Major Freddy?"

"You bet, Commandant."

"And when you are finally in position, you signal the Ops Room[28] here that the B Team may leave the base. They may not know where you purportely landed and they will have to go and seek you – and try to wipe you out."

Major Ferguson-Smythe sits at attention, stretches by holding his arms straight over his lap and declares: "Will do, Commandant!"

"The exercise continues through the following day, Wednesday. Until one of the teams gets overwhelmed – that's according to the referees. We add the finishing touches during Wednesday afternoon and evening. The area where we operated has to be cleaned up and everybody must be back here at Rooikop at supper time. Thursday is used to clean equipment, to wash vehicles and to do a post mortem. And then we go to bed early on Wednesday night because nobody would have been able to close his eyes the previous night.

"Every group must have a medical team to deal with possible injuries. There is, after all, always a few troops who do stupid things and then get hurt. Of cause, their mates may also get hurt. Doc, get your medics ready and see to it that your blood boxes[29] are serviceable."

Me: "Right, Commandant."

---

[28] "Ops Room" – short for operations room, the headquarters of the base.
[29] "Blood box" – SADF slang for a field ambulance.

"Sargeant Major van der Merwe, do you have enough ratpacks[30] so that each troop can be issued with one for the time he won't be able to eat in the mess?"

Sargeant Major "Vên" van der Merwe: "Commandant, the QM store is full. We also have enough beer for the barbecue afterwards. There are more than enough thunder flashes and blanks and illumination flares for the troops to make some loud bangs and to illuminate the world so that it may look and sound like World War Three or Armageddon."

"Okay, Sargeant Major, we needn't simulate Armageddon this week. Anyway, you mentioned the barbecue. That will be on Thursday night after the end of the exercise and the battle was won – by whomever – and everybody is back in the base and had some rest. Sargeant Major, you must see to it in good time that there is enough provisions for Wednesday evening because the troops will be hungry after all the action."

"Right, Commandant."

Captain Wollie Wolmarans, commander of Alpha Company, gets up and asks: "Commandant, what will happen with the civvy trafic during the time we are fucking each other up? If our lot are attacking from the beach and the Bravo Team is ready to hammer and smash us and make mash of us, then all the action will be exactly on both sides of the coastal road. How are we going to prevent the civvies with their cars and trucks and motor bikes not to get caught in the cross-fire? It won't do to stop the war each time as an old lady in her jalopy comes cruising along."

"Captain, it's a good thing that you ask that question. I have already spoken to the South Wesr African Police and the traffic cops. All the traffic between Walvis and Swakopmund will be rerouted to

---

[30] "Ratpacks" – boxes containing rations for at least one day.

the road behind the dunes, the road next to the railroad track. That means that all the action is to take place on the western side of the ridge of dunes. That's on the area between the dunes and the sea. You may use the road next to the railway line, but only on condition that you don't interfere with the civilian traffic in any way."

While I leave the conference room, I remember that the two commanders of the opposing teams cannot bear each other. Freddy Ferguson-Smythe is a stiff aristocratic Englishman who is proud of his grandfather who was a British major general during the Second World War. Majoor Tinus Theron has the nickname of "Shell-Shock". It is his favorite expression that he uses all the time and that became his nickname. Some troops transformed that to "Shout-Shock" and "Shit-Shock" because of his habit of critizing everybody and everything with a loud voice. He regulaly uses very spicy language and can often be very rude – in contrast with the aristocratic Ferguson-Smythe who always behaves himself very correctly, never swears and who is always painfully neatly dressed. I can imagine that these two are eager to outwit each other with this exercise. The referees may perhaps even decide which one of the two qualifies for promotion.

Major Ferguson-Smythe waits for me outside the conference room: "Doc, I want to reserve you now as a member of my A Team. Your side-kick can lead the medics of the B Team. We are going to retire to the HQ of Charlie Company right now to get our plans ready."

"Right, Major. Will do. I must go to the sick-bay, first of all, to tell my people about the exercise and to make sure that my assistant knows that he will be the doctor for the B Team."

I am grateful for this arrangement because I get along much better with Ferguson-Smythe than with Major Shell-Shock or Shit-Shock.

While I reach Major Ferguson-Smythe's office a little later, I am joined by a group of other men – three other company commanders, company Sargeant Majors, and platoon commanders.

The major informs all theose present about the manoevers awaiting us, as explained to us by the commandant. He takes in position in front of a map of Walvis Bay and vicinity: "Men, here is the area in which we are going to operate and attack the other team, here between Walvis Bay and Swakopmund. I think I know how we can manage things in order to outfox the B Team. I will discuss all the finer points with the company commanders afterwards. And also with you, Doc. You know something about warfare with those parabat wings on your shirt.

"Gentlemen, you all know that the big secret of warfare rests upon two legs – the surprise element and attack at the enemy's weakest point. We must figure out how we are going to do it. For the surprise element, one has to be mobile and fast so that your enemy doesn't expect you at a certain spot. This also depends upon measures to mislead your opponent so that he expects something different from what will really happen. One has to have good intelligence about your enemy to identify his weak points. Fortunately, we know the people against whom we must wage war. We will have to guess what type of plans they will concoct and how they will move.

"We will have the initiative because we will be the attackers. The other team can only react to what we are doing. That provides us with a nice advantage. We must imagine ourselves in the position of the other team and calculate how they they will deploy their men. And then we may see how we can lure them into a tasty and tantalizing and tempting trap, or something of the sort. Do I make myself clear?"

All the heads nod affirmatively and a few grunt "Yes".

"If I were Major Theron, I would establish observation posts on various points on the dunes behind the beach – that is, after we have supposedly landed on the beach and got dug in. Perhaps also somebody on top of Rooikop Hill, here next to the base. And, of course, on Dune 7, the highest point in the area. These spotters will certainly be transported on the road behind the dunes to prevent us from seeing them. Every OP will certainly have a radio, night sight equipment and binoculars to see where we have been concentrated. And then they will have to establish comms with Major Theron to inform him what they are seeing and then he will send his troops to that point to get us in a vice grip. Do you agree, that's what Major Theron is most likely to do?"

Everybody agrees.

"He will certainly leave an element at this base to guard this place and to deter us from capturing the place if we could succeed in breaking out of his grip. Do you agree that is what he will do?"

We all agree once again.

"All right. Now we have a good idea regarding the possible plans of the B Team and how Major Theron's brains will grind out a strategy. The question is now: how are we going to surprise them? Where are we going to exploit their weak points? Do you agree that is what we have to deal with this next?"

All heads nod affirmatively and most men smile.

"I want to reorganize our companies somewhat. We are going to operate in two groups. The sipport company with its mortar platoon, LMG[31] platoon, and the assault pioneers is part of the one group. The rest of this group will consist of troops who are not very fit. The second group must consist of men who are strong and fit, who can move far and fast without allowing their tongues to drag on

[31] LMG – light machine gun.

the desert sand. They will be our surprise element. They will be strengthened by the anti-tank platoon of the HQ Company with their RPG-7 rockets. We are not allowed to use vehicles, but then wheeled vehicles are not really suited for travelling on the soft and smothering sand of the desert or through the mud of the wetlands just outside town, at the bird sanctuary. These will be men who move on foot, are more mobile in these circumstances. Howe does that sound? Do you agree that is what we must do?"

We all smile and growl: "Yes!"

"Doc, you're a parabat. You are frightfully fit and fast. You leave all the wounded troops, dead corpses, disabled deserters, paralyzed persons and cripled casualties in the care of your medics. I give you an expanded section of all the best athletes and you will be given a special job. Right so?"

"Gee whiz, Major! OK. I'm ready. Just tell me what I must do."

"We will get to that. Later."

"Thanks."

"Our first task will be to divide the two groups. One group consists of most of the HQ Company and a company consisting of all the unfit men, all of those who are not G1K1. That's the men with spectacles. The overweight men. The men with diabetes, lung cancer, heart problems, and psychiatric disorders or whatever. Let's call them the X-Ray Company. The other two companies become Yankee Company and Zulu Copany. They are the fit and strong men. The three company commanders, me and the commanders of Alpha and Bravo Companies, will assemble our troops and mix and scramble ans reorganize the companies before we leave tomorrow night. Doc, you are with us at that time so that we can provide you with an expanded section of top athletes who will be selected there and then. More or less fifteen or sixteen men.

"After that, we can inform the troops about what is expected of them before we get onto the vehicles. If we do it today, our plans will certainly get leaked – and we don't want that. It must only happen tomorrow. Do tou agree?"

Everybody smiles and says 'yes", except for me.

Me: "Major, may I suggest that we mix and reinvent the companies only after we have left the base? It's possible that the other team may see what we are doing and then guess what our strategy will be."

"Makes sense, yes, it makes sense. The men must get onto the vehicles here and we stop at the other end of the town to perform the reorganization and jumblng there."

A lot later, I return to the sick-bay to inform my assistant, Lieutenant (Doctor) Giles Groenewald, a national serviceman, and the medics and other personnel about our tasks.

Afterwards, I ask my admin-assistant, Corporal Jackie Kotze, to come to my consulting room: "Jackie, you've had basic training, if I'm not mistaken?"

"Yes, Doc. I know everything about marching. I can also shoot with a rifle if it's necessary."

"Have you ever worked with radio's?"

"Doc, yes, I know the radio alphabet: Alpha, Bravo, Charlie, Delta, Echo, Foxtrot, Gholf, and so forth."

"But do you know how to tune a radio to the right frequency? Can you make comms[32]?"

"That was also part of basics at George.[33]"

"Have you ever used night sight equipment?"

"We were also trained in George with that."

---

[32] "Comms" – communications.

[33] Female members of the SA Army were trained at the Women's Training College at the town of George.

"Wonderful. How far can you count? From one to one hundred?"

"Up to ten million. Just give me enough time."

"We don't have so much time. Annyway, you won't get much sleep Tuesday night, if any. Kobus, you husband who is the second-in-command of his company, won't be at home for a short period of time, as I have explained to you all. He is part of the attacking team. And you are going to help him and that means that you won't be sleeping during the night from Tuesday to Wednesday, either."

"Ooooh! What must I do?" She giggles excitedly.

"You're going to be my spy in this base. Also Major Ferguson-Smyth's spy. He's in command of the team of attackers. Your call sign is Juliet Kilo Zero. Your initials. My call sign is Mike Sierra One. That's the abrecviation for Number One of the Medical Section. Do you have that?"

"Fantastic. It sounds like fun!"

"You will tell us how many men are left behind in the base to look after the place when the rest move out to attack the attackers on the beach. You will let us know where they are taking up positions."

"Must I flirt a little bit with them to divert their attention from any attackers who may come in this direction?"

"Hell, no! Kobus will most certainly strangle you to a slow and painful death if you do something like that."

"May I tell Kobus that I am going to be a spy?"

"Hell's bells, no! Spies work in secret. Nobody must know they are spies, except for their contacts. That's me and the major. Can you keep your mouth shut?"

"That will be extremely difficult. We women like to babble and gossip. But I will keep these lips of mine tightly glued together.

I may even insert a zipper between my lips. Doc, will you make me a sergeant if I'm a good spy?"

Walvis Bay, Tuesday, 14 November 1978

During the late afternoon, just before sunset, the troops belonging to the attacking team assemble on the parade ground – each one kitted out with his fire-arm and a rucksack contianing water bottles, a ratpack and a sleeping bag.

Major Ferguson-Smythe roars: "All right, men. Get onto the vehicles!"

All of us mount the Buffels and Samils, section for section and depart from the base. We enter the town of Walvis Bay and turn right onto the coastal road in the direction of Swakopmund. Directly after the last houses of the town, the convoy stops and all of us get assembled next to the road. The companies get scrambled and stirred and reorganized into three new companies – out of sight of anybody at the base at Rooikop. I get my bunch of a dozen super fit athletes – mostle members of the first rugbt team of the base.

The four newly constituted companies get each a spot to get comfortable on the desert sand, a short distance away from the road. It's the major's plan that we all get a few hours' sleep before the "attack" is actually to take place. He wishes to do his thing with rested troops. In the meantime, we are sure, the B Team will stay awake the whole night so as to be ready to move out at any momnent, as soon as they get the signal to pursue us. They will, therefore, already be tired when they have to grapple and wrestle with us.

I get Jackie on the radio and ask: "Mike Sierra One here. What is going on over there, Julliet Kilo Zero?"

"All of them look extremely bored. They stand around, waiting for better times. Some of them have already smoke their tenth cigarette of the night."

Walvis Bay, Wednesday, 15 November 1978

It's still dark at three o' clock, apart from the full moon, and Major Ferguson-Smythe blows his whistle to wake up everybody. He gives everybody thirty minutes to make some coffee and then to get onto the vehicles according to their new companies to get deployed on the beach.

It's twenty-to-four when we depart and a quarter of an hour later the two companies with fit men and my tem of top athletes are download at Long Beach, the piece of beach directly north of the harbor in the bay. The rest of the attackers, the men with disabilities, together with the supporting company with its mortars, machine guns, and assault pioneers, have to be dropped just before Swakopmund on the beach – as far away as possible from Walvis Bay to give them enough time to get dug in before the defenders come to grips with them. They have been ordered to behave in such a manner that the OP's of the "enemy" can see them where they are getting dug in on the beach.

Just when the vehicles return afer having dropped the men at the furthest point, Major Ferguson-Smythe sends a message to the Ops Room at the base that the "landing" has just taken place. And now we wait that the B Team gets moving. The drivers of our vehicles are ordered to move about 500 meters beyond the point where the road to the base branches off and to park at an open field inside the town. The drivers have to come back as fast as possible and join the companies with fit men. These companies must then run towards the bird sanctuary just outside the town and hide themselves between the reeds of the area and make themselves invisible.

The major makes sure that one of the referees moves into hiding with the two companies with the fit men. The other referee was left with the group near Swakopmund.

From Jackie I get the message that the defenders have just left the base. Right in front, there are two armored cars and two Buffels and they are followed at a distance by the rest of the vehicles. She will be able to tell me how many men stayed behind at a later stage.

It has to be assumed that the first four vehicles carry the men who have to establish observation posts on top of the dunes, together with a protective element.

After having informed the major of Jackie's news, I and my team start in the direction of the base, but not along the road. We move through the desert and pass the foot of Dune 7 to reach a point north of the Air Force base to approach Rooikop hill from behind. The distance from the point on Long Beach where we started to our objective is nine or ten kilometers.

On our way, I establish comms with Jackie again. She informs me that two platoons stayed behind in the base. They stood at attention on the parade ground to receive orders where she could see them clearly and count them. There are about sixty-five men with the 2IC of their company in command. They stand guard at the gate or march in pairs outside the base to keep the place safe.

We succeed in reaching our destination, the foot of Rooikop hill, after ninety minutes of hard marching and jogging over the soft desert sand. I call Jackie again: "Do you know if there are any guards on top of Rooikop hill?"

"Yes, Doc, two men went up there."

"Dammit, don't use names over the air!"

"Sorry, Doc."

I decide to ignore Jackie's little mistake. It's unlikely that somebody is watching our frequency.

All thirteen of us ascend Rooikop from the back side just when the day starts breaking in the east. Suddenly, we see fireworks and hear loud bangs from the direction of Swakopmund. It's clear that the combat group of Major Shit-Shock started to attack our men. I doubt whether the B Team can come out of the scrap without scratches, because the two companies on the beach were supposed to spread out on both sides of the coastal road. The vehicles of Major Shout-Shock's team would, therefore, have ridden into some sort of a trap or an ambush.

My team climbs Rooikop Hill in the light of the moon, as silently as possible. About ten meters from the top, we stop and I and one of the men, Second Lieutenant Chris Carstens, slide slowly nearer to see where the two guards are. We pass the water tower on top on both sides. The two chaps who are supposed the stand guard are fast asleep with their backs against the water tank. We kick them awake and we make gestures as if we are cutting their throats.

"All right, guys, you are now officially, totally, and finally dead. Killed. Exterminated and terminated. You are no longer involved in this exercise. You remain seated where you are, just like dead corpses and don't do anything anymore. Give me your radio and fire-arms and other equipment. Come, sit quietly so that I can draw black crosses on your cheeks."

Next, I inform Major Ferguson-Smythe that we have occupied Rooikop hill and that we can observe the whole base below us.

Somewhat later, the "battle" at this side of Swakopmund has ended and the major informs me that our men have managed to "kill" or "wound" about half of the members of the B Team. The A Team surrendered, though, after having "lost" many men and because their ammo got used up. The whole lot of them are now travelling back to the base on the vehicles of the B Team. But they still have to go past the bird sanctuary with its ambush …

This is the signal that I and my team must leave the hill and occupy the base.

Daylight has arrived and we hear loud explosions and illumination flares being shot into the air from the direction of the bird sanctuary. The B Team entered a trap and they are being shot at from two directions.

Our first task is to disarm the ten men guarding the gate, to mark their cheeks with black circles and to lock them up in the troops' mess. One of my men guards them to prevent them from escaping. I creep to the Ops Room where I switch the base's siren on for a few seconds. Thereafter, I get onto the public address system of the base: "All the troops outside the base, return immediately! Repeat: all men return immediately! Report at the Ops Room!"

In the meantime, the remaining eleven men of my team take up positions just inside the gate, under command of Lieutenant Carstens. They keep their rifles ready.

While the men from outside return in drips and drabs, they are systematically captured and disarmed. When all of them have been taken prisoner and marked, I inform Major Ferguson-Smythe that the base belongs to us.

In the meantime, my spy, Corporal Jackie, joined me with big bright eyes.

"Jackie, without your help we would never have been able to capture the base. You were wonderful. Thank youm very much."

She giggles: "It was a pleasant job. I was able to move between the men who stayed behind and they never thought that I was the spy of the A Team. May I tell Kobus now?"

"Only tomorrow at the barbecue that will be held. Then Major Ferguson-Smythe may perhaps mention your name as a valuable member of the attacking team."

A quarter of an hour later, all the vehicles of the B Team enter the base with laughing members of the A Team who shout at me: "The lot of them were shot rather quite dead. We captured their trucks and Buffels and now all those disarmed corpses must march back to the base while getting blisters on their feet! And we liberated all their POW's and we could remove the black marks from their faces."

I congratulate them.

After more than an hour a long column of "prisoners", "wounded" and "fallen" members of the B Team reach the base under the watchful eyes of a few guards. They are the members of the B Team who were overwhelmed at the ambush. By this time, the expected easterly wind from the interior started to blow and that causes a suffocating and stinging sand storm. The poor "prisoners", "wounded" and "fallen" of the B Team pulled handkerchiefs, shirts and underwear over their heads to keep the most unwelcome sand from their eyes, noses, ears, and mouths.

Major Shit-Shock is one of those who was captured and marked with two big black spots on this cheeks. When he notices me, he charges like an angry bull at me: "Doc, you were not supposed to take part in the battle. You must have stayed with your ambulance. I feel like hitting your fucking head off your bloody body."

Major Ferguson-Smythe intervenes: "We haven't broken any rules. The commandant pertinently said that we may use people from the HQ. If you can't behave yourself, I will ask the Meat Pies[34] to handcuff you and keep you in the DB until you can be court martialled."

Commandant Fourie, the leader of the team of referees, steps nearer: "Major, you had better acknowledge that your team was beaten fairly and squarely. You came a very bad second. Now, listen to sound advice and keep yourself in check."

I locate my assistant, Giles Groenewald, and ask him how many real injured men there were.

"Only one man who broke an arm.There he sits in my ambulance."

During the afternoon, friend and foe jump again onto some vehicles to clean up the battlefields and to fetch the parked vehicles in town. We are amazed to find a few men of the supporting company who are still holding their position on the beach. One of them has a machine gun and the other holds a 81 mm mortar pipe.

Their leader explains: "We were so well dug in that the B Team never saw us and never caught us. And then the whole bloody lot drove off without us. And now we sit around on this beach and wait for better days. I hope nobody will think that we went AWOL."

---

[34] "Meat Pies" – Army slang for Military Policemen or MP's.

Another troop smiles: "You guys could have left us here. We are having a lovely holiday, here on the beach. We only miss a few bikini-clad girls here. That would have made this whole exercise the climax of my national service!"

Walvis Bay, Thursday, 16 November 1978

Commandant Fourie, the leader of the team of referees or judges, takes the word just before the whole of Two SAI starts supper with the barbecued steaks:

"Commandant van den Berg and all the members of Two SAI, thank you for a pleasureable reception that we received from you. There cannot be the slightest doubt that Major Ferguson-Smythe was by far the best commander of his troops. We are unanimous in our opinion that a great future awaits him in the military world. We recommend that he be admitted to a course for unit commanders at the School of Infantry at Oudtshoorn next year. His employment of the surprise element and misleading of his opponent was right out of the manual. He relied on good intelligence.

"The wooden spoon is awarded to Major Theron. We hope that he hasn't contracted serious shell-shock from this episode. What we find surprising, is that he didn't realize that there were still two companies hiding somewhere after he had captured the two companies on the beach. It was evidently his plan to lock up his prisoners and then go out again to hunt the rest and hoped that his

OP's on the dunes would tell him where they were – and then he was caught in a classic ambush.

"Special mention must be made of Lieutenant (Doctor) Scholtz who succeeded in taking over this base with only an extended section while the men were battling each other elsewhere. It's not too bad for a medical officer. He admits that he wouldn't have achieved anything if he hadn't planted a spy here in the base. Any successful military action depends upon accurate intelligence. Corporal Jackie Kotze, the wife of Lieutenant Kobus Kotze, was the Doc's spy. I hope her husband gives her a smack of a kiss to congratulate her.

"Its clear that Corporal Jackie is a girl who one cannot tackle without gloves. She certainly was the octopus of Exercise Octopus."

All the men whistle and give applause – except for Major Shell-Shock who sits with an angry scowl on his face. Lieutenant Kobus Kotze gives his wife a hug and a smack of a kiss and that causes more whistles and applause from the men.

After we have eaten, Jackie approaches me where I am talking to Commandant Fourie. After I have introduced her to the commandant, she says: "Commandant, the identity of spies have actually to be kept a secret. After all, they work in secret to uncover the secrets of the enemy. You have endangered my life now by disclosing my identity. Until toninght, not even my husband knew that I was the Doc's spy."

"I'm sorry. I apologize."

"Something else, Commandant. I wondered, what are we going to do if a dozen terrorists of Swapo landed here somewhere to sow amuck and start to kill people, as they regularly do in Ovamboland? Will we be able to stop them? I am sure they have spies all over the place here and that they have their tentacles all over the place with lost of friends. Just like an octopus with its eight arms."

"Corporal, would you like to follow an officer's course to become an intelligence officer? Some of the most successful spies in history were women."

"OK. That sounds exciting. But will that mean that I will have to jump into bed with the enemy's generals to hear their secrets and plans? My husband will throttle me to a slow and painful and cruel death if I have to do that."

8. OPERATION OXYGEN

Etale, Ovamboland, Monday, 8 July 1979

It is impossible not to feel lonely without my wife, here where I am sitting in a company base – Etale, not far from the border between South West and Angola.

My lovely wife, who completed her house docotr's year as medical practitioner in Swakopmund, was transferred to the state hospital in Oshakati, Ovemboland, at the beginning of this year. Fortunately, my outoppie, a retired brigadier in the Surgeon General's office, knew enough people in the personnel section and he could arrange a transfer for me to the sick-bay at the military base at Oshakati, officially known as 10 Field Hospital, where I am deployed as a medical officer. This arrangement works very well because the state hospital is directly across the road from the main entrance to the Army base.

We find this set-up financially advantageous. We live in a military house in a Defence Force base and we receive "danger pay" because we live and work inside the Operational Area.

Oshakati's Army base is the headquarters of Sector One Zero and this sector comprises the whole of Ovamboland. It is the busiest secctor in the whole of South West because the terrorists of Swapo's military wing, PLAN, concentrate mainly on specifically this area to sow evil and mayhem with their insurgents.

During December last year, I said good-bye to the military base at Walvis Bay. The occasion was also the farewel to Warrant Officer Ertjies Esterhuizen who retired. He was the regimental sergeant major or RSM. I believe his farewell words at the farewell ceremony will be remembered for a long time. He declared: "Commandant, when people ask me nowadays how I am, I can immediately reply: 'My point is pointing into the wind, but unfortuantely, there's also wind in my point!"

The office of the Surgeon General became a separate part of the Defence Force last week and it is now known as the South African Medical Service. This is a new service branch, independent from the Army, Air Force, and Navy. Only a week after the new dispensation came into effect, Commandant (Doctor) Flip Venter, the commander of the sick-bay at Oshakati, informed me that I had to relieve the medical officer at Etale for a month. This is a base near the border and it lies next to the road to the north. It often happens that units moving to or from Angola on that road, spend a night at Etale. The quack there is, therefore, often rather busy. Unfortunately, the doctor – of all people! – forgot to swallow his malaria pills and now he lies here in the sick-bay at Oshakati with malaria. Amd now I must take his place.

Therefore, I am now far away from my wonderful wife. She accepted the situation stoically and said: "We Germans here in South West are tough. We can deal with anything!"

I report to the commander of Etale, Captain Danny Claasen and he leads a company from Number Three South African Infantry Battalion from Potchefstroom. He is a pleasant guy, but the company sergeant major, or CSM, Warrant Officer Ockie Olivier, is a devil of a man – especially because he suddenly doesn't have any authority over my medical orderly, Lance Corporal Louis Lancaster. Since the day that the Medical Service became a separate branch of the Defence Force, Lancaster decided that he could not be bothered by the barking and swearing of the CSM anymore.

It doesn't take long before I dicover that I landed within a difficult situation. I make myself at home in the medical tent, which I share with Lancaster. After I have unpacked my things and organized everything, I start a conversation with the medic.

"Doc, do you see that fenced-off piece of land in front of our tent? That's civvie territory. Nobody who's standing there, is allowed to salute. It doesn't belong to the Army. Saluting is strictly forbidden! The same applies to the interior of this tent. It's medical territory."

Etale base, Sector 10

"Who said that?"

"Doc Hamilton, your predecessor. He explained that the Medical Service is no longer part of the Army. We are now our own boss. The Army cannot shunt us around anymore."

I decide to keep the status quo for the time being and wait to see how things develop.

During supper, all the men are wearing their browns – but not Lancaster. He's wearing shorts and a T-shirt. There are thunder clouds on the CSM's face, but he seems to realize that he is powerless.

After we have returned to our tent, Louis introduces me to his brother: "Doc, this is Lance, my twin brother. He's the store man. He can find anything you may need and get it for you."

"How does he manage that?"

"He's a Lancaster. We both are known as Magician Number One and Magician Number Two. We are not going to divulge our secrets. Let me show you everything that Lance has scored for us."

He shows me a big fridge. I open the fridge. On one shelf there are a number medicine bottles and the rest of the space is taken up with soda drinks and beer. The freezer is filled with ice cubes in trays.

"We sell this on he sly. At a profit. The troops may only drink it here, otherwise the CSM will confiscate it all. But he has no say here. We are the Medical Service."

I ask: "How did you manage to get into the same base?"

Lance answers: "Oh, that was easy. I was initially a driver – in a convoy en route to Angola. I have already heard the most horrible stories about the bad road conditions. My convoy stays in this place for a night and I ask the store man whether we can exchange places. Louis organizes also with the previous doc that I be declared G3K3 – unfit for active duty in enemy territory."

"Hoe did you manage that?"

"I tell the doc that I am deaf in my left ear. I can't hear anything on that side. He tests my hearing. And really, suddenly I can't hear anything on that side. Not a thing."

Louis: "And that's how my brother joined me. Nobody can prove that he's not deaf in one ear. Now he's officially a G3K3."

I can't help to laugh: "You earned your names. Magician Number One and Magician Bumber Two. Who's Number One?"

Louis: "I am. I was here first. He came afterwards."

Etale, Ovamboland, Tuesday, 10 July 1979

The daily prayer parade is being held at eight and the chaplain takes care of that. The officers assemble on one side and I look at the rows of troops to see where my medic is. I can't see him. When

I return to our tent, I find him busy at the medicine locker.

"And why weren't you at the prayer parade?"

"That's only for the Army. I'm a medic."

"The chaplain is here for all of us. Tomorrow, you are going to be there with a clean uniform, the same as me. And I request you in a friendly manner to get dressed in clean browns for the brunch at ten and supper at six."

"OK, Doc. If you say so. How about a Coke? Ice cold."

I pay willingly for my cold drink because I am rather thirsty.

Shortlky afterwards, a troop arrives at our tent after he had bumped his head against an iron bar and the blood flows from an open wound. Louis says: "Doc, you're the anethetist. I will treat the wound and do the stitching. You give him his pain shots and then I will take over."

Louis' skill is amazing. After he has shaved the troop's hair very neatly, he cleans and disinfects the wound. Finally, he closes the gash with delicate stitches.

"You impress me. Where did you learn to work so neatly?

"My dear mother. She's a teacher. Domestic science. Her forte is neadle work."

"Louis, have you ever thought of becoming a surgeon?"

"Yes, often. I battled to become a medic. They wanted to make a signaller out of me, but I put up such a racket that they transferred me. I hope I will be able to pay for my studies one day by working as a waiter."

"I'm sure you will be a very good doctor."

Etale, Ovamboland, Wednesday, 18 July 1979

CSM Olivier stops at the entrance to the medical tent and salutes me. I get up, walk out and take a stand outside the the little fenced-off area. There I reciprocate the CSM's saltue while I hve to control myself not to laugh.

"Sergeant Major, I don't know which one of us two is correct, but I think I have to maintain the arrangement of my predecessor that saluting is not allowed outside or inside this tent. That's why I got out to stand here."

"Doc, I can't help it. I must uphold all the rules – and these rules also concern the Medical Service. I salute all officers, including those of the Air Frce and the Police and the Prison Service."

"All right, then. You keep on saluting but don't expect me to reply with a salute when I'm here. We parabats are also sometimes upstairs and we bend the rules sometimes."

"Doc, I'm actually here to thank you. You managed to convince that medic of yours to get dressed properly. He even stood at attention this morning when he spoke to me."

Dirctly after brunch, the two Lancasters approach me. Lance speaks: "Doc, tomorrow is Thursday. Then we must go to Ondangwa to fetch supplies. Coming with us?"

"Yes, please."

"Doc, okay/ You must be ready just after the prayer parade. We are taking two Samil Twenties with a squad as body guards. My driver's licence is still valid and I drive one of the trucks."

Etale, Ovamboland, Thursday, 19 July 1979

In Ondangwa, I visited my colleague in the sick-bay while my medic and his brother, the store man, did their work to get supplies. The section troops that escorted us must do all the loading. And now we are back at Etale. Two troops carry the boxes with the medical supplies for Lance Coorporal Lancaster into the medical tent. When he starts to unpack everything before storing it, I ask him to show me what he got. My mouth hangs open from amazement.

"Lancaster, how in hell did you manage to procure all this stuff? Black market? You are better equipped that many state hospitals."

"Doc, that's my secret. You must know the right people and do them some favors. Then you get anything you want or need. I believe I have the best dispensary of all the bases here on the Border. You must also see what Lance brought back. Boxes full of ice cream powder. Toningt, the base will guzzle ice cream. He also brought a bottle or two of whiskey for the captain. Tonight the captain will entertain us again with all the songs he knows."

"It seems as if you can perform magic."

"That's not all. Lance also begged three lumps of rump steak for the three of us from the kitchen in Ondangs and we grill those tomorrow night. With beer."

"Louis, I think that you and your brother will get ahead in life. You know how to look after yourself. Beware, though, that you don't get involved with illegal things, because you will be caught."

"Doc, me and Lance must look after our mom one day when she's old and she cannot look after herself anymore. Our father ran away when we were still small. She only has the two of us. We can't look after our mom if we sit behind bars. So – it's the straight and narrow road for us."

"Lancaster, with men like you we can't lose the war – even if you sometimes make your own rules."

Etale, Ovamboland, Thursday, 26 July 1979

Supper today contains pleasant surprises. We are fed steak with a mushroom sauce and each man receives two pancakes with cinamon suger afterwards. Everybody is delighted with the change in rhe cooking skills of the kitchen staff.

Afterwards, I ask Louis: "Did you have anythinbg to do with the fact that we had this most delicious menu tonight? I think I can detect something of your activities."

"No, Doc. Lance is the man who did most in this regard."

"Tell me."

"You see, we were joined by a squad of campers a week ago. You must have noticed them. Old men who did their initial national service a few years ago. We needed a mortar squad to handle our 81 millimeter mortar in the mortar pit and these men turned up. They were supposed to stay in the base the whole time and never go out on foot patrols. They got extremely bored. Their corporal, Callie Calitz, requested to go on orders to the captain. He complained that the food in this place taste like shit and he and his men volunteer to do kitchen service. According to him, preparing food is second nature because he claims he owns a restaurant in civvie street – which is, of course a lie, but the captain doesn't need to know it. I find him two cookery books at the sick-bay in Ondangs. So the mortar boys become cooks and they conspire with Lance to have all sorts of extras to be delivered from Ondangs."

"And that's how we got this most delicious supper toninght?"

"Yip. Tomorrow night we will get custard slices for pudding."

"How will that happen?"

"Lance brought them a dozen ostrich eggs and a few other goodies this afternon, including a few liters of fresh cream. They used one half of these giant eggs to bake pancakes. Tomorrow the rest will be used to manufacture custard slices."

"Well, well."

"And we will have a choice. Custard slices with brandy sauce or whiskey sauce!"

Etale, Ovamboland, Thursday, 2 August 1979

The twins departed this morning with their escort and again without me to fetch supplies from Ondangwa. They return during the late afternoon and Louis invites me to see what he has brought.

"Doc, here is something that can save lives. I'm sure you will like it. It will be very usefull, I'm sure."

He removes a cloth from a trolly with two wheels on which a sylinder is affixed. With a proud smile, he announces: "This is a supply of Oh-Two. For seriously wounded guys – to keep them alive longer until they can be operated upon."

"Oxygen? Really? Where is the coupling for the patient's nose or mouth?"

"Here. In this bag on this side. Wonderful, isn't it?"

"You really are a magician. Where dit you get it?"

"Doc, the secret of success in life is to have networks. You must know the right people."

Oshakati, Ovamboland, Sunday, 7 October 1979

It's already two months since I've left Etale and the impossible twins, but in a certain sense I still miss them. It is, though, much, much more pleasant to have my loving, glorious German wife with me.

It's Sunday today and it's my turn to handle emergency cases at the sick-bay in Oshakati. After all, the war doesn't care whether it is a week-end or a holiday. More or less at eleven I hear a helicopter landing on the landing spot next to the sick-bay. Three of my medics run out to go and help. Five minutes later they are back. One of them opens doors and the other two help to carry a stretcher. Next to the second medic who carries the stretcher, I see my old friend, Louis Lancaster. He pulls an oxygen cylinder on wheels along. The oxygen mask covers the face of the patient and I can't, therefore, see his face.

Aerial photograph of the sick-bay (aka 10 Field Hospital) at Oshakati with the heli pad in the background

Louis calls out when he sees me: "Doc! Scrubs!"

I jump to disinfect myself and to put on sterile operation overalls. Louis joins me and does the same.

"What happened?"

"Shooting accident. In the chest. A stupidsod, a fucking fool was cleaning his rifle without removing the round from the chamber. And then he pulls the trigger – and this is the result."

In the operating theater I start preparations to remove the bullet from the patient's chest. To Louis, next to me, I say: "You can stitch the wound afterwards. You do it better than I do."

While I inspect the wound to decide on the best way to remove the bullet, I notice that the patient's heart has stopped beating and that he doesn't breathe anymore – in spite of the oxygen. I remove the oxygen mask and look into the lifeless eyes of Lance Lancaster.

9. EXERCISE LAND MINE

Concor Base, Tuesday, 8 January 1980

It is again necessary for me to do substitute work – this time at the Concor base in the area of Five One Battalion with its headquarters at Ruacana. I arrived last Friday as a passenger on a Samil 20 truck as part of a convoy en route to Ruacana.

A young doctor doing his national service was stationed here but he became naughty by looking for sexual favors from some of the troops. That caused an untenable situation and he was transferred somewhere else. I was sent here in his place on short notice.

Concor base during the 1980's. The medical tent is on he far right of the photo. Behind it are the ablution blocks with the water tower. The tent on the left was occupied by the chaplain. The outlook post on top of the scaffolding was called the "Aapkas" (Monkey Cage). The scaffolding doubled as a radio antenna and the headquarters tent was directly next to it.

It is a company base with about one hundred and fifty members. The base wasbuilt about a year ago to giard the important water purifying plant neerby. The commander is Major Danny du Rand and he was relieved to welcome to his base a professional medical officer with parabat wings and a member of the Permanent Force. He even suggested that I accompany one of the platoons when they patrol the open stretch along the border with Angola to pick up the tracks of insurgents. It is now the rainy season and there is enough water for the terrorists when they try to slip into Ovamboland. Patrols all along the border are supposed to pick up their tracks and pursue them on foot or on vehicles.

The major explains that his men are at Concor since last July and that they have already scored a number of heads – that's how he calls the fallen terrorists. I seriously consider the possibility of joining such a hike because I love my sports – running and parachute jumping. During the few days I was here, there was no need to perform any medical work. The troops are healthy and the hygiene in he camp is adequate.

This afternoon, a Landrover (called a Garry by the troops) arrived and a captain and a sergeant got out. Major du Rand sends a troop to call me and introduces me to Captain (Doctor) Swanepoel and Sergeant Swanevelder.

"Doc, is it possible that our guests can sleep with you in your tent toninght? I don't have any other accomodation for them."

"They are welcome, of course – especially because both of them are pill tiffies[35]. Are there cots for them?"

I look at Swanepoel: "Colleague, what is the reason for your visit? Why are we honored in this way?"

Major du Rand replies on their behalf: "They are here to give our troops some guidance regarding the dangers of land mines and the necessity to fasten their seat belts when they travel on a Buffel."

---

[35] "Tiffie" – Army slang for a mechanic. A "pill tiffie", therefore, is a member of a medical team who "repairs" the troops with pills.

Me: “That’s certainly necessary. I have treated quite a number of men at the sick-bay in Oshakati who were not properly fastened while travelling on Buffels or other vehicles that detonated land mines. Some of those men lost fingers, feet, teeth, toes, and even noses and necks.”

After supper, after it became dark, all the troops in the base at this moment are ordered to proceed to the parade ground and to sit down. A large white sheet is hung between two trees and Sergeant Swanevelder operates the slide projector. Doctor Swanepoel does the talking.

“Men, what I’m going to show you will perhaps save your lives. You are aware that Swapo has the ugly and nasty and filthy habit of planting land mines in places where they suspect that members of the Defence Force will pass with vehicles. When such a land mine goes bang beneath a Buffel or a Samil, the vehicle is thrown into the air. If the men in those vehicles are not fastened properly, they are also shot into the air. They don’t have parachutes to give them soft landings and they often get hurt rather badly when they come down again.”

He describes the types of land mines used by Swapo, which the Soviet Union donates to them, and Sergeant Swanevelder shows some pictures of these land mines. Swanepoel mentions that the Russians gave frightening nicknames to some of their land mines, such as “Black Widow”. The troops also see how the sappers locate these land mines and render them harmless.

“Do you have a section of assault pioneers here?” the doctor asks.

The hands of ten men are held up into the air.

“Okay, you guys. Your training is rather similar to that of the sappers. How many land mines have you lifted?”

The corporal in charge of the section gets up: "Captain, we have lifted more or less twenty mines – all of them on the dirt road here next to the camp that connects the highway with Onesi further south."

"Right-oh. Then you know what I'm talking about. The big question is now: what did the Defence Force do to minimize the danger of land mines – apart from locating those horrible things and digging them out?"

Some slides are shown to demonstrate how vehicles were adapted and designed over time to make them more mine resistant. Initially, ancient Bedford trucks were loaded with sand bags to prevent them from being thrown into the air too easily. The Hippo followed later. It's a mine resistant vehicle built on the chassis of a Bedford that got a base in the form of a V on its bottom. The goal with that was to deflect the explosion of the land mine to the sides to prevent the vehicle from being shot upwards. Later still, the Buffel and the Casspir appeared. Many trucks of the Samil series also received V-shaped bottoms.

And then the most important part of the lecture is given. Pictures are shown of men who didn't fasten their seat belts while travelling on Buffels and other vehicles. The land mines that exploded under their vehicles caused less damage to the vehicle due to its V-shaped base, but it often happened that the Buffel or truck got overturned – and then the men got injured. The troops see pictures of men who lost hands, feet, or their lives when their skulls were cracked and sqaushed.

Captain Swanepoel asks me if I want to add anything. I utilize the opportunity: "Men, the biggest asset of any organization is its personnel. If a van develops a flat tyre or when a trucks develops a few wrinkles, we can fix it. If our troops, though, lose parts of their bodies, we can't replace those parts. There are no stores where spare parts can be drawn from to replace damaged body parts. I'm sure you don't want to look like the men of whom you saw some pictures. I recognized two of them because it was my unpleasant task to operate on them and relieve them of utterly damaged parts of their bodies, like feet, fingers, or something. They were lucky that they weren't sent home in body bags."

After the lecture, the officers and senior NCO's retire to the saloon to socialize, while the troops watch a video in their part of the saloon. The lights are switched off at ten when the generator stops. By that time, all of us are back in our tents.

Concor Base, Wednesday, 9 January 1980

Shortly after midnight, a violent thunder storm breaks out and wakes me up. I and my guests hastily fasten the side flaps of our tent to keep the streaming water out.

Shortly after I have crept back into my sleeping bag again, a ttroop with a torch comes looking for me. While getting upright again, I ask: "Yes, man, what is it?"

"Doc, I have a horrible cough. Do you have medicine for me?"

I get up and switch my big torch on to scrutinize the troop better.

"How did you get so wet? Don't you have a bivvy[36]?"

"My bivvy lies in my tent. I forgot to take it along when my shift at the entrance started."

"Are you doing guard duty? In this rain?"

"Yes, Doc. I will only be relieved at two-oh-hours."

I feel the boy's forehead while he is racked by yet another coughing spell.

---

[36] "Bivvy" – Army slang for a bivouac shelter, which may be used as a rain coat.

"This tastes like fever. That bad cough has almost the sound of bronchitis. You can't keep on standing around at the gate – not in this weather. I will call another troop to replace you and then you go and get dressed in dry clothes and crawl into your cot. Here are some coughing louzenges and other pills. I'm booking you off. You are to come back to me during the day and then I will again see how you are doing."

"Thanks, Doc."

"What's your name? Who are you?"

"79657775 Bravo Tango Lance Corporal William Wolfaardt, Doc."

I grab my rain cout and run to the nearest tent with troops. I shake the first man I find awake: "Troop, do you want to earn two extra beers?"

"Hêy, who are you?"

"I'm Doctor Scholtz. I have just now given the man who does guard duty at the entrance sick leave. He is too ill to stay there. You are going to stand guard. In his place. We can't leave the gate unguarded. And tomorrow you get an extra beer and the day after that another one."

"Okay, Doc."

"And then you report to me tomorrow during the day so that I can see who you are."

In the meantime, buckets full of water are pouring down from heaven, thunder flashes shoot brightl bolts and loud explosions are heard due to huge electric discharges in the clouds. It rains as it can only rain in the African bush. I slide back into my sleeping bag and I manage to fall asleep again.

Directly after brunch, which takes place at ten, our two guests announce that they must travel furthery. Major du Rand stops them: "The road between the gate and the highway hasn't been swept yet. We must task our section assault pioneers to do that, first thing."

"Major, we can't wait. We must get on our way. I also don't believe that any terr would have ventured outside with this terrible storm of last night. We will be safe. We get onto the hard-topped highway over there and we will be Okay."

The two guests get into their vehicle. They have already loaded their lugage. Both salute the major and he reciprocates.

I go to look for my patient of last night, but before I can find him, I hear a huge explosion. It is immediately clear to me that somebody must have been hurt and I run back to my tent to grab my first aid bag.

It sounded as if the bang came from the direction of the gate. When I arrive there, I look outside. Thee Garry, the Landrover of our two guests, is lying on its side. I warn the few inquisitive troops coming up behind me: "Stand back. Don't go onto the road. There may be some more land mines!"

It's clear that the land mine got detonated by the front wheel on the right hand side of the vehicle so that it landed on its left-hand side. Before a rescuing effort can be organized, Captain Swanepoel starts with a big effort to climb out through the smashed window above him. Sergeant Swanevelder follows. Both are covered in blood.

I realize: "Here is some work for me …"

Ruacana, Wednesday, 16 January 1980

After the board of inquiry heard all the testimonies in the conference room at Ruacana and a meeting was held behind closed doors for thirty minutes, the chairman of the board, Commandant Theuns Terblanche, gives the verdict:

"This board finds that the two injured members, Captain (Doctor) Swanepoel and Sergeant Swanevelder, are themselves responsible for the injuries they have sustained during the land mine episode on 9 January. It is clear that the Swapo terrorists utilized the opportunity to plant land mines outside the Concor base during a heavy thunderstorm and when the gate was not guarded. It was extremely simple to dig a few holes into the muddy road and to plant the vehicle mines. The rain erased their tracks. The board laments the multiple injuries sustained by Captain (Doctor) Swanepoel and Sergeant Swanevelder – amongst others, the eye that the captain has lost due to sharp glass shards and the sergeant who lost two fingers on his left hand – but finds that it must be ascribed to the negligence of Captain (Dctor) Swanepoel, since he drove off despite the warning by Major du Rand."

I can only shake my head in amazement. How is it possible that the captain, who lectured the troops very eloquently against the dangers of land mines, could become a victim of the same type of trap? His head must have been full of useless noise.

10. OPERATION SNOTKLAP

Oshakati, Ovcamboland, Tuesday, 1 April 1980

It is already after nine in the evening when I stumble into our home. I have already phoned Hannolore at six to tell her that I won't get home for supper. A number of casevacs had arrived by chopper and I informed her that I will order a few sandwiches from the mess to consume between operations and treatments.

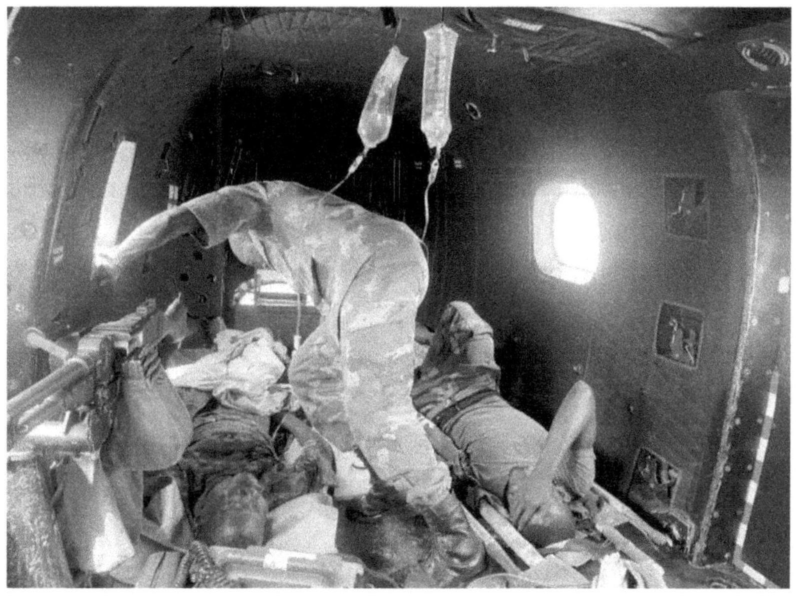

Hannelore: "I think I've heard that chopper as it landed. It was shortly before six."

After I have gotten ready for the night and I join my lovely wife in bed, she asks: "Were those casevac cases serious? You needed a long time."

"Yea, rather. But that wasn't all that made my tired. It was that new medic or pill tiffy who reported here this morning and who had to help me later with those operations."

"But aren't you supposed to have a theater nurse to help you with that?"

"Yes, but there's often a medic or two available to do odd jobs. Sometimes, one of them take over from the nurse if her hands are too full."

"Now, what's the problem with this new medic? How did he manage to make you so tired?"

"Yes, you may ask. The guy's name is James Jackson. When he came to my consulting room this morning to introduce himself, he lay emphasis on the fact that his name must be pronounced as 'Dzaims' – as in high English, even if he's a 'Boer'[37] boy from the Eastern Cape countryside where all the people are Afrikaans-speaking. He also explained that the name can be pronounced as 'Yahmis' in Afrikaans, but that he is actually just 'Dzaims'. He also added that James is the English for the Afrikaans and Dutch 'Jacobus', but that nobody addresses him as such. He is simply just 'Dzaims'."

"Now, what is so special about this Dzaims who isn't Yahmis or Jacobus?"

"He's hopelessly too cheeky for his own health. Glib with ht lip. Constantly delivering compulsive comments. Usually something stupid or silly or senseless. In the end, I couldn't endure it anymore and I warned him: 'If you're not going to shut that trap of yours, I will close it with a thick kick or a 'snotklap'[38]. Do you understand?"

"Did he reply, if anything?"

---

[37] "Boer" – this word literarily means "farmer", but it is often used for an Afrikaans-speaking person.

[38] "Snotklap" – an Afrikaans expression: to slap someone across the face so that some snot will fly in all directions.

“He remained as cheeky as ever and told me: ‘Doc, I know you can give me a thick kick or give me a ‘snotklap’. I saw those wings on your browns, telling me that you are a parabat. You must know something about giving thick kicks.’”

Hannelore laughs: “And what other pieces of profound wisdom did this this pill tiffy throw about, there in the theater, so that you wanted to provide him with a thick kick?”

“Let me start at the beginning. Shortly after five o’ clock, while I was completing my day’s work, including admin, and wanted to lock the door of my consulting room, I got the message that a chopper was on its way with four serious casualties – men who were bleeding.There was a skirmish or a contact or something somewhere. I was the only available doctor and that meant that I had to stay and deal with these casualties. I, one of the nurses, and Dzaims got the theater ready so that we could start immediately when the first man was brought in.

“The first case was a terr of Swapo. Ugly gunshot wound. On his stomach, left side. He’s bleeding profusely and I order Dzaims to determine his blood group. It’s O-positive. Dzaims fetches a bag of blood while I and the nurse stabilize the man. He is coupled to the bag of blood and then Dzaims starts with his tricks and witticisms.”

“What did he say?”

“Terrible nonsense. He was watching me while I was stitching the open wound and tells me: ‘Doc, I want to show you how good I am with a needle and gut.’

“I ask: “And how do you want to show me?’

“He answers: ‘Doc, I’m going to sew this terr’s upper lip to his loewer lip. Then he won’t be able to lie and swear anymore.’”

“Hannelore laughs again: “And what did you do then?”

“I tell the theater nurse to make sure that he doesn’t lay his paws on any needles. I couldn’t stop him myself because I was busy stitching the wound.”

Hannelore: “And what else?”

“The second patient was another wounded Swap. I had to amputate his hand, at least the shattered part that remained of it. The fool held too long onto a hand grenade before throwing it after having drawn the safety pin. Then it exploded while his hand was above his head at the end of his extended arm. Due to some or other miraculous reason, he didn’t really get injured any further – only a few superficial scratches as the schrapnel hit his head and shoulders. The medic of the team that caught him took care of those while they were waiting for the chopper.

Hannelore: “Any other juicy nonsensical clever ideas from Dzaims?”

“Yes. He said to me: ‘Doc, I don’t think we must give this terr a bag of blood. I’m sure he was born without a blood group. I will phone the mess immediately and order a bottle of brandy. Which they will deliver. I will drip that into him, instead of blood. He will sleep for the next three days and stay asleep.’

“And then I asked the wise guy: ‘And how much of that bottle will you throw down your own throat, Dzaims?’

“He replied: “Doc. No, nothing. I’m a very generous chap.’

“And then the third patient came – one of our troops. He has an ugly wound, at a very strategic spot. His male instruments were shot to shreds, somehow or other.

“And just there, Dzaims speaks out: ’Sorry, my man. We will have to cut off that pecker of yours, together with the goolies. You will never be able to make use of those again. But relax, we will steal a set of them from one of these terrs. We will remove it on the sly while he's asleep and do a transplant on you. There will, though, be a little problem – whose children will it be?'

Hannelore: "Yes?"

"That's just where the theater nurse loses her temper and tells Dzaims to shut up, otherwise she will see to it that his own male instruments would be transplanted onto the poor wounded troop. She also consoled the troop: 'We will do our best to save your masculinity and your water works. Don't listen to this fool of a mindless maniac of a medic.'"

Hannelore: "And the fourth patient?"

"Yes, it was again one of the Swaps. Head wound. Not too serious, except a part of his left ear was shot away. Dzaims gives this wound one look and declares: 'This guy has almost kicked the bucket already. Hole in the head. Nobody can survive this. I think we ought to help this poor soul to reach heaven a little sooner. Or perhaps the hot place.'"

"The nurse asks him: "Yes, wise guy, how do you propose that we do that?"

"This infantile and almost insane medic replies: 'I propose that we push a thunderflash into his throat so that it explodes inside his esophagus. We have, though, to pull a sheet over him to prevent the blood from getting splashed and splattered all over the place. I don't like cleaning up blobs of blood.'"

Hannelore: "And that was when you threatened to give him a fat big thick kick on his bottom side?"

"Exactly. I almost hit him with hammer blows or kicked him in the groin. Fortunately, my hands were filled with other things and that prevented me from assualting a troop, which is, of course, irregular and illegal. His first remarks may perhaps have been humerous, but I can't handle such bloodthirstiness and lack of empathy and humanity. Just tomorrow, I will see to it that he is transferred somewhere else where his wise cracks may perhaps be appreciated."

Hannelore: "Or where somebody else may give him a real snotklap."

11. THE 'KOTSKOETS' AND THE FLY SPY

Eenhana, Ovcamboland, Friday, 11 April 1980

It happens that I am tasked to help somewhere else again. This time, it's at Eenhana, the HQ of Five Four Battolion, on the eastern side of Sector One Zero.

The medical officer at Eenhana, a two-pip loot[39] doing his national service there, was wounded when the fighters of Swapo attacked the base yesterday and he had to be evaciated. The officer commanding the sick-bay at Oshakati, ordered me to fly immediately to Eenhana and to help the helpless medics there with all the less seriously wounded men.

"Only for a week or so, until we can get another national serviceman to fill the gap."

And now I am flying from the Ondanhwa airfield in a DC-3 Dakota, an old crate dating from the Second World War, to the landing strip at Eenhana. Therev are a number of civilian passengers on board – wives and children of Permanent Force personnel at Eenhana who live in Oshakati and are allowed to visit their spouses and fathers every second week-end.

We are flying just above the tree tops to avoid any possible Russian hand-held anti-aircraft missiles – Sam-7's – fired by Swapo terrorists who may have evaded our patrols. By flying low, the plane will not be visible from afar between the trees and there won't be any time to aim and fire a missile.

---

[39] Men who were called up for their national service after having obtained a professional qualification, such as medical practitiners, teachers, engineers, lawyers, or ministers of religion, usually received the rank of lieutenant with two stars on their shoulder straps after having received the appropriate training.

All passengers are supposed to stay on their seats, strapped in, due to the air turbulence created by the heat from the hot earth below us. It is, though, impossible to the keep the children on their seats and they start chasing each other along the aisle.

Suddenly, a little girl stops in frond of her mother, sitting next to me, and she throws up her whole lunch onto her mother's lap. The shaking airplane must have been too much for her.

The mother gives a shriek, but it's too late. Her clothes are messed up. The little girl – about five or six years old – runs away and continues with her game as if nothing really happened.

Of course, the interior of theplane suddenly smells less pleasant and I wonder who will have to clean up afterwards.

I am reminded of why the the Dakota has earned her nickname of "kotskoets" (vomitting coach). As a trained parabat, I am fortunately not prone to air sickness or sea sickness.

Eenhana, Satruday, 12 April 1980

At Eenhana, I was given the tent of the previous military officer. He – or perhaps one of his predecessors – has put up a notice board proclaiming: "Consulting hours – 08:00 – 10:00 and 14:00 – 16:00. I see no reason to change this arrangement. That gives me a rest period after brunch at 10:00 during the hottest time of day.

All the men who had lesser wounds were already patched up by the two medics when I arrived yesterday and there is very little else for me to do in any case.

After brunch, I amble over to the tent of the chaplain, a young man who is doing his second year of national service and who is ministering to the folks who occupy Eenhana from time to time.

He tells me: "I'm sure that you must have met our battalion commander, Commandant Desmond Duncan."

"Yes, I had to report to him immediately after my arrival."

"Well, I don't think I am guilty of malicious gossip if I tell you to steer clear of this man."

"Why?"

"Well, we all don't think he realizes that we are in a war situation. He runs this camp as if it is a training unit. Nobody may move around at walking pace, as you did when you came to me. We must all run. And when two or more men are moving in the same direction, they must do it in unison with one of them calling out 'Left, left, left' or something similar the whole time. We are all supposed to take part in physical exercises every morning at five – except over week-ends. Keep yourself ready on Monday for that. It was his decree that you must have fixed consulting hours at your medical tent."

"I know that every army needs disciplne, but it may be overdone sometimes."

"Exactly. Fortunately, I am a fitness nut and I like all the exercises and runs we have to take. He makes sure that every man in the base, who is not out on patrol, writes at least one letter to his parents in the States[40] every Thursday so that it can be taken back by the Dak[41] the next day. If anybody is caught out who doesn't obey all his rules, that poor chap is fined four hundred dollars, deducted from his monthly pay."

"Thanks for warning me. I will write a weekly letter to my old man next Thursday, although I phoned him from Oshakati three days ago."

"And you know, of course, that you may not seal the envelope. I am the official censor and I must make sure that nobody gives any military secets away, such as where we are situated or what we are doing or achieving or messing up."

"And what do you do if you find any military secrets in the letters of the troops?"

"Ignore them. I only scratch out obscene and blasphenous expressions."

Eenhana, Thursday, 17 April 1980

The 2IC of the Eenhana base, Major Mike McLachlan, brings a corporal to my tent.

"Doc, this is Corporal Jerry Jennings, the fly spy who is visiting us for a few days. Since we don't have any other accommodation for him and he is part of the medical and sanitary works, it may be best for him to sleep with you."

"Do you expect me to sleep with this corporal? I'm a married man and I'm totally straight!"

"That's not what I mean. Sorry. We will get a cot for him somewhere. Only till Monday. Then he starts visiting the company bases around us."

"Okay."

---

[40] "The States" – Army slang for South Africa.

[41] "Dak" – Army slang dor Dakota.

The corporal dumps a bag on the floor and salutes me.

"Doc, thanks for providing me with a roof over my head, even if it's only a canvas roof. Give me some time to fetch my other gear."

Jennings leaves and I follow him to help him with his gear, if necessary. He came with his own Garry as part of the weekly convoy that travelled from Grootfontein, via Oshakati and Ondangwa, with provisions and personnel. We carry cans of insexticide and a spray pump back to the medical tent. Mosquitoes and flies are a real pest here inside Dark Africa and specially trained men are tasked to lessen the inpact of these pesky insects, especially because the mosquitoes may spread malaria.

Jennings: "Doc, I was told that Eenhana is only a few kilometers from the Angolan border."

"That's right."

"And I was told that Swapo terrorists revved this base a few days ago."

"Exactly a week ago."

"How many men fell?"

"None. Only a few got hurt, although the previous doctor had to be casevaced because he was the only serious casualty."

What did they use to attack us?"

'Russian mortars and Russoan rockets. We call these rockets 'Red Eyes'."[42]

"When will we be attacked again?"

"Heaven alone knows. Perhaps also a few Swaps who are planning something. I could be toninght, for all I know."

---

[42] "Red Eyes" – Army slang for the Russian BM-21 Grad missile system supplied to the Angolan Army.

The eyes of the poor corporal grow wide and wild: "What must I do if we're attacked?"

"Hide under your bed and pray. And make sure that you have a dry pair of trousers ready."

Eenhana, Friday, 18 April 1980

Last night, the poor frightened fly spy hid his nine milimeter pistol under his pillow when going to bed. His R1 rifle stood ready next to his bed. He repeats the procedure tonight.

It is clear that the poor young man has never slept in a base in the Operational Area. At least once a week, a firing plan is put into action – just to let Swapo know that we are ready for them. During this time, a few 81 millimeter mortar boms are shot to explode at a predeterimined spot outside the camp where the explosion won't cause any damage. Illumination flares are shot up to light up the whole environment. All base personnel are supposed to rush out and occupy bunkers and other safe places. This routine has to be followed regularly as part of drills to be ready whenever a base is being attacked.

And tonight a firing plan is being put into effect shortly before midnight. The mortars go bang and their bombs roar a few seconds later when the strike the earth.

The poor fly spy jumps out of his bed, totally bewildered. Before he can do anything, I grab his pistol and rifle, to prevent him from shooting wildly into the air. I lay those on my bed and I grab the panicked man by the arm.

Before I can do anything to calm him down, he starts looking for his fire-arms and shouts: "Doc, these terrorists have stolen my guns. What must I do?"

"Don't panic, no need to panic. No need to shoot anybody or anything. These bangs are only part of an exercise."

Eenhana, Sundayday, 20 April 1980

After a short religious service led by the soul tiffy[43] in the open air and brunch afterwards, I stroll over to the landing strip where a flight of Alouette helicopters, converted into "gunships" by the installatin of a twenty millimeter canon firing through the open door, are being kept. My training as a parachute soldier made me curious about anything that flies.

One of the pilots, Lieutenant Williams, smiles at me: "Doc, do you want to take part in a little exercise? I see you're a parabat and you can't be afraid of flying."

"What is this exercise about?"

"My twenty mil gun got some hick-ups and got jammed. We want to test it after having fixed it. We embezzled the commandant of the Army camp out of a supply of twenty mil rounds. He thinks we want to use them somewhere inside Angola."

I get into the seat next to the pilot and his gunner takes a seat behind us. We get airborne and after a flight of two minutes, we start to circle around a big scrapyard. The place is filled with mangled Russian equipment – brought back from Angola to prevent the Angolese, Cubans, and Swapo from repairing them and using them again.

For the next five minutes, the gunner, Sergeant Olly Olivier, blasts the wrecks until all his ammo is used up.

When we land again, both crew members declare their satisfaction with the performance of the canon. Olly starts to clean the gun again.

I decide to spend a quiet Sunday afternoon with the Air Force chaps. They tell me about the way they helped the Army recently

[43] "Soul riffy" – Army slang for a chaplain.

when the Eenhana base was revved. Three teams of trackers and pursuers were tasked at first light the next morning to chase those terrs. While one team was following the tracks made by the fleeing terrs, the other two teams would follow on vehicles. Whenever the team on foot became tired, they were relieved by another team. They had to move fast because the terrs had a head start of a few hours. They were only sighted on day four of the chase. At that stage, the help of the gunships were called in to do their work from the air. The whole gang of terrorists was witped out.

Me: "Those terrs must have been dead tired after having been chased for four days. But I know that they inject themselves with all sorts of drugs and things to keep going. I believe they were only caught when the effect of these drugs had worn off and they couldn't go on any further."

Lieutenant Williams: "Although we can't approve of what these terrs are doing, we must salute them for the guts they have."

When I return to my tent shortly before supper, the RSM, Sergeant Major Pierre Prinsloo, waylays me: "Doc, we needed you this afternoon, but we couldn't find you anywhere. There was somewhat of an emergency."

"What happened?"

"That fly spy became totally bezerked, mentally disturbed, agitated, and unhinged when he heard that gunship testing her gun. He ran out of the base with his rifle, screaming bloody murder. We had to chase him and lock him up. The commandant has ordered him to return to Grootfontein in his Garry with a section of troops in a truck to escort and guard and protect him."

"Did he shoot at anything with his rifle?"

"Yes. Look at your tent. He emptied a whole magazine into the air, ripping holes in the canvas, before running away. You will have to shift your cot if you don't want the rain drops to fall on your head or your feet."

When I appear in the mess for supper, Commandant Duncan tells me: "Doc. I want to see you directly after supper."

While I consume my grub, it strikes me that I've missed my consulting hours this afternoon and that the commandant must be furious about this omission.

I was right. When I enter the ops room where the commandant is sitting behind a table, I salute him while standing at attention. He also salutes and immediately fires away: "Doctor Scholtz, you are fined the sum of four hundred bucks."

"Why, commandant? What did I do wrong?"

"It's what you didn't do. You didn't write a letter to your parents on Thursday. I saw you strollihg about this afternoon instead of jogging. And you missed your consulting hours today."

"Commandant, my presence was needed at the Air Force detachment on the landing strip."

"You left the base without permission. Four hundred bucks. To be deducted from your pay at the end of the month. It will be paid into our regimental fund."

Eenhana, Tuesdayday, 22 April 1980

I am still stuck at Eenhana, despite the fact that I was told that I would only have to stay a week before being relieved.

After supper, the officers usually retire to the officers' club to socialize and to consume some alcoholic beverages or other liquid refreshments. After I've enjoyed the company of some of the men for about an hour, Sergeant Major Prinsloo approaches me: "Doc, the commandant requires your presence at your tent. Immediately."

I rush to my tent where I find the commandant sitting on my chair.

Before I can salute, the commandant whines:"Doc, this tooth is killing me. I know you're not a dentist, but you're the second best."

"Commandant, you will have to allow me to look at the offending tooth."

"Just do anything to help me. This pain is killing me."

"Commandant, I will gladly help. But you owe me four hundred bucks."

"For what? You get a fucking fixed salary for your work on military personnel."

"That doesn't apply to consultations outside the official consulting hours. Four hundred bucks in cash, up front."

"All right. I dn't have it withme now, but I promise to bring it later tonight."

After I have illuminated the inside of his mouth with my torch, I notice a huge abscess on his lower jaw, next to one of his molars. I give him a hefty pain injection. While I give the injection time to take effect, I disappear. At the workshop of our tiffies, I borrow a pair of pliars.

In the kitchen, I disinfect the instrument in a pot of boiling water and I return to the suffering commandant. His jaw has become totally anesthetized and I pull the culprit of a tooth.

I order the commandant to rinse his mouth with a antibacterial mouth wash and I hand him his tooth. It is, after all, his property. For good measure, I hand him a box with painkillers and a box with antibiotics – just in case.

The commandant struggles to speak because his tongue is partly paralyzed and he thanks me profusely for helping him. Thirty minutes later, he returns and hands me four bills of one hundred bucks each. He doesn't look happy, despite the pain pills.

12. OPERATION OMELETTE

Oshakati, Ovamboland, Friday, 16 May 1980

My quiet and lazy Fri Matt 3:11–12day morning is suddenly interrupted when two helicopters arrive outside our sick-bay at Oshakati, the headquarters of Sector One Zero in the Operational Area. Ten wounded men are carried into our building.

Today, three medical officers are doing duty. The four most serious cases are immediately taken to the operating theater, while I get three men to treat in my consulting room with the help of a nurse and a medic. The other three are given to a colleague.

The first one has a broken left leg. I cut the leg of his trousers open to reach the lower leg. He explains: "Doc, this happened when I jumped from our Buffel troop carrier and landed with my left foot on a loose stone. That made me fall down and somehow this blooming leg just gave notice."

I give him pain injections and set the leg, while the nurse and the medic fixes his leg in a plaster cast afterwards.

Number Two has serious bruises on his face and the skin is on his right cheeck is almost peeled off. He complains of a broken rib. I ask: "How did this happen?"

"Doc, our bloody Buffel hit a land mine and was overturned. Somehow, my seat belt got loose and I was thrown onto the dirt road and this is the result."

I disinfect his facial wounds and direct the medic to apply some ontment and give the man some pain pills. The broken rib must take care of itself.

The third man has three gun shot wounds that grazed his left thigh, his left hip and his neck. Fortunately, no bullets have to be removed and I treat the wounds after the boy – a corporal – has gotten rid of his browns.

Me: "Was there an ambush, or something?"

The corporal: "Yes Doc. I was in the last Buffel. We were in a convoy on our way back to Rundu when the Buffel in front of ours struck that loony land mine and got overturned."

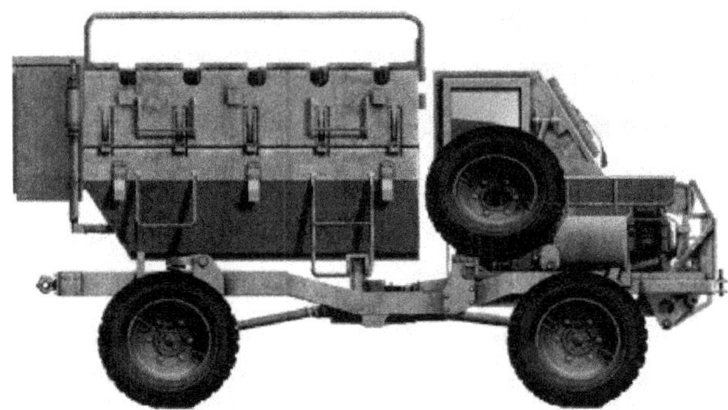

Buffel Armored and Mine-Resistant Personnel Carrier of the SA Army. The V-shaped bottom under the seats of ten troops doubled as a water reservoir.

Number Two: "That's where I got thrown out and fell on my face."

Number One: "I was on the last Buffel. After the Buffel in front of us detonated that land mine, I jumped off. It was stupid, because I should have stayed on the Buffel and be protected by the armored side plates."

Me: "Was there shooting?"

The corporal: "Yes. They were waiting for us. Hiding in the bush at the spot where they planted that bloody land mine."

Me: "And how did you manage to get shot? Didn't you stay on your Buffel and shoot from there?"

"No, I was so angry at these cowardly Swaps that I stormed at them where they were hiding in the bushes. I don't know how I managed it, but I shot three of them before the rest got a fright and fled. As fast as possible. With wet pants, I believe."

"You're a brave man. No wonder you got these wounds, because those terrorists were certainly shooting back at you."

Number One: "Doc, that man deserves a medal. A golden one. He saved our lives by chasing those terrs away."

Me: "Didn't you get help from the other Buffels?"

The corporal: "It took some time for them to wake up and turn around. There were fifteen Buffels in total in the cursed convoy. And then only the second last vehicle got bowled over."

Me: "Didn't you realize that it amounted to suicide to run directly towards those people who are firing at you?"

Number One: "Doc, of course it was stupid of our corp to do that. But he saved the day. And the funniest part of it all is that we're not even trained infantry soldiers."

Me: "From which outfit are you?"

The corporal: "We are from Six SAI from Grahamstown. Delta Company. We did duty the last six months at a spot called De Put[44], right on the border between Sector One Zero and Sector Two Zero. We were on our way back to Rundu after another company arrived at De Put to relieve us. We should actually have been taken to the sick-bay in Rundo, but the chopper pilots decided that Oshakati is somewhat nearer and that's why they brought us here."

Number Two: "Doc, you won't believe it, but these other two guys aren't trained infantrymen. They are members of the Catering Corps – cooks, chefs, potato peelers, coffee brewers. That's why the kitchen staff travelled in that very last Buffel because nobody thought they would be caught in an ambush. For a guy trained to man a stove and wash dishes and prepare omelettes, that corporal didn't do too badly by shooting three terrs."

Me: "Yes, congratulations with your most successful omelette of today. But your own egg was almost cracked. "

---

[44] "De Put" – this name can be translated as "The Well". There wasn't really a well at that spot, only a bore hole with a diesel pump to provide water for the military base and a nearby village.

13. OPERATION SCEPTIC

Oshakati, Ovamboland, Monday, 30 June 1980

My parents came to visit us in Oshakati for a whole month to assist my dear wife Hannelore with our first baby, little David, while I was away to participate in an operation in Angola as a medical officer. I arrived home this afternoon after the end of the operation and now I and my father, retired Brigadier David Scholtz, sit on the veranda and we chat while we are both nursing an ice cold beer.

My dad: "It seems as if you have seen enough sunshine while you were gone."

"Without any doubt."

We remain silent again.

"And how was it?"

"What?"

"The operation."

"I haven't been in an operation theater for quite a while."

Pa laughs: "You know very well that's not what I mean. How was the operation?"

"A big, bloody, blooming bugger-up."

"Yea?"

I take a sip of my beer, look in another direction and stay silent.

After a minute, my outoppue says: "You called it a bugger-up. Can you tell me more?"

"I am actually too angry and I feel like hell. Ach, Okay, here's the story."

My pa sits on the edge of his chair's seat to demonstrate that his ears are wide open.

"Pa, you know the South African Defence Force. You also experienced the Secnd World War almost from day one with the

German Wehrmacht and the terrible Waffen-SS. You know about warfare. Things can easily go haywire. And when things start to run askew it may develop into a huge hell hole. That's what happened with this ops. That's my story."

I stay silent again and I sigh.

My Pa tries again: "What was this operation called?"

"It was Ops Sceptic. It made me very sceptic about the ability of our intellgence people to provide us with accurate and intellugent intelligence. Afterwards, a few officers grumbled that a better name would have been Operation Septic. It really amounted to a stupid septic disaster. We also wonder whether the staff officers who do the planning know what they were doing. Brigadier Witkop[45] Badenhorst got this job from the politicians, after all, to assemble a whole brigade, consisting of four battle groups, each one comprising a whole infantry battalion with extra armor, artillery and engineers, to go and smoke Swapo out somewhere in Angola."

"Witkop? I remember hin as the commander of the Infantry School at Oudtshoorn when he was only a colonel."

"Yes. He's a brigadier now and commander of Sector One Zero, the whole of Ovamboland. He was supposed to be in command of Operation Sceptic while sitting in his air-conditioned office in Oshakati, while we were battling and wrestling and fighting with the flies, with the mosquitoes, with the dust, with the heat, with Swapo and with the Angolese. He devised the most wonderful plans for us – which had no chance of working properly. Extremely idealistic, but unrealistic, unworkable, impossible to execute. Based on guess work and wishful thinking and hopelessly bad intelligence."

"How's that?"

---

[45] "Witkop" – an Afrikaans nickname for somebody with white or blonde hair and it may be translated with "Blondie" or "Whitey".

"The word 'intelligence' is a hell of a mistake in this case because it contained absolutely no intelligence, plain common sense. Let me start from the beginning. A few weeks ago, Commandant Flip Venter called me. He's the commander of the sick-bay, here at the HQ of Sector One Zero. He tells me that Four-four Parachute Brigade of Bloemfontein requested that I be part of the medical team for two parabat companies for this operation. They still remember me from Ops Reindeer last year when I helped the parabats at Cassinga. That's why I asked you to come and assist Hannelore with the baby while I was away."

"I enjoyed the time with you here and I appreciated the time with my grandson. I'm glad his mother speaks German with him. I also do."

"Thanks. Anyway, I had to report on the first of June at the Eenhana base. Flip Venter provided me with a Casspir field ambulance and two medics. One of these medics was an old friend, Lance Corporal Louis Lancaster, whom I got to know last year at Etale. The brigade then holds an exercise to get us ready for the ops. The plan was that the strongest battle group would attack Chifufua from the south. This headquarters of Swapo was given the code name of Smokeshell and afterwards we spoke about the battle of Smokeshell. Our two parabat companies were supposed to be taken by celihopter to the north of Chifufua. (My pa smiles at my pronunciation of 'helicopter'.) We had to divide into six ambush groups, each one of platoon strength. The expectation was that the Swaps would flee when the main force attacked them during the early morning from the south and then they would stumble upon our ambushes. That would have caused a blooming blasted blood bath."

"Was there such a blooming blasted blood bath?"

"No, damn it … I will get to that. It was furthermore planned that one of the battle groups would already cross the border on 25

May to establish a temporary base in the bush at Mulemba. That spot is about ninety clicks[46] from the border and about halfway to Chifufua. The other three battle groups were then supposed to deploy from there in different directions. These three groups got underway very early on the tenth of June. Our group was supposed to hit Chifufua the same morning with a bit of 'Blitzkrieg'. It was also planned that the two parabat companies would get onto the choppers at Mulemba and then get off the choppers again somewhere north of at Smokeshell so that we could prepare our ambushes."

"Did it work that way?"

I sniff and roll my eyes a few times. "Witkop Badenhorst and his Kindergarten of staff officers thought our battle group would be able to jog the ninety kilometers to Smokeshell from Mulemba in a jiffy. I'm sure not one of those guys knows anything about bundu bashing[47]. We had to struggle through dense bushes and loose sand and lost many valuable hours. Something not one of those planners ever did in their lives. Sometimes we progressed only at ten kilometers per hour. Afterwards, one of the chopper pilots told me that when they got airborne at Eenhana to proceed to Mulemba, the rear guard only reached the border at the time the first vehicles reached Mulemba. That was how slowly we proceeded."

"And it was supposed to be a surprise attack?"

"And it was supposed to be a surprise attack, as Pa said. Every single member of the local population, as well as the Swaps, knew very well we were coming."

"And how much behind schedule did the main force arrive at Smokeshell?"

---

[46] "Clicks" – Army slang for "kilometers".

[47] "Bundu bashing" – Army slang for bashing with military vehicles through dense vegetation and bushes.

"These guys were supposed to attack shortly after eight. The Air Force dropped lots of bombs on this base exactly at eight. To no avail because most Swaps had performed a vanishing act long before that.

"Nobody knew about their subterranean bunkers and none of our bombs could penetrate those. And then our main force arrived at Smokeshell only during the late afternoon – many hours too late. There was a little bit of resistance, but the attackers had to step down when it became dark."

"And what happened with your ambushes?"

"Exactly nothing. We remained in Mulemba and played with our toes

"Yes?"

"Yes. Poor planning. I'll get to that shortly. Anyway, our battle group continues the following day with the cleaning up of the place. And they request another battle group that had another target, to forget about that and help them – and that messed up the other battle group's program. And in the meantime, we sit and wait for better days, there at the temporary base at Mulemba."

"Did these two battle groups achieve anything worthwhile at Smokeshell?"

"'A few heads. Also a few boxes with paper work and a few Russian trucks that Swapo had left behind. After all, the Russians will certainly replace those trucks, so it's not a big loss for them."

"Did the parabats get some work later on?"

"Because our plans didn't work as planned, we sat around at the HQ of the battle group as some sort of a reserve force, but we were almost never called upon to do anything. Fortunately, I and my medics slept in the Casspir – in the lap of luxury, on mattresses. In any case: the plan was that the whole operation was supposed to be over after a week, but the politicians in Pretoria decided that we must stay longer and look for other Swapo targets to strike. It happened to happen that way."

"Oh, you did find other bases?"

"Yes, but all of them were empty or almost empty. The Swaps saw and heard and smelled us and made tracks with their boots in the soft sand timeously."

"With the result that they can continue at another time with their evil deeds, hey?"

"Exactly. So that they can continue with their evil deeds at another time. We were hanging around in Angola till last Sunday and then we drove back again. I was able in all that time to fix the ailments of a few men in my ambulance. To put the cherry on top of the cake, the Angolans decided to pick a fight with us. They even managed to shoot down one of our choppers. In the end, we lost seventeen men during this month. Almost the worst happened when the Ratel infantry fighting vehicle of our commandant struck a land mine. It was almost a hell of a mess because the chief of the Army, Lieutenant General Constand Viljoen, was also in that Ratel. What the hell he was doing there the devil alone knows. Fortunately, nobody got hurt. Swapo lost in total something like one hundred and eighty members, against our seventeen. We, therefore, had something to show for all our troubles, but it could have been much, much better. The problem is that Swapo can absorb those losses rather easily."

"During the Second World War, we sent thousands upon thousands if the Russians to their graves, but they could also absorb their losses – which the Germans couldn't do."

I sigh and stay silent again after I have fetched fresh beers for both of us.

Pa breaks the silence: "You wanted to tell me why you never laid your ambushes."

"Ah, yes. It will certainly never be possible to eradicate stupidity and idiocy and lunacy from mankind. I am thinking to go and specialize next year in neurology in order to understand the human brain better. There was this stupid, simple, sluggish sot of a staff sergeant who misunderstood his orders and thought he knew better than anybody else. Our angry captain almost assaulted the fucking fool afterwards, but he got a hold on himself just in time."

"What was the poor staff sergeant's crime?"

"This foolish…, eh…, foolish fool was in charge of the logistical echelon. He was the boss of the truck drivers who had to transport all our ammo, food, water, and fuel to wherever those were needed."

"And?"

"And then this thick-headed and brainless idiot decides that the tanker with fuel for our choppers is not necessary – and he leaves it behind in Eenhana. He argued that our vehicles only needed diesel and gasoline – not aircraft fuel. When our helicopters wanted to get refueled at Mulemba to take the six ambush groups to a point north of Smokeshell, there was no fuel for them. And then we sat there while playing with our toes. That caused the whole plan to fall flat."

My Pa sighs: "Yeaaa…"

Me: "How about another beer for you, Pa? From the fridge."

14. OPERATION KLIPKOP

Oshakati, Ovamboland, Friday, 11 July 1980

After a hard day's work in the sick-bay in the military base at Oshakati, which houses the headquarters of Section One Zero of the Operational Area, my father joins me for a beer on the veranda at our home after dark. My father is a retired brigadier and medical practitioner and he understands my occupational world.

I start the conversation: "Swapo threw a few bombs, yet again, on the power station at Ruacana and they even tried to rev the military base at Ruacana with rockets and mortars."

"Is that their way of taking revenge because you blasted them last month in Angola?"

"It seems to be the case."

"And now you will have to do something to stop ths nonsense?"

"Precisely. But of course, not me personally, but the SADF. And that's why I want to ask you to stay another few weeks here to help Hannelore with little David. I received orders this afternoon that I must report at Ruacana on Wednesday, 23 July, with full kit."

"What is the plan?"

"How must I know? We will certainly be informed in due course. But my boss, Commandant Flip Venter, speculates that we are going to rev Chitado – with the parabats on account of the fact that specifically I received orders to take part in something as a medical officer. There are not many other medical officers with parachute training. The name of this ops is Operation Klipkop.[48]"

"Chitado? Where's that?"

---

[48] "Klipkop" – Afrikaans for "stone head". It may be applied to a stubborn person, but also to a stony hill.

"It's a small place a few kilometers across the border inside Angola and more or less thirty-five clicks west of Ruacana. That's the nest where these Swapo lice and bugs and cockcroaches are being hatched."

"You mentioned Operation Klipkop?"

"I don't know where Army HQ finds names for all their operations, but I think this name is appropriate. Chitado is just across the river from Kaokoland and it's very hilly over there – in contrast with Ovamboland that is one big flat sandy plain. There are apparently a few stony hills in those parts."

"Do you think that a number of stone-headed staff officers at Sector One Zero are planning this ops?"

"Don't know. Hopefully not."

We enjoy our beer in silence after this.

"Pa, the mention of stone-headed staff officers reminds me of something else. I have always had an interest in people's heads. I always wanted to know why people can be so stone-headed. I applied to specialize in neurology at the Medical Faculty at Maties[49]. I have received news today that I have been accepted. It's a course of four years. I am tired of devoting most of my time and attention to troops who are bleeding or have malaria or who need headache pills. It became rather boring."

"Why not surgery?"

"Pa, I knew you would say that because you are a specialist surgeon. I see enough cases of troops who became "bossies"[50]. That's how the men describe somebody who has shell-shock. The Americans call it 'post-traumatic stress disorder'. I want to do

---

[49] "Maties" – the nickname for students of the University of Stellenbosch and for the University itself as well.

[50] "Bossies" – Army slang for shell-shock or post-traumatic stress disorder, acquired during the Bush War in Namibia.

some research in this regard."

"But then you must specialize in psychiatry."

"Neurology and psychiatry overlap a lot. But in this regard I want to know something from you. Who are the people at the office of the Surgeon General with whom I can talk to get a redeployment or transfer to Two Military Hospital? If I want to swot furhter at Maties I have to get a clinical assistantship. Two Mil looks like the right place for that."

"I will arrange that for you. I will also enquire whether a position as a civilian medical practitioner for Hannelore at Two Mil is possible. For this German daughter-in-law of mine, I will do anything. Then she can be seconded by the South West Administration to the Defence Force – which is also a gevornment service."

On my own, I think that my outoppie must be in love with my beautiful German wife – she looks very similar to his first wife in Germany where he studied before the Second World War. She was killed by an American bomb during the war.

I answer enthusiastically: "Hang, Pa. That will be wonderful. And then we will be much nearer to you over there in Gordon's Bay.[51]"

"Grand! Very grand!"

Oshakati, Ovamboland, Friday, 1 August 1980

My dad is sitting with me and we are enjoying Hannelore's chocolate cake and coffee.

"Pa, thank you very much that you were here to help Hannelore and little David."

"Always a pleasure."

After we have swallowed our coffee, my dad asks: "Did you have lots of work? How many wounded?"

---

[51] See map on page 6.

“Only one guy who was bleeding. He will make it.”

“Any corpses?”

“’A few men of Swapo and a number of Angolese don’t live anymre. Perhaps two dozen, or even more.”

“Oh.”

When I don’t talk any further, my father asks: “And what did you accomplish with Operation Klipkop?”

“Our men flattened the base at Chitado. Totally. And a number of terrs were brought back as POW’s.”

“Exactly what was there?”

“A base of Swapo and a base of the Angolese Army – with a big ammo store.”

“Please, tell me more. Was it again an ops thought out by stone-headed chaps at Sector HQ?”

“Not really. Fortunately not. We were a company of parabats who were flown in in two shifts by five helicopters.

There were also five chopper gunships. Alouette Three’s, each with a twenty millimeter canon. These egg-beaters were not really desig-ned as gunships and the can-nons were added later and they shoot through the open side door. When a whole salvo is shot, the recoil is so heavy that the chopper is thrown back in the air. But is works well in any case.

“The first wave parabats sat down behiund some trees and bushes where the Swaps couldn’t see them and shoot at them. Those forty men stormed the base and only one of our boys got wounded. The place was taken within two ticks. The gunships kept the defenders so busy that they had no opportunity of shooting effectively at our men. When the second wave of forty more men landed after a while, they only had to help to clear out the place."

"In other words: the attack was a total and unpleasant surprise for the enemy?"

"Totally."

"And then you destroyed the base, as you said?"

"Everything went up in shards and pieces and fragments and slivers and bits when we blew it up. We completed everything before lunch time."

"Did you blow yourselves up in the provess of destroying that lot?"

"Of course, not. We left explosives with time switches inside the ammo store and the place flew sky-high only after we had left with the choppers. The shock wave rocked the helicopters somewhat."

"And the war is going on and on?"

"The damn war is going on and on. It seems as if nobody is willing to stop. Hannelore says she's glad that the war is going to stop for me when I start my studies next year. She thinks I am tired of this war and even became somewhat bossies due to all the violence and bloodshed and dead corpses that I have witnessed."

"I think I've contracted some shell-shock myself after four years of uninterrupted fighting against the Russians. Perhaps you can do something to my head after the completion of your studies."

"Speaking of those Russians. They will only compensate Swapo for all their losses. The war will go on and on."

15. OPERATION COBRA

Oshakati, Ovamboland, Friday, 7 November 1980

Hannelore and I arrive simultaneously at home – both of use spent after an ardious week – I did my thing in the sick-bay of the military base and she was busy in the state hospital across the road from the military base.

Me: "And how was your day? Busy?"

Hannelore: "More or less. The usual. Kids who got burnt, old people with chest problems, pregnant women – the usual lot. And yours?"

"It was Okay. My job alternates between very busy directly after a military operation and rather quiet times when there are not many clashes. But I, nevertheless, had a very interesting patient today. He arrived yesterday with a number of rather serious aches and scratches and cuts and bruises and I had to check up on him again today."

"And?"

"The man then told me his story. He is a lieutenant in the artillery and he had to man an OP somewhere in Angola while sitting in a big tree with binoculars and a radio."

"An OP?"

"That's an ovservation post. That's the guy who sits near the target and who informs the gunners per radio whether their bombs are falling on the right spot."

"Isn't that a very dangerous job?"

"According to this chap, it was extremely dangerous. He got into this big tree – that's what he tells me – so that he can see far. Just after he has made himself confortable on a fork in the tree, he discvers that he is sitting on a cobra. He grabs the snake behind its head and ties it into a big knot. That, allegedly, prevented the snake from lifting his head to bite him."

Hannelore laaughs: "Really?"

"That's what the man tells me. But that's not all. Because he climbed into this tree, early in the morning, just after first light, he didn't realize that the tree was the resting place for a troop of lions during the hottest part of the day. When the sun started to heat up and after he had thrown the snake from the tree, half-a-dozen lions came to relax and rest under that tree."

"Which, of course, makes it dangerous to leave his seat in the tree?"

"That's exactly what he tells me. He says that he developed a serious need to relieve himself during the day and he emptied his bladder from high up in the tree – directly upon the head of the big male lion below him. This chap didn't like the stream of warm yellow fluid and he gave a loud angry roar."

"Do you believe what the man told you?"

"There is more to come. He comes to the realization that he has chosen the wrong tree for an OP and that he must move away. Fortunately, a troop of elephants came that way and they chase the lions away. One of them starts rubbing himself against the tree and shakes the tree. He falls from the tree and lands on the back of one of the elephants. This animal gets a fright from the unexpected load on its back and starts running away. After about a kilometer, the elephant manages to shake him off onto a bush with thorns – and that's where he got so badly hurt."

"Can you believe this man?"

"Well, he has all these scratches and cuts and bruises that he can show for his experience."

16. EXERCISE DILEMMA

Oshakati, Ovamboland, Saturday, 15 November 1980

Hannelore and I rest a little while of all the hard work to pack our household in preparation of our move to Cape Town.

My beautiful German wife remarks: "It's wonderful what you Pa has been able to arrange for us: a transfer for both of us to Two Mil in Wynberg. It helps that the state pays for our relocation. It's not so nice that the removal contractor won't pack all our crockery and other valuable stuff and that we have to do it ourselves."

"I had a medic at Etale who said that success in life is dependant upon the networks you have. It does seem as if this is true in the case of my Pa. He knows a lot of people in the personnel department of the Medical Service where he worked before his retirement."

"I'm sure he didn't bribe anybody. But is just works that way that one is inclined to do a little more for your friends that for outsiders."

"Exactly."

"On the one hand, I'm relieved to be able to get away from this war, but on the other hand, I also say farewell with a heavy heart."

"Yes, we made lots of friends. When will we ever see them again?"

"Not only that. Remember, I was born in South West. I grew up in this country. This is my country. There in the state hospital, I saw how these countrymen of mune are suffering."

"Of course, they suffer. After all, a whacking war is being waged here for the last fourteen years. Many of them received gunshot wounds or lost body parts due to land mines."

"Not only that. They are torn apart by conflicting loyalties."

"How on earth can anybody feel loyal towards those terrorists who kill, maim, and rape, wherever they go?"

"Dave, this is Africa. These people experience the world very different from us with our European background."

"I realize that. But how can you be on the side of a party whose members maim paople, abduct peole, kill people and rape people?"

"Let me explain. During the time that I've worked here in the state hospiatl I managed to gain the confidence of a number of black nurses. They told me a lot. The Swapo fighters are in many cases their brothers, cousins, friends. Sometimes also their sisters and nieces. Of course, they won't like it when some these fighters are shot dead by our troops. In many cases, they can't even have a funeral because this brother, cousin, friend, or sister was buried somewhere in Angola in a mass grave after they were blown up by the bombs of our Air Force or our soldiers."

"These terrs blooming well deserve that. They were all trained to sow death and destruction to satisfy the lust for power of their leaders. We can never allow that."

"Of course, the civilian population in these parts suffer under the onslaughts of these terrorists. But they also suffer from the onslaughts by the Army and especially the 'Koevoets'[52]."

"Yes, I must agree: the Koevoets are supposed to be Policemen who have to protect the population. But I am sure that you must have treated more than one member of the local population

---

[52] "Koevoet" – the Afrikaans word for a crowbar. This was the name of a special Police unit that hunted terrorists and often went too far in their treatment of the local population. The members of this unit were popularly called the equivalent of "crowbars".

who was on the receiving end of the thuggish and tactless treatment by these bullies."

"Exactly. Just as they are trampled upon and maltreated by their own people. But that's their own people. The Koevoets are commanded by white officers. They are strangers – not their own people."

"Do they hate al white people?"

"Actually, only the South Africans whom they regard as occupiers of their country. They don't want to be a province of South Africa. They see that many other former colonies throughout Africa gained independence and they wish that for their own country. They accept me because I was born in this country. The South African government forces apartheid upon them and they experience that as very humiliating. They want to manage their own affairs without any force from outside."

"The South African government has already agreed to grant independence and self-government to South West. But we can't allow it when the country is taken over by a gang of allies of the communist Soviet Union. If Swapo gains the upper hand here, it will become just as bad as in the countries behind the Iron Curtain. The leaders of Swapo are just a bunch of Stalinists."

"I dn't think the ordinary people here are communists. Communism is alien to their Africa culture. According to their culture, it is a matter of fact that one follows a strong leader. A strong leader demonstrates his power by committing acts of terrorism and violence and eradicaing his opponents. That's how he gains respect."

"All right, even if all the supporters of Swapo won't embrace all the doctrines of communism, the Soviet Union and her lap dog, Cuba, will get a foothold in our back yard. We can never allow that because it will only lead to misery and poverty. Our Defence Force is fighting here with the purpose of preventing such a destiny for these people. Angola already has a communist government and the poor people are living in horrible conditions there."

"We both understand that. But I have my doubts whether these people will ever see it that way. And that's why they continue with the struggle. And that's why their young people slip over the border to get trained as fighters in Swapo's camps in Angola."

"We try our best to convince them that it will be best to support us. We build hospitals, schools, roads, reservoirs – you name it."

"Granted. But they think that it's anyway our duty. They don't experience it as a favor. But then I am struggling with a huge dilemma. I often get patients who are actually secretly fighters of Swapo. My nurses point them out to me."

"And it's your duty to report them so that they can be arrested and stand trial."

"It's my duty as a medical professional to aleviate pain and suffering and to do nothing that could harm my patients. The essence of our medical code of ethics, after all, boils down to the following: 'Do no harm'."

"That's a damned dilemma."

"And then I only have the word from my nurses that patient A, B, and C are actually terrorists. The moment I report patients A, B, and C to the Police, I will lose the confidence of my nurses."

"That's definitely a damned darned dilemma."

"We say good-bye to this place over a fortnight and then we are going on holiday of a month on my dad's farm and at your folks' place in Gordon's Bay before we start just after New Year's Day at Two Mil and you start with your course in neurology at Maties."

"Halleluyah."

"And then you can start to get rid of your own shell-shock. You were involved in far too many battles. You have seen too many people who have been killed, maimed, wounded, or damaged. You're not the cheerful and playful young maan to whom I got married."

"'A very valid point. Thanks."

"It can only be a good thing if you become a qualified neurologist and understand how people's brains work. You will be able to understand your own shell-shock so much better."

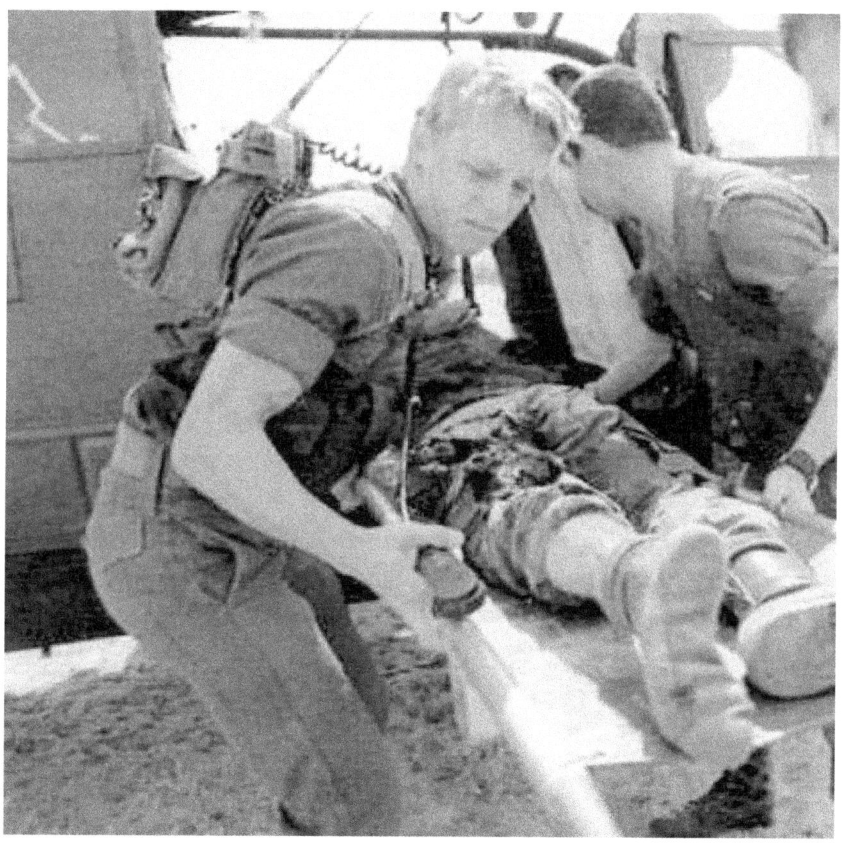

"As well as rhe shell-shock of thousands of troops and civvies. This bloody war messed with the heads of too many people."

“And it will be your task to help people to get rid of all their ghosts, nightmares, and anxieties. Perhaps you will be able to discover the mechanisms behind shell-shock.”

“There’s still a long road ahead before I will be able to call myself a specialist.”

Hannelore suddenly smiles: “You just mentioned a specialist. Do you know what is the difference between a general practitiner, a specialist medical practitioner and a psychiatrist?”

“No. Please enlighten me.”

“Okay. The general practitioner knows a little bit about everything.. The specialist knows everything about a little bit. And the psychiatrist makes sure that his patients tell him everything.”

I laugh as well: “And in the meantime my brain tells me that he wants coffee and cookies before we strat working again.”

“And little David tells me it’s time for his bottle.”

17. OPERATION ASKARI

Wynberg, Cape Town, Monday, 28 November 1983

The telephone in my consulting room at Two Military Hospital in Wynberg, Cape Town, rings. I'n very busy with an urgent case and I ignore the ringing. If it's really something urgent, my receptionist will take a message and I will phone back as son as possible.

After the phone has stopped ringing, it starts ringing again. I feel annoyed because my receptionist knows that she must take messages when I am busy with a patient. Very impatiently, I pick up the reeiver and bark: "Yes, what is it?"

"Please hold on for Commandant Flip Venter of Oshakati."

Immediately, I sit up straight, at attention. He is my old commander at the sick-bay in Oshakati and if he phones me here in Cape Town, it must be something urgent. After ten seconds the voice of the commandant comes through. After we have enquired about eachother's health and welfare, he asks: "Man, is it possible for you to jump on a plane to Ruacana immediately? I will see to it that a signal, together with a travel order, will be sent to you as soon as possible. Issued by the general in Windhoek."

"This is bloody unexpected. What the devil must I do at Ruacana, of all places?"

"I get the feeling that another big ops is brewing again. Rumors have it that it's called Ops Askari. The tactical HQ of the task force contacted me urgently because they need a doctor. One of the men who joined them during the tactical exercises was involved in an accident and got seriously hurt. He had to be moved to One Mil. Now they need a replacement, pronto, immediately, as in yesterday. Because this ops is due to start very soon. Can you come? I immediately thought of you because you have lots of operational experience. Apart from that, you're a parabat."

"Commandant, this is a sudden unexpected surprise. I don't know. I'm sitting here at Two Mil and quite a number of the medical officers are planning to take leave over the Christmas period. I was seconced to Casaulties for this time, although I'm actually a clinical assistant at Neurology."

"I will see to it that a signal is immediately sent to your commander – by the commanding general – that you will have to be released. It looks like a medical state of emergency here. I can't lose one of my medical officers – I have anyway not enough of them at the moment. The Citizen Force members whom we have called up, all somehow or other nanaged to get exemptions and I must rely on a few unexperienced national servicemen. You had better come."

On my own I think that this commandant is risking much with this telephone conversation. A call from the Border to Cape Town passes through at least three exchanges and somebody in one of these exchanges could easily have overheard us and betray the planned operation called Operation Askari and which is due to start from Ruacana very soon.

I answer nevertheless: "All right. I'm coming. I actually don't have a valid excuse because the exam for my third year of my course in neurology is something of the past and I passed everything. All that remains is that I complete my thesis and pass the final exam next year before I can call myself a specialist neurologist. I don't have plans for the holidays that would have to be cancelled because I was supposed to do duty during the whole of December, working at Casualties. Okay, send those signals."

Ruacana, Monday, 5 December 1983

My arrival at Ruacana yesterday afternoon was in the nick of time because the task force, of which I was to be part, took to the road this morning. I was told to become part of the artillery component. I and two medics travel in a Casspir ambulance.

The commander of the artillery, Major Len Lightfoot, explained to me last night what the goal of the operation is: "It's the plan that we must give Swapo and the Angolans such a fright that they start running away from southern Angola. The Angolans are providing Swapo more and more with aid and protection and we can't wrestle and grapple with Swapo without interference and meddling by the MPLA. Our fight is actually only with Swapo – not with the Angolans. But now we are forced to attack Angolan bases. We hope to give them such a fright that they will wet their pants and run away. Then we also get rid of Swapo at the same time. Our goal is to gain control over the southern parts of Angola. But I don't think we will be able to hold onto those parts indefinitely. The government doesn't have the money and the resources to conduct too many large-scale operations over an extended period of time."

"How big is the task force? Do we have enough men and equipment?"

"Man, there are quite a lot of us. Not all of them got assembled here. As I understand it, we have five combat groups. We are, therefore, something between a brigade and a division, or an outsize brigade. Here at Ruacane, we have three combat groups. There is Combat Group X-Ray. It's basically Six One Mechanized Battalion Group, plus extra armor and artillery. We travel along with them.

"And then there is Combat Group Victor. It consists of a group of Citizen Force members, about one third of Eight Two Mechanized Brigade. Combat Team Tango is somewhat too big for a combat team, but they also cannot be regarded as a complete combat group. Furhter to the east, there are four companies of Three

Two Battalion[53] on Buffels, as well as Combat Grup Manie, which will operate more or less on their own."

"Thanks. Now I know. And I guess my job will be to patch up the men of the artillery of X-Ray who are bleeding and to feed them Panados."

"Yes, more or less."

"And malaria pills."

We cross the Kunene, which forms the border with Angola, at Calueque and our first destination is Xangongo where a tactical headquarters – a Tac HQ – is to be established under the command of Brigadier Joep Joubert.

Xangongo, Sunday, 11 December 1983

When we reached Xangongo tthree days ago, it became clear that all Angolese soldiers and Swapo fighters had left the place long ago. They must have known about our advance. It's a sizable town on the banks of the Kunene River and there's a landing strip for light aircraft. The town consists mostly of shabby and seedy shacks.

We push on early this morning to conquor Quiteve further north We cross the Kunene again at Xangongo to move on the western side of river northwards. The river flows basically from the north to the south at this point.

---

[53] 32 Battalion consisted for the most part of Portuguese-speaking Angolans who previously belonged to the FNLA and were recruited by the SADF. They were known in Angola as "Os Terríveis" (the Terrible Ones) and was the most feared unit in the South African Army. They were known as excellent guerilla fighters. Although its base was inside Sector 20, it wasn't part of this Sector. It was larger than a conventional battalion, consisting of more than a thousand men.

Quiteve, Monday, 12 December 1983

We attack Quiteve during the early morning hours. 'Attack' is certainly the wrong word because we find this place also desolate. Any Angolese soldiers or Swapo fighters who could have hidden here, have disappeared a long time ago. That's what we hoped for. We do find, though, a big amount of loot – ammo, weapons, food and vehicles. And paper work.

Lightfoot informs me that Battle Group X-Ray is supposed to advance this afternoon in a south westerly direction – doing bundu bashing. Combat Team Tango is supposed to move further northwards and attack Mulondo, while we are attacking Cahama. It is thought that a whole Angolese brigade lies dug in at Mulondo and the major wonders whether Tango will achieve anything.

While we are getting ready to leave Quiteve, two Angolese tanks from the north suddenly try to surprise us. The aid of the Air Force is quickly summoned and two Mirages see to it that one tank is blown up. The other one quickly gets out of the way.

Cahama, Friday, 16 December 1983

We reached Cahama yesterday evening after a difficult drive through the bushes and rough terrain. The bundu bashing damaged a number of our vehicles, but fortunately not my ambulance. Cahama is about eighty kilometers to the south west of Quiteve. According to our intelligence, Cahama contains a Swapo headquarters, together with an Angolese brigade and a Cuban battalion. It seems to me that we have collided with a rather strong force. Our real enemy is Swapo but it's impossible to smoke these terrorists out without letting fire and flames rain down upon the Angolese and Cuban units.

Major Lightfoot asks me when we encounter each other during first light: "Doc, will you get afraid when our guns start spitting fire and vomiting sparks here all around you?"

I laugh: "Major, you must please excuse me when I get so afraid that I wet my pants, due to all the shocks. I bought these parabat wings at a flea market (and I point to the wings on my left breast). I didn't really work for them."

The major laughs more than I do: "Doc, do you really think that I would fall for that one? Look here, you must have noticed long ago that we have three batteries – guns and rocket launchers. One battery consists of those new G-4's, self-propelled howitzers. We are going to boil and burn and broil and bash the Angolans and Cubans from different directions. We have enough bombs and rockets to continue shooting the shit out of them for many days."

"I'm glad that I'm not now cornered inside Cahama."

"Our men are ready to tackle them from the east and the north – the directions from where they won't expect it."

During the day, our guns roar and rumble and the rockets scream and shout. I stay busy with a few wounded men who are being carried to my ambulance. They got hit because the Angolans shoot back, although not very accurately.

Cahama, Saturday, 31 December 1983

Although our artillery managed to silence most of the Angolese aritllery, were are still sitting outside Cahama after a fortnight of fighting. The enemy refuses to give up or run away, although we make it almost impossible to do so because we besiege them from all sides.

A few days ago, a few tanks tried to drive us away, but our agile armored cars, the Ratel 90's, ran circles around them and wrecked a few of them rather badly and permanently.

The Ratel 90 armored car, armed with a 90 mm anti-tank gun.

The fast flaming birds of our Air Force flew over a few times and dropped exploding eggs onto the Angolans and Cubans. I believe that a great number of them suffered so much pain that funerals had to arranged for them.

General Constand Viljoen, former chief of the Army and presently chief of the Defence Force, visited us the day before Christmas and urged us to carry on with our efforts to drive the enemy out of Cahama. We only have time till New Year's Eve because there is much international pressure to force us to abandon Operation Askari.

General Constand Viljoen

Our commandant explained to him that it would be suicide to send in our infantry to capture the town because our men would have to attack over open terrain, filled with land mines, where they would be swatted like flies, even if they attacked in our Ratel infantry fighting vehicles. The enemy is simply too well dug in that we can dislodge them, although we must have destroyed almost all of their tanks and bigger artillery pieces.

They still have, though, a number of 23 millimeter anti-aircraft guns and heavy machine guns with which they can penetrate the light armor of our vehicles.

And today, right on New Year's Eve, we get the order to stop the siege of Cahama and to retreat to Xangongo. The idea is that we throw in the towel and submit to international pressure.

Major Lightfoot: "Doc, it doesn't seem as if we achieved any of our goals. My gunners did their thing but they couldn't do more than that."

According to Major Lightfoot, the same thing happened to task force Tango. They were not able to make the enemy frightened and they also received the order to withdraw.

Cuvelai, Tuesday, 3 January 1984

Our orders are suddenly changed. Major Lightfoot tells me that the new orders expect of us to get as fast as possible to Cuvelai and not to proceed to Xangongo and return to South West Africa as originally ordered. Our new task will be to aid the struggling task force Victor at Cuvelai. It seems as if the politicians in Pretoria suddenly decided that we must not be satisfied with failuers and blunders at Cahama, Mulondo and Cuvelai.

We must struggle through dense bush country and we manage to travel the distance of 180 kilometers between Cahama and Cuvelai in three days. The whole X-Ray task force is exhausted and we hope to get some respite to regain our breaths and catch up on sleep before we go into action again.

When we arrive during the late afternoon at Cuvelai, the major tells me that the men of Victor, who are all members of the Citizen Force who were called up for a camp, regarded the whole outing as a camping holiday and did almost nothing. It was their task to scare the Angolans, Cubans and Swaps to such a degree that they would all disappear with their tails between their legs, but they achieved "flippin' nothing". It appears that they didn't even try.

Major Lightfoot: "These chaps grew soft in civvie street. Their discipline is lousy and they've forgotten all they were taught during their two years of national service."

Later during the evening, when the major has returned from an order group, he is angry, agitated, and annoyed: "The brigadier ordered those campers to be the speer point of our attack on Cuvelai tomorrow. Their officers flatly refused. He threatened them with a court martial, but they just laughed in his face because a court martial will only be possible much later. And should he arrest them now, there won't be anybody to lead the troops. That left him in jam street. And he needs to overpower Cuvelai now, immediately, as soon as possible, pronto, so that the Angolese and Cuban troops can be chased away. The end result is that X-Ray, as tired, spent, and tattered as we are, must lead the attack tomorrow."

Me: "It's clear to me that civvie street made those campers lazy and rotten. They probably came from different units and don't know each other well. X-Ray consists basically of Six One Mech and these men were working together for the last few months."

"Exactly."

"And I observe that the men of Six One Mech got excellent training, even if I am not familiar with the artillery."

"Exactly."

Cuvelai, Wednesday, 4 January 1984

Major Lightfoot informs me that Cuvelai is occupied by a strong force. There is an Angolese brigade, as well as two Cuban battalions and three battalions of Swapo. "We are going to giv them hell," he promises me: "Doc, do you have your bandages, ointments, headache pills, and injections ready? I think a few of our men will develop some aches and pains."

"I'm ready and my medics are ready."

Our Air Force arrives shortly after dawn: Mirages and Impalas. The bombs rain on Cuvelai. Even before the last bomb has fallen from the heavens, our artillery lets loose and pieces of exploding metal are showered over the Angolans, Cubans, and Swaps. Our mechanized infantry in their Ratel-20's infantry fighting vehicles attack directly afterwards and they sow death, destruction, and disaster onto the defenders.

In my ambulance, I listen over the radio to the messages coming in. I count five Angolese tanks that were destroyed by our Ratel 90's. One of our Ratel 20's filled with troops is, however, hit by the gun of a Russian T-54 tank and shot to bits. Four survivors are brought to my ambulance and they tell me that seven of their mates were killed. These four boys got wounded badly and they still tremble from the shock.

The Ratel-20 infantry fighting vehicle. It is armed with a 20 mm canon and carries a crew of eleven men

One of them tries to hide his shock with this remark: "Doc, our mates were blown to pieces. How are we going to know which hands and feet belong to which head? How the hell will anybody be able to sort out all the bits?"

After I have tended to the men in the ambulance, I get out to watch more of the battle. There is an Alouette III helicopter whose pilot is defying death by flying low over the Angolese positions. With that, he forces the Angolese anti-aircraft guns to shoot in his direction, thereby betraying their positions. Our artillery takes them out in no time.

During lunch time the remaining defenders decide that they've had enough and they break out to flee in a northerly direction – exactly what we wanted to achieve. They leave all their equipment behind – tanks, cannons, ammo, vehicles, everything.

I ask Major Lightfoot: "Are our boys going to pursue them on our Ratels?"

"Our men are too tired. That would be too much for them. But, don't worry. A nice and nasty and noxious surprise is waiting for these fugitives. I've received the message that our own Askari's, the black Portuguese of Three Two Battalion, the 'terrible ones', are waiting for them at Techamutete, a few clicks from here. Lots of blood, brains, brawn, bowels, and shit will be blown all over the place."

During the afternoon, I hear that our men picked up the bodies of three hundred and twenty enemy fighters here at Cuvelai.

A sergeant complains towards me: "Doc, you will have to deal with many men with blisters on their hands."

"What do you mean?"

"I'm in charge of a platoon whose members have to dig a deep hole where we have to park all these corpses. The men are not used to work with spades and picks and their soft hands will develop lots of blisters."

"It will also not be pleasant to pile all those dead bodies into a big hole. Order them to fasten handceherchiefs over their mouths and noses to keep the flies out."

Cuvelai, Thursday, 5 January 1984

While I'm busy looking at the wounds of a number or our men, a lonely airplane of our Air Force, a DC-3 Dakota, flies low over our position. Two parachutes open under the plane while she turns around to fly back. Its clear that she didn't drop people, but big boxes or crates. Our commandant immediately jumps to the spot where the crates land. He orders the men of X-Ray to assemble in their companies, batteries, and squadron, as if on parade.

He opens the boxes and asks his 2IC to help him with the distribution of the contents. As every man passes, he is given a very welcome tin of beer with compliments of the chief of the SADF.

The troops call this beer "Number Seventeen". If one holds the tin upside down, one can read the name "NO17". If the tin is held uprifgt, the name "LION" appears on the label.

Gordon's Bay, Sunday, 19 February 1984

We are visiting my parents during this weekend at Gordon's Bay where they are currently living. I and my dad, a retired brigadier, are sitting on the veranda while we are watching the waters of False Bay. Each one is fondling a Number Seventeen.

"Pa, thank you, again, that you've taken care of Hannelore and little David when I had to go to Angola on short notice."

"We did it with pleasure.I enjoy speaking German to my daughter-in-law and my grandson. I will help her eagerly with anything. By the way, have you noticed that your wife is expecting again?"

"How do you know that?"

"Any fool can see that. You don't need a degree in medicine to notice something like that."

"Oh."

After we have stayed silent for two minutes, my outoppie asks: "What do you think of that agreement we reached with Angola in Lusaka last week?"

"It looks good on paper. We could convince the Angolans to talk to us because we whacked them not too gently last month at Cuvelai. We promised to pull all our troops out of Angola. There are still four companies of Three Two Battalion camping out at Tehamutete to make sure that the Angolese troops and Swapo fighters don't return. They are being aided by some men from Unita. The Angolans promised on their part to get a firm grip on Swapo and to prevent them from crossing the border to South West. On paper it looks all right."

"Will it work?"

I grin: "Forget it. The Angolans will rapidly forget what they have promised and we will have to fight once more against them and Swapo, somewhere deep inside Angola to keep the terrs out of South West. Then our gains in Angola will all be for nought."

"And the Russians will compensate them for all their losses – tanks, trucks, big guns, AK-47's, the whole tuti. I saw during the Secpnd World War that the Russians just keep on coming and coming. This will happen again."

"Hmm. Hmmm!"

18. EXERCISE TRAUMA

Gordon's Bay, Wednesday, 12 December 1984

My parents, my German parents-in-law, my elder sister, my brothers and their families are assembled on the veranda of my father's home in Gordon's Bay. A big barbecue fire has been ignited and we enjoy the pleasant early evening air while we look over False Bay.

Today was a very special day because the degree M.Med. (Neurology) was awarded *cum laude* to me in Stellenbosch this morning.

I wore my step-out unform with medals for the occasion – of course, together with the academic gown. This was the first occasion when I wore three stars on my shoulders and now I am Captain (Doctor) David Scholtz. My promtion was approved directly after the results of my course as a medical specialist were announced.

My dad, a retired brigadier of the South African Medical Service, as well as a trained surgeon, is the host. My brother Pieter, who works as a medical practitioner and virologist, wants to know what the topic of my thesis was.

I proudly announce: "The title is 'Eye Movements for the Treatment of Post-Traumatic Stress Disorder'".

Pieter finds the title incomprhensible: "How on earth will eye movements cure soldier boys of their trauma?"

Me: "If you apply it crreectly, I might help a lot."

My dad: "During the war, when I was attached to the much-feared German Waffen-SS, I saw many men who were suffering from shell-shock. In other words, post- traumatic stress. In may cases, I had to amputate an arm or a leg, inside a terrible and timeworn tent for a theater, not far from the ront lines. Others lost an eye or were maimed in another manner. Many boys blew out their last breaths while I was still busy with them and they called for the last time for their mothers. But the war was simply too much for others, even if they were otherwise unscathed. It often happened that I had to embrace and hold a crying young man on account of his nightmares and fears. Some of my colleagues were not able to endure it any longer – they simply saw too much blood, death, pain, shit, suffering, and tears."

Me: "Pa, were you able to do something for these suffering souls?"

My Pa: "I wished I knew how to help them. I left these men in the care of our chaplain, a Romish priest with whom I had strong friendship ties. All he could do, was to pray for these boys and perform the last rites, where applicable. It seemed as if it helped when they confessed their sins towards him and he gave them absolution."

Pieter: "Pa, you actually told us very little about your war experiences. I would have liked to hear more of that."

My Pa: "I think that I've contracted quite a bit of shell-shock myself. Most veterans don't like to talk about their experiences and exploits. It's too painful, these memories."

Me: "That's what I also found – especially when I did interviews for my thesis. During my service at the sick-bay in Oshakati, as well as during operations, I saw many men for whom the war just became too much. And not only young men, national servicemen. Also members of the Permanent Force, men with many years of service. The problem with many of these men was that they started drinking and get soaked in an effort to get rid of all their noxious and nasty nightmares and terrible trauma."

Pa: "That's what I also often saw. But, of course, the alcohol doesn't really help."

Me: "Precisely. Actually, it only aggrevates the pest of a problem. And that's how I got the theme for my thesis. All the doctors, medics and social workers feel powerless to do something about this state of affairs. The troops often said that somebody became 'bossies' if he had contracted shell-shock. Even the psychologists didn't know what to do with these cases."

Pieter: "What did the psychologists do in these cases?"

Me: "They conduct group sessions where half-a-dozen men sit in a circle and tell their stries about their fears and accidents and near brushes. The theory is that it will help if they see that they are not the only guys who had bad experiences and trauma. It is supposed to help if you let off some steam and share your feelings with other by talking about those."

Pa: "Does it help?"

Me: "My investigation showed that it helps almost bugger-all. If one compares the men who attended these sessions with men who didn't get this treatment, they are all after a few weeks still at exactly the same point. Those who improved wuuld have improved anyway without these group sessions."

Pieter: "How did you go about to do your investigations?"

Me: "Fortunately, I did my clinical assistentship at Two Mil. I was able to study more or less sixty, seventy cases of post-traumatic stress disorder."

My dad:"How did you know which men to use for your study?"

Me: "They were referred to me by general practitioner, social workers, chaplains and so on. I had to discriminate between genuine cases being 'bossies' – and men who were merely 'slapgat'[54]. I divided the genuine cases into five groups: Group one got lectures about techniques to deal with sress, but they didn't receive any other treatment. Group two took part in group sessions with a social

[54] "Slapgat" – an Afrikaans expression that can't be translated directly; it means something like lazy or loafing.

worker. The men of groupt three were fed antidepressants by a psychiatrist. The fourth group received sleep therapy where they were sedated for a whole week. And group five was the men on whom I perfrmed eye movements. I should actually have had a sixth group where the men could be treated with hypnosis, but the psychologists at Two Mil didn't want to do it because they told me that they had already tried it and it didn't really help."

Pieter: "Which group got the most benefit from all these types of treatment?"

Me: "The only group that improved substantially was group five, the boys who did eye movements. I gave questionnaires to all the participants before the time. Afterwards they completed the same questionnaires again. With those, I wanted to determine whether there was any improvement over time. I wanted to know how often they got nightmares, how high their anxiety levels were, how their lives got changed by the accidents or other traumatic experiences, and so forth.

"The results of the analysis of these questionnaires were interesting. The men who only received lectures improved only marginally. Group sessions were a waste of time. A few men were afterwards really in a worse state because they were exposed to the trauma of other guys. Antidepressants didn't help and all it did was to blunt the emotional life of those men. Most of them also suffered nasty and ugly and unwelcome side-effects. The men who were put to sleep showed very little improvement. But I could see promising results with those who did eye movements."

Pieter: "Lok here, as a medical prctitioner I know something about the eye. I can hardly imagine that eye movements will do anything to lessen the fears and anxieties of people."

Me: "You must remember that the eyes are actually part of the brain. The retina, at the back of the eye, is directly linked to the occiputal lobe at the back side of the brain. On their way there, the optical nerves make contact with the amygdala, the alarm system of the brain. When the amygdala registers some or other danger, the person reacts immediately, inter alia to secrete stress hormones to deal with the sudden dangerous situation. If you step on a snake, somewhere in the bush, you jump very fast, very high, and very far. It's an automatic reaction. Only afterwards, you realize that you stepped upon a puff-adder or a cobra and that he could have been dangerous."

Pa: "And when the bombs explode all around you and your mates are being shot dead, then your amygdala kicks in and becomes active, I suppose?"

Me: "That's right, Pa. But your amygdala can also become over-active if he registers too many shocks. Some people are just more susceptible than others for trauma and in their cases the amygdala becomes hyperactive more easily. I came to the conclusion that it is necessary to switch off the over-active amygdala in men who became bossies in order to pull them out of their trauma."

Pieter: "And you do that with eye movements?"

Me: "Exactly. You must have heard of REM-sleep, I guess? When one sleeps during the night, your sleep goes through several stages. One of them is REM sleep. That is the abbreviation for 'rapid eye movements'. That's when you are dreaming and your eyes are moving around while you are watching the action. The amygdala is anatomically part of the hipocampus, your short-term memory. While you are sleeping, and especially during REM sleep, the contents of your short-term memory are being transferred to the temporal lobe, directly next to it. That's your long-term memry. I figured that if one could interfere with this process of transferring memories, then one can lessen the anxiety element of traumatic memories and switch off the amygdala in the process."

Pieter: "And that's why you simulate REM sleep by these eye movements?"

Me: "Exactly. You are hitting the little nail directly on its little head. One of the functions of REM sleep, while you are dreaming, is precisely to process negative experiences. I ask the man with shell-shock to retrieve his memory of a shocking experience. He must re-experience it as realistically as possible. Then I take up a position in front of him and instruct him to follow my hand with his eyes while if move my hand to and fro and up and down in frond of him. He must keep his head still and only move his eyes. With that, I simulate REM sleep and that helps the man to process his fears, anxieties and shocks – more or less as if he is asleep and dreaming."

Pa: "And it works?"

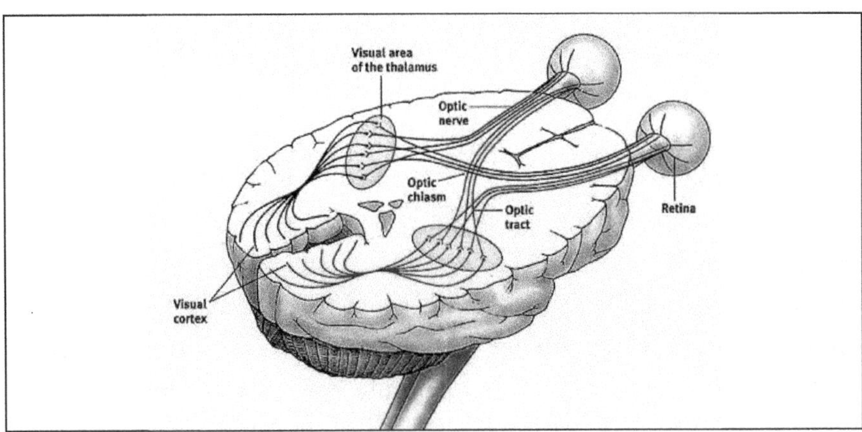

Me: "Rather a lot. It's in any case better, far better, than the other techniques. The process has to be repeated a few times to achieve the desired outcome. One neads many repetitions to, as it were, reprogram the brain."

Pieter: “And if you influence the hipocampus with these eye movements, then it also has an effect on the amygdala that is attached to it?”

”That’s right.”

Pieter: “Have you included any people outside of Two Mil in your investigations?”

Me: “Not directly. I had, though, a very interesting conversation with an old lady in Fish Hoek. She is Aunt Annie Patat[55] Theron, originally from Ceres and the Patats of those parts. After the Second World War, she had the task of looking after a dozen men who were extreme cases of shell-shock. On a government grant. I mean, the government grant didn’t cause the shell-shock, but it paid for her time and expenses.”

Pa: “What did she tell you?”

Me: “Interesting stories. There was this guy who hid in the toilet the whole day and who shouted that the Germans were coming. And then there was this man who boiled pots full of water on her stove every day. Just in case the medics needed it for sterilizing bandages and medical equipment. Another chap hid under his bed every time when an airplane flew overhead. And yet another man made Aunty Annie Patat mad by asking her ten times per day: ‘Nurse, where did you hide my rifle?’.”

Pa: “Poor guys!”

Me: “And another poor soul asked her at least three times per day: ‘Nurse, when will this war end and we get peace so that I can go home?’ And that was more than a year after the end of the war.”

Pa: “It’s only an act of grace that I didn’t develop that type of condition. Hey, I must go and attend to that barbecue fire before

---

[55] “Patat” – literally, a sweet potota. It is used as a nickname in this case.

all the wood has burnt down to a heap of ashes – just as these poor guys got burnt out."

After supper, my outoppie asks: "And what are your plans, now that you are officially a neurologist? Are you resigning from the Defence Force and start a private practice?"

Me: "Hannelore and I have decided to put in applications to be posted back to Oshakati. There, at Sector One Zero, I will be able to treat the traumatized troops so much earlier. The sooner, the better, before they get transferred to somewhere else. Hannelore wishes to return to South West. That's where she was born, after all."

19. EXERCISE SHELL-SHOCK

Gordon's Bay, Friday, 14 December 1984

We are visiting my parents in Gordon's Bay for the weekend. During dinner, my father says: "I have just the right patient for you on whom you can apply your new technique."

"Pa, it's the weekend now and I want to rest and relax with you. When must I see this man?"

"It's an old friend of mine and I've invited him to visit us here tomorrow afternoon. Then you can hear his story and perhaps do something for the man. He complains of serious shell shock that he could not get rid of, forty years after the Second World War. Please, do it as a favor for your beloved gray-haired 'outoppie'."

"Then, all right. Where can I work with the man if I think that it will be possible to do something for him?"

"We may perhaps prepare one of the bedrooms for you."

Gordon's Bay, Saturday, 15 December 1984

My dad introduces me to Brigadier Karl Krause, an old Air Force officer who has retired nine years ago already. His wife Sonja is with him.[56]

Within a short period of time, my father, Brigadier Krause, his wife Sonja, and Hannelore chat excitedly in German. I try my best to follow them.

My dad explains that he met Brigadier Krause and his wife in 1938 at a holiday resort in the Alps. That was during his honeymoon with his first German wife. Krause was at that time a young pilot in the German Luftwaffe, despite being a South African citizen. His wife was a student in Berlin at the time. He flew bomber

---

[56] See the novel SHELL-SHOCK.

aircraft during the war – against the British, against the Russians, against the South Africans in North Africa and against the Americans in Europe. During the war, they encountered each other on two occasions. When my dad returned to South Africa in 1948 after having received amnesty for fighting on the German side, he bumped into Krause again. They saw each other again a few years ago when my dad had to operate on his old friend for a third time – this time, in Two Mil. After that, they kept contact with each other.

My dad: "I'm actually jealous of my friend. He has three things that I never could get. I received merely the Iron Cross, Class One. He has the Knight's Cross to the Iron Cross, the Oak Leaves with the Knight's Cross, as well as a death certificate to prove that he fell during the war. His wife also has such a death certificate."

Me: "Golly! It's no wondet that you contracted shell shock. I will also get it if I held my own death certificate in my hands."

Brigadier Krause: "It's a long story how that happened. Anyway, I and my wife were indirectly and remotely involved in the attempt on Hitler's life on the twentieth of July 1944. We feared for our lives and we had to simulate our deaths to enable us to flee to safety without being pursued. That's how we obtained our death certificates. I wanted to frame them and hang them on the living room's wall, but my wife threatens to hang me instead if I should try anything of the sort.

"We reached Turkey and later Portugal along a circuiteous route before we moved to Angola and South West after the end of the war."

Sonja Krause: "At the end of the war, both of us held the rank of major – just as your father. My husband was in the Luftwaffe and I was with the 'Sicherheitsdienst'[57] or SD of the SS. I was actually a spy during the war."

Me: "Heavens! Did both of you contract shell-shock?"

Brigadier Krause: "Actually, yes. I was shot down three times and every time I was able to crawl out of the wreck alive. I was wounded twice and if it wasn't for your father, I would have lost a leg. I had to sink ships, shoot tanks out, bomb buildings and airfields, evade anti-aircraft fire and fighters and flee for my life in the end, a few months before the end of the war. It happened regularly that Russians, Americans, and Brits dropped bombs upon me and my base and it's a miracle orchestrated from the highest heaven that I am still alive today. Dozens and dozens of my friends and colleagues didn't make it. I had to observe how their air planes hit the earth and explode, with them still inside.

"In addition, I was responsible for the deaths of hundreds, yes, thousands of people. I think I won't ever be able to forgive myself, although I know it was war."

Sonja Krause: "I also encountered dangerous situations often. To be a spy, one needs guts in your insides and some insides in your guts. And then you always had to keep your presence of mind and stay as cool and stiff as a block of ice from the North Pole. It wasn't easy. Both of us still get nightmares about the war. It is still difficult to talk about it."

Brigadier Krause: "We cannot risk returning to Germany. Somebody there sued us for a gigantic amount of money. My brother-in-law was able to deflect the case by presenting copies of our death certificates dating from 1944 to the court and, fortunately, the court fell for that. But should we arrive there as living people, we will be charged with fraud, lies, perjury and theft and be locked

---

[57] "Sicherheitsdienst" – German for Security Service, the intelligence branch of the SS.

up because of all those. My wife still gets the horrors on account of that."

Sonja Krause: "The so-called theft actually occurred in Switzerland. A German court cannot lock us up for that. As a spy, I had several forged passports with which we could move all over the world, but their expiry dates occurred long ago. It's sad because I would have liked to go and visit my two brothers in Berlin with assumed names."

Me: "Goddness gracious me! It sounds as if both of you have acquired a hefty dose of post-traumatic stress disorder. Perhaps, I can help. I don't think it will work over here. I still have consulting room at Two Mil before I move back to Oshakati in January. Can you come thither sometime next week? Phone me on Monday and then we can can organize an appointment. I will do my best to help you to experience your first Chrismas withut nightmares, anxiety, and fears"

"Tops."

Afterwards, Hannelore tells me: "Thank you that you are prepared to help those poor folks. It's clear that they went through hell."

Me: "Just as many of our troops on the Border."

Hannelore: "Our troopies perform service of a few months at most, there on the Border. They participate perhaps in one battle – or two or three contacts at most. These people survived in the shadow of Death for many years, just as your dad. They had to flee for their lives. You must help them."

20. OPERATION SHOWER

Ruacana, Friday, 1 November 1985

It is part of my duties as neurologist at the sick-bay at Oshakati, Ovamboland, the headquarters of Serctor One Zero of the Operational Area, to visit the headquaters of the six battalions in the sector from time to time. There are the following six battalions: Five One Battalion (Ruacana), Five Two Battalion (Oskakati), Five Three Battalion (Ondangwa), Five Four Battalion (Eenhana), One Oh One Battalion (Ondangwa) and One Oh Two Battalion (Opuwa). At each of these headquarters, I must pay attention to troops who may be suffering from post-traumatic stress disorder. In Army slamg this condition is called "bossies", with reference tp the fact that the troops contracted this condition in the bush of the Operational Area or in Angola.

Troops who have taken part in battles or contacts with the enemy, the terrorists of Swapo or the Angolese Army, sometimes suffer from this disorder – especially if they witnessed lots of violence and bloodshed.

Somebdy who suffers from post-tramatic stress disorder is usually plagued by nightmares and flashbacks during which the traumatic experience is usually being relived. The patient's life is being ruled by all sorts of fears and anxieties and he is mostly over-cautious – very afraid of a repetition of the tramatic experience or something that may resemble it.

Medication doesn't help for this condition. During my training as neurologist, I managed to develop a method to quieten down the alarm system of the brain. During a period of two or three days when I visit a battalion base, I usually see about a dozen boys whose fears I have to conjure away. It is also my duty to weed out the malingerers who pretend to be "bossies", just to get out of the war.

I explain to my patients that they may be grateful that our Defence Force has sympathy regarding this condition. During the First World War, it happened that soldiers were executed by a firing squad as cowards or deserters when they contracted shell-shock and refused to fight any further or ran away. We understand this better today and there are methods to lessen the suffering and pain of a patient.

Yesterday, I arrived at the headquarters of Five One Battalion in the far western parts of the Sector at Ruacana and it is my intention of moving back to Oshakati under the protection of a convoy vehicles the day after tomorrow.

I was given a spot to sleep in the tent of the chaplain – called by the troops a "soul tiffie" or a "Bible tiffie" – the Reverend Cobus Coetzee, a part-time chaplain of the Citizen Force whose home unit is a commando in the Free State. He was called up for a camp of six weeks and this is his frist experience of the Border War. He is in his fifties and he approaches his work with great sincerity and enthusiasm to provide spiritual comfort to the troops.

After the day's activities, the officers and senior NCO's congregate as usual in the officers' club of the base. Unfortunately, there are those who endeavor to drown their fears and anxieties with alcohol – which doesn't help, of course. I join this group for the company. There are always interesting people to get acquainted with. The fact that I am a member of the Permanent Force and a professional soldier helps that I am easily accepted in this group.

This officers' club is, just as many other structures at bases at the Border, partly underground and in the form of a bunker that is surrounded by walls of sand bags. One has to descend on a flight of steps, consisting of sand bags, to reach the floor of the bunker. The roof, consisting of a number of heavy tree trunks, covered by a piece of canvas and some more sand bags, rests on thick logs planted into the earth. This reinforced roof must protect those inside from possible mortar bombs fired by Swapo insurgents.

I notice that the Reverend Coetzee doesn't spend some time in the club. I ask the adjutant, Captain Mielies Myburgh, where the chaplain is.

"Doc, do you notice? He is sitting over there, outside, and peering through one of the ventilation gaps of this bunker. He has a note book and he writes down how much every officer drinks."

"Doesn't he realize that he's welcome to join us, even if he only drinks a soda?"

"The poor old guy has alcohol on his brain. He arrived here three weeks ago and at every church parade so far he rants and raves about alcohol abuse. During chaplain's periods, he warns about the dangers of drinking. And he finds enough ammo in the Bible where drunkenness and insobriety are condemned as serious sins."

"As a medical practitioner, I can confirm that alcohol abuse is bad for your health. But a mouth full of beer, wine or spirits on occasion may help against high blood pressure. Humanity has been using wine and beer since the time when agriculture was invented. Jesus was also somebody who enjoyed his wine."

"We suspect that he will lay a complaint against us at the sector commander when his time of service is over. For that purpose, he is gathering statistics."

"I don't think the brigadier will pay much attention to this guy. The brig also enjoys his drinks."

"It sometimes happens that some of the men drink too much here and then they have to be carried to their beds. Perhaps that outoppie has a valid point because you can't wage war with a bunch of alcoholics. When these guys pass out you can explode a hand grenade under their beds and they won't wake up."

"It will be interesting to get scans of their brains, with all the alcohol-soaked parts all shrivelled up"

Later, I notice that a group of younger officers and a few sergeants leave the club together and disappear into the night. One of them who stumbles past me, mumbles something about a"secret operation".

Three minutes later, I hear a terrible scream and a howl and it sounds like the voice of the chaplain. He even uses a few unacceptable and unchristian and uncouth expressions. The remaining men in the club start laughing heartily and merrily.

I ask the merry RSM, Regimental Sargeant Major Gary Gamble, why everybody laughs. "Doc, you weren't part of this conspiracy when this secret ops was planned. A few men decided that they had enough of the espionage by the padre[58] regarding their drinking habits. You ought to know, it's not really possible to buy a beer. You can only rent it. Half-an-hour after you've swallowed it, you have to return it – by emptying your bladder. These young men

[58] "Padre" – the official form of address of a chaplain in the SADF.

all drank lots of beer before the start of the secret ops and they got onto the roof of this bunker. From there, they gave the poor padre a hot shower, which he will never forget in his life!"

Oshakati, Sunday, 3 November 1985

After my home-coming from Ruacana, I tell my loving wife, a civlian medical practitioner, of the episode at the club in Ruacana. She laughs out: "I'm sure that you had another patient with shell-shock after this secret operation!"

21. OPERATION BLOOD AND BRAINS

Oshakati, Sunday, 10 November 1985

Although the war never stops, it is possible to visit a weekly Sunday church service in he troops' mess at the HQ of Sector One Zero, led by an Army chaplain. It is always a bilingual and non-denominational service, because it has to cater for adherents of all brands of Christianity. There is also an interpreter available to translate for black worshippers whose Afrikaans and English are not quite up to standard.

The Scholtz family prepared to go to worship our Creator today, together with other HQ personnel. Just as we are leaving our prefab home, my new commander at the sick-bay, commandant Tom Taylor, phones. My presence is urgently needed at the sick-bay. I greet my family and I ask Hannelore to tell me afterwards what he chaplain said.

Commandant Taylor is relieved that I am able to help at short notice, "Look here, Dave, you need to fly to Concor Base in the area of Five One Battalion, to the far west. There's a troop with a serious case of epilepsy – or so it sounds. There isn't a doctor at the base at this moment – only a medic who is a corporal. He radioed Sector HQ with the request to speak to a doctor. I was phoned and requested to tune in to his frequency. According to what he told me, it really seems to be a serious case of epileptic fits.

"Fortunately, we have you as a neurologist. Since it seems to be an emergency, I already contacted the air base at Ondangs[59] to come and pick you up and fly you out. If it's necessary, casevac the troop and then we must decide whether or not to send him to One

---

[59] "Ondangs" – the popular nane for Ondangwa in Ovamboland where the largest air base in the Operational Area was situated.

Mil. That chopper is already on its way. Get you medical bag and wait for that chopper at the landing zone outside."

"Commandant, I actually hoped to spend a peaceful Sunday with my family. Hannelore has already defreezed some steaks, but that will have to wait. Give me five minutes to pack my bag. Will you please phone Hannelore later to tell her to expect me back for dinner?"

When we land on an open spot outside the Concor Base – a place I know from the past – the commander, Captain Pete Pretorius, greets me and he takes me to the medical tent where I find the patient and the medic.

The medic: "The doctor to whom I spke over the radio confirmed that this must be a serious case of epilepsy. I've given the chap a strong sleeping pill and he's lights out at the moment. That was to prevent him from falling down again and perhaps hurting himself again, as he did last night when he was doing guard duty at the entrance."

Since I can't examine a sleeping troop, I ask the captain for two men to fetch the stretcher from the helicopter.

Ten minutes later, the troop is fastened onto the stretcher and we carry him to the chopper. Lieutenant "Jakkals" (Jackal) Jones, the pilot, starts the helicopter, but after a minute he kills the engine again.

"Doc, this thing won't fly. Some warning lights came on. I will have to radio Ondangs to send a repair vehicle with some tiffies and spare parts to fix this crate before we can leave. That will perhaps only be tomorrow."

"Jakkals, I'm in your hands. I'm sure the good captain will be able to provide each of us with a bed for tonight."

The captain: "Yes, you can take the cots of the two platoons that are out in the bush at this moment. Welcome to you guys. I will organize a few troops to stand guard at your chopper to keep unwanted elements away."

An hour later, the captain sends a troop to call me. He says: "Doc, I don't know what these two black rascals want. I can't understand what they say. They just apeared at our gate and the guard brught them to me. Perhaps they need some medicine or something."

With signs I ask the men to strip so that I can examine them. They have some scars from old wounds, but no new wounds or any other visible ailments. They don't seem t be feverish ir sick. I tell the captain to give them some food because they seem to be hungry.

We are stuck with the two guys. They refuse to leave. The captain asks me whether he should bind their hands and feet and hand them over to the Police since they may be Swapo spies. I convince him that they seem to be peaceful enough.

Just at that moment, the CSM, Warrant Officer Barney Barnard, brings the interpreter, an Ovambo man with the name of Africano, to the tent where I examined our two guests. Since it is a Sunday, he had the day off and visited the nearby village for some company. He immediately ask the two men want they want and he reports to us: "These guys tell me they are Swapo fighters. They want to surrender because they don't want to get killedby our troops. They hid theur guns and two land mines in the bushes across the road."

The captain immediately orders a squad of his resting men to take a Samil-20 truck and deliver these men to battalion HQ at Ruacane after their guns and land mines have been retrieved.

During the late afternoon, Captain Pretorius greets some more guests. The lieutenant in charge of a platoon from One Oh One Battalion, the Ovambo Battalion, asks where he and his troops can spend the night inside our base instead of in the bush. Permission is granted.

They arrived in four Casspir armored landmine-proof personnel carriers, which are also used by Police patrols. The lieutenant, Karl Kruger, declares that his men are used to sleep in the open air and they don't need tents.

My practiced eye detectes a serious alcohol problem with this lieutenant and I conclude that his supply of brandy or whatever must be depleted and that he wants to make use of the duty-free stocks of this base.

My hunch proves to be correct. During supper, Kruger has already downed three cans of cold beer. Afterwards, Captain Pretorius invites me, the chopper pilot, and Kruger to join him and his officers in their saloon. Kruger orders one brandy 'n Coke after the other and he starts to speak in a load voice. He boasts about all the "heads" he and his platoon have already notched up. They haven't had any successes the past three months and that makes him depressed and sad. His language is typical Army language will all the current very uncivilized words and expressions.

He looks at me: "Doc, I'm sure you must have soft hands. Have you ever handled a gun or a machine gun? You medical people are certainly too fucking afraid to chase a terr like we do."

Captain Pretorius: "Havem't you noticed tha parabat wings on the Doc's shirt?"

Kruger: "Probably bought at a flea market."

I only laugh because I know it's no use arguing with a man under the influence.

Kruger looks at the chaplain, a young man doing his compulsory national service with the rank of lieutenant: "Padre, it's easy to preach to these troops if you sit the whole time on your arse in a base. I'm sure you haven't left this bloody base since you came here with dozens of body guards to hold your bloody shaking and trembling hands."

The chaplain only smiles, but Captain Pretorius comes to his Defence: "Look here, Karl, this padre will lick you on any foot patrol through the bush. He's as agile as an ostrich and as tough as a hippopotamus.He has the endurance of a racing horse. He played rugby for his university's first team. We returned last week from an ops in Angola where he went along. On foot. For a whole fortnight. He carried the same load as all the other troops. We struck a contact and he shot one terr. He's one hell of a shot. The silly Swap got the bullet between his eyes, at the top of his flat nose. The bush behind him was splashed with blood and brains and pieces of bone."

Kruger: "That's only one body. I have dozens of them on my record. The trouble is, it's getting more and more difficult to score any hits. I haven't collected a single scrotum during the last two or three months."

Captain Pretorius asks the loquatious Kruger: "And how many Swaps have you caught alive?"

Kruger: "I don't believe in catching them. It's far easier just to shot them. Dead, quite dead, really dead."

The captain: "Well, we caught two of them this afternoon and they were sent to Ruacana just before you came. That's much better than collecting heads or scrotums, as you do. Any way, I'm going to bed. Good night, all of you."

All the other officers follow him. Nobody shows any appreciation for the way Kruger was talking, boasting, swaering, and drinking.

I decide that Kruger must be a serious case of post-traumatic stress disorder who self-medicates with alcohol to drive all the ghosts and demons and devils away. The poor man's life consists of looking for heads and nothing more.

Oshakati, Tuesday, 12 November 1985

It was only possible to get home yesterday afternoon. Hannelore kept the steaks and we grilled them last night.

The troop with the epileptic fits was sent by the Flossie to One Military Hospital in Pretoria. When he woke up after the strong sleeping pill had worn off, he told me that he had a nasty fall during his basic training when he fell on his head and was unconscious for almost an hour. To make sure how much brain damage, if any, was caused by that fall it was necessary for him to get a good brain scan done at One Mil.

Hannelore phones me just after lunch: "David, please come and help me. Tell your commandant that you are urgently needed at the state hospital across the street. When you come, I will tell you more."

Ten minutes later, I join Hannelore in the operating theater of the state hospital in a sterile gown, a sterile cap on my head and with sterile hands and sterile gloves.

Hannelore takes me to a young Ovambo woman on the operating table: "Gun shot woumd, in the head. I can't remove the bullet. Look at these X rays; they shows you exactly where the bullet got stuck inside her head. I know you're not a neurosurgeon, but you're the next best. How will you be able to remove that bullet?"

In inspect the X rays taken from various angles.

"I don't want to cut open her skull. That will just cause more brain damage if I have to dig the bullet out that way. That bullet has to come out through the same route that it got in. Let's hope that I will be able to get a grip on that piece of metal with the first try."

After twenty minutes, I drop the bullet into a bowl and Hannelore helps me to stitch up the wound.

"I'm afraid that her sight will be impared. The bullet penetrated the back of her skull and got stuck in the occipital lobe. How did this happen? Do you know?"

"Yes, actually a sad story. Her boy friend, a corporal of One Oh One Battalion, lured her into a Casspir of which he was the section commander."

"Was?"

"Yes, was. He's no longer with us."

"Yes?"

"A sad story. His girl friend jilted him and preferred another man. Somehow or other, he got her into this Casspir. There must have been a fight or something and then he shot her with his rifle. When he saw what he had done, he shot himself. According to his platoon commander, he set his rifle on automatic fire and pulled the trigger. At least six bullets went through his jaw, his nasal cavity and the frontal lobes of his brain."

"Who told you?"

"This corporal's platoon commander who heard it from some medics who were called to the scene. A certain lieutenant Kruger.

You will find him at the workshop over there in your base where he supervises the claning of his Casspir. I'm sure, he can tell you more."

After we have made sure that the patient was taken care of and that her chances of survival were not too bad, I go looking for this Lieutenant Kruger.

I'm not surprised when I find the same man who visited Concor Base on Sunday night.

He tells me: "Doc, nice of you to come and have a look at my Casspir. I haven't seen such a mess in my life. Blood and brains all over the roof of this vehicle and on the fucking seats. I don't know how we will ever be able to clean this bus. And that blooming corporal is no longer there, otherwise I would have given him the hiding of his life for messing my vehicle like this. Blood and brains all over – his girl friend's and his own."

Ondangwa, Friday, 27 December 1985

Today, I am seeing patients in Ondangwa, a neighboring town to Oshakati. It is where the most important base of the South African Air Force in the Operational Area and the headquarters of One Oh One Battalion are situated.

One of my patients today is Commandant Welgemoed, commander of One Oh One Battalion. He complains about a frequent migraine, for which ordinary pain killers don't help.

"This blooming war is giving me these headaches and ulcers and high blood pressure."

I try to console him: "No war is ever pleasant. My dad fought during the Second World War and that made a psychological wreck of him and some of his friends."

"Some of my men are also psychological wrecks. The day before yesterday, right on Christmas Day, one of my platoon commanders blew out his own brains."

"Oh, yes?"

"Yes. It was the commander of one of our Romeo Mike teams.[60] He only lived for getting kills. During the past few months he didn't achieve anything, but I think that was because he drank too much. That made him slow, dim-witted, angry, reckless, and depressed. It was a huge disappointment and humiliation for him that his team couldn't show anything the last few months and then he blew out his own brains."

I shake my head, almost in disbelief, because I suspect that I know who this chap was. I ask: "Who was he?"

"A certain Lieutenant Karl Kruger. The blooming fool chose to kill himself inside one of our Casspirs. Blood and brains all over the place. Was it really necessary to create so much of a mess and muck? And the trouble was, he had no relatives to bury him. Both parents are dead and no other family. Poor chap. We will have to bury him here somewhere."

"I met him once or twice. Actually, a tragic case."

"I won't ever forget all that blood and brain tissue in the Casspir. That must be one of the reasons for my horrible, hideous, horrific headaches. The scene in that Casspir haunts me, even if I am a professional soldier."

"That lieutenant had the same experience when one of his corporals did the same thing. The sight must have given him nightmares and drove him over the edge. This war really messes with people's heads and minds."

---

60 "Romeo Mike" – the abbreviation RM stands for the Afrikaans expression "Reaksiemag" (Reaction Force or Reaction Team).

22. OPERATION CANDLE

Oshakati, Friday, 16 October 1987

Colonel Viljoen enters the conference room where I and four other men are sitting. He starts without any prelimenaries: "Gentlemen, you are going to take out a big shot of Swapo for us. Not take out as in taking out for real, but taking out as in taking out. You are going to dig him out of Angola and bring him back as a POW, a prisoner of war. You are going to take him out of his hide-out so that he can be tried as a murderer, rapist and terrorist. Of course, we also want to hear what he can tell us about everything.

"Gentlemen, welcome to Operation Candle. This ops has been ordered and approved by the politicians and the generals tasked me, as staff officer: operations at Sector One Zero, to plan this operation."

I interrupt him: "Colonel, I'm a medical officerr It's my job to take care of the wounded, crippled, and sick troops. All the medical and psychological wrecks. How must I get involved in this ops?"

"Doc, you are going to be the most important man in this small combat team that has to do this little job for us. It will be your task to render Mister Klemens Karupu, one of Swapo's battalion commanders, harmless so that he can be abducted on a stretcher and brought back here in a chopper."

"Is it the plan that I sedate him, or something like that?"

"You are going to put him to sleep, gently. With anesthetics, of course. You need not sing him a bed-time song or read him a bed-time story."

"And if he refuses to lie still while I try to administer anesthetics? It will be rather difficult to give him something to sleep if he wriggles and wrestles and fights back and refuses to give his cooperation."

"Yes, I know, I know. But first of all, you and your team will deliver some sleeping gas to him and the girl who will probably share his cot with him. Then he won't feel anything if you give him a little injection."

"Oh."

"Doc, with those three pips n your shoulders, you will be the senior officer on this ops. After all, you were also trained as a parabat. Whatever you say, goes during this ops. The tactical commander will be you, Captain Joos Jooste (and he looks at the man sitting next to me). Captain, it will be your job to look after the safety of the Doc and the POW. I will provide you with four carriers for the stretcher and three more men to act as sentinels and body guards. Together with the Doc, you will be a team of nine men.Ten, with the POW."

Jooste: "When must we go and fetch this terr?"

"In fourteen days' time. On Saturday morning, 31 October, very early. Your ops will coincide with another ops, Operation Firewood. Firewood will draw all the attention away from your clandestine action. As you probably know, there is since August a big operation going on in Angola against the Angolans and the Cubans. We try to help Jonas Savimbi of Unita and that draws all the attention. The plan with Ops Firewood is to blow Techamutete and a task force consisting of some parabats, recces[61] and members of One Oh One Battalion will do the job. That's an important rat hole where the terrs are hiding. And at the same time you are going to pay a social visit to Lubango at Swapo's HQ to take Comrade

[61] "Recces" – the nickname given to members of the Reconnaissance commando's, the special forces of the SADF.

Karupu out and transport him ever so gently on a free chopper ride back to us. All expenses paid.You will also get a free flight."

Joos: "How do we get there?"

"On a truck."

"And where do we get the truck?"

"Sector provides it. With the compliments of Swapo. You are going in one of the trucks that we have looted from them – at the same time when our boys are going to smoke out Techemutete. And then you simply drive a little further on, until you get to Lubango."

"Colonel, with all due respect, but Lubango is Swapo's HQ. The place will be overflowing and overcrowded with terrs and guards. How will we ever get inside?"

"Captain, easily. The surprise element. Nobody will expect you. With Swapo uniforms for the seven black members of your company at One Oh One Battalion and Cuban uniforms for the two whiteys."

Me: "It's against the Geneva Conventin to parade all over the place in the enemy's uniforms."

The colonel: "To hell with the Geneva Convention. Anyway, you're not going to hold a parade in the middle of the night over there. The politicians argue that Swapo doesn't respect this convention and we're only following their example. But you just won't get caught. Nobody will know that you will be parading in Swapo's atire. You are going to travel with one of their trucks, in any case. Your camouflage will be perfect, therefore. On top of that, it will be new moon, a week before Operation Candle. At the time when you will be moving in, you will have a half-moon for the first part of the night and at the time when you remove the comrade from his comfortable cot, it will be pitch blach dark. It might even be cloudy."

An Air Force Captain who is sitting here, asks: “I suppose it’s my chopper that will have to bring this team back, or am I mistaken?”

“Captain, yes, you’re not mistaken. Gentlemen, I think you have met Captain Nelson of the Air Froce?”

Me: “Yip. We did.”

The colonel: “There is still more than a week left before your sight-seeing tour into Angola is to start. This will give you enough time to assemble your team and to practice all your moves and actions and steps. During this time you must also inform me what type of supplies and equipment you will need – and then we fly those in, from wherever, if needed.”

Captain Jooste: “And may I assume that this sergent-major is the man who has to see to it that our truck is in a running state and roadworthy?” (and he points at the man sitting next to me.)

“Gentlemen, that’s Warrant Officer Kellerman of the Tiffies, in case you haven’t met him yet. He will get your truck in tip-top condition for you. Even with new tyres. He just won’t do some pannel beating.”

Me: “If that damn truck has too many dents and scratches and cracked wind screens, she won’t qualify for a roadworthy certificate.”

Kellerman: “The cops in Angola are not famous for being finicky about those things. And that’s where you will be travelling.”

Me: “How are we going to know where this comrade is sleeping?”

“Major Paul Potgieter of Intelligence will show you everything (and he points at the major). Aerial photo’s. Road maps. Everything. He will also provide you with the necessary paper work so that you can pass as Swaps or Cubans. Major, are you ready to do your thing?”

The major nods his head.

Me: "Colonel, while we are going to be a team of only nine men, our fire power won't be terribly great. What do we do when we are attacked? If shooting should start, it will wake up every terr within a radius of two hundred clicks. I suggest that we defend ourselves with tear gas, should it be necessary. That will slow down our attackers considerably and give us a chance to get away in the dark. The tear gas won't make lots of noise, except when our pursuers start shedding tears and howl on account of that."

The colonel: "Doc, brilliant, yes brilliant. That's a tactic that we haven't used in this war so far and, therefore, we don't have any stocks. I will immediately send a signal to Pretoria for them to beg some tear gas cannisters from the Police and forward those to us with the Flossie on Monday."

Captain Jooste: "May I choose the men from my company myself? The men to take along into Angola?"

"Captain, I leave that in your hands. It will be a good thing if you can take former terrs who know Lubango. Perhaps, and preferably, men who have caught a dislike in Comrade Karupu."

Ruacana, Monday, 26 October 1987

We are nine men who are sitting in a truck that we have scored from Swapo. We are still wearing our browns for the time being – our South African combat uniforms. But we keep bags filled with Swapo and Cuban uniform pieces ready.

We are armed with Russian automatic rifles and other pieces of armament, as well as forged papers purportedly ordering us to travel to Lubango. Our seven black members who speak the Quanyama dialect of Ovamboland will do all the talking along the way.

All our black team members are former Swapo terrorists who absconded or surrendered after becoming disillusioned. At One Oh One Battalion, they learned some Afrikaans. I chat with them while we are crossing the Angolan border at Calueque to travel in the direction of Cahama.

One of them tells that he and his sister were abducted by Swapo while they were still school children. His sister was so badly raped by Comrade Karupu and his body guards that she was maimed for life. Another one tells that Comrade Karupu accused him of espionage for the South African Army. Fortunately, he could escape before he was caught, tortured, and locked up. Yet another one saw with his own eyes hoe Karupu became so angry at a friend of his that he smashed his eye with a blunt stick, leavind him blind in this eye.

It is, therefore, clear: we have a number of men who all have a grudge against this comrade. They are eager to be on our way to Lubango with some sort of a motive to be part of this expedition.

Our journey takes us past Cahama, a Swapo stronghold.

Lubango, Friday evening, 30 October 1987

There were three road blocks during our journey to Lubango, including one at Cahama. Sergeant Ndjolonimus, our driver, could convince the Angolese soldiers every time that we are genuine Swapo fighters with two Cuban instructors, who have to report at Lubango. On my documents I am named as Sergeant Luiz Domingo.

Lubango is a big town, almost a city. There is a military air field and also a big base of FAPLA, die Angolese army. On our way, we heard and saw Russian Mig fighter, flown by Cuban pilots, clearly on their way to attack our men to the east.

We were given the assurance that the biggest part of the Angolese army was busy in the east, in the vicinity of the Lomba river, where our South African forces kept them busy. When we entered the town shortly after dark, we weren't surprised to see very few security measures. Over the radio of our truck we could hear what the password for the night is and with that we could hoodwink the only road block in this town.

It's clear that the Angolans and Swapo don't expect to be attacked here. Our Air Force bombers have downloaded some bombs here in the past, but the place never experienced a surface attack.

Swapo's headquarters and training camp is to the north of the town and to reach those parts, we drive through the eastern parts. We find an abandoned ruined building and we stop there to eat our last provisions from our ratpacks. It is our plan to move again after the moon has disappeared behind the horizon at midnight

.

Lubango, Saturday, 31 October 1987

We managed to sleep a few hours and now we are travelling further. Sergeant Ndjolonimus knows the place quite well and at about 01:00 we pass the house in which Comrade Karupu is supposed to stay. The Swapo camp is not really a camp and consists of a number of free-standing buildings with lots of space between them. We observe a few lights in some of the buildings or huts, but it's dark at Krupu's place.

Our driver parks the truck behind a neighnoring building and we get off as silently as possible. Captain Joose and his three guards spread out in four directions to keep watch. I and the four carriers creep as silently as possible nearer to Karupu's abode, while I hold my medical bag and the other men carry a collapsible stretcher. Everyone has a gas mask ready.

Everything proceeds very smoothly, almost too good to be true. Karupu's home seems to consist of four rooms. Every room has an open window and I blow a hefty dose of sleeping gas into each one. It ought to work within minutes.

Corporal Djolomien, a small lean man, enters through one of the window with his gas mark over his face. We don't want to break down doors and cause a racket. A minute later, he opens the back door for us and we slide inside with our gas masks to prevent us from falling asleep.

We find Karupu in a naked conditions next to a young girl – whose is also clothed the same as Eve before she and Adam made clothes from fig leaves. Corporal Djolomien lights a candle on a table with a box of matches he finds on the table, although there is a switch for an electric light. As usual, I disinfect a spot on the shoulders of both occupants of the cot with a sterile swab and I inject a hefty dose of Ketamine into their bodies. It is an anesthetic that will keep them asleep for a number of hours and will ensure that they won't remember anything of the whole episode.

I mumble softly: "Do you see this candle? This is the candle after which our operation is called." The men grin silently.

I warn the men: "Do you see this half-a-bottle of whiskey? Don't touch it. I don't want to struggle with drunken stretcher bearers."

The men get the stretcher ready and cover it with a blanket with which we will cover Comrade Karupu. I will never as a medical practitioner be able to expose a patient in public in a naked condition and, thereby, trampling upon his human dignity. There are leather straps with clasps with which we fasten the prisoner's legs and upper body to prevent him from falling off and getting hurt.

We carry the stretcher outside and I keep my stetoscope ready to make sure every so often that the prisoner's heart is still beating. He is a heavy man and I don't know in which condition his heart is. When we get outside, I flash with my torch in the direction of the truck. Two minutes later we hear how the truck is being started and driven in our direction. I leave the back door of the house open to allow all the sleeping gas to escape. We don't want any traces of it to remain and give our game away.

It's easy to load the stretcher with my patient onto the truck. We depart to keep our appointment with the helicopter.

After we have travelled two hundred meters, Sergeant Ndjolonimus suddenly stops and Captain Jooste, who sits next to him, jumps out. He runs to a fairly large building, evidently the sleeping quarters of some Swapo fighters. He throws a tear smote grenade through one of the windows and runs back while making all sort of obscene signs with his fingers and giving a cruel churckle.

We travel on the highway in a north easterly direction and exactly twlve kilometers from the home of Karupu we leave the road for another kilometer in a northerly direction by doing bundu bashing through the dense vegetation. We find the helicopter waiting for us.

We get airborne ten minutes later and thirty minutes later we land at an open spot in the Angolan bush where a fuel truck with bright lights is awaiting us. It takes half-an-hour to refuel the helicopter. During this time, I pay attention to the POW. He starts groaning and tries to wriggle free from the leather straps holding him. I give him another hefty dose of Ketamine.

The problem with Ketamine is that it causes hideous hallucinations. I wonder what type of nightmares Karapu is getting from my sleeping draught and that must be the reason why he groaned and fought the straps.

I and Jooste get the opportunity to talk for the first time. I remarkp: "Joos, this was far too easily done. I'm afraid that something will still go wrong."

Joos: "Doc, you know Murphy's law. If something can possibly go wrong it will certainly go wrong. I was never in any ops where everyting turned out to work according to plan. I must agree, Everything went far too easily and smoothly. It's almost too good to be true. It wasn't even necessary that we throw some tear smoke to make the tears roll over the cheeks of our pursuers. I just couldn'r resist the temptation to spoil the sleep of a lot of Swaps with that tear smoke."

Me: "All that is still necessary for Operation Candle to be a resounding success is that we get aiurborne again and land at Oshakati. I can only wonder what the Swaps will think when they find the cot of this comrade empty. Will they think that he abscnded and left his darling to hold the baby?"

"Yes. I wonder myself. Will they perhaps connect our lonely

truck in the bush with his disappearance? How will they explain the tear gas? That was perhaps stupid of me."

The chopper lands in Oshakati shortly after daybreak. A Casspir ambulance awaits us.The POW is taken to the sick-bay where he is placed on a comfortable bed. The men who accompanied us disappear and three armed guards occupy chairs in the POW's room. I am armed with a stetoscope, a thermometer, and a blood-pressure apparatus and I wait that my hand-cuffed and chained patient wakes up. He is connected to an oxygen cylinder.

It has been agreed that I will call Colonel Viljoen and Major Potgieter as soon as the patient regains consciousness.

Oshakati, Monday, 2 November 1987

I sat guard next to Karupu's bed the whole of Saturday and the whole of Sunday, although I got a few hours of sleep in-between.

The sun has just risen on this Monday morning when Colonel Viljoen appears.

"Doc. What's wrong? Why haven't you informed me that this piece of rotten humanity has woken up? I see his eyes are open. What's going on here?"

Me: "Colonel, I'm afraid I have a little bit of bad news. A slight, little mistake, I must confess."

"Yes?"

"See, I'm a qualified neurologist, as you know, Colonel. I know everything about the human brain. It became apparent, already on Saturday, that something is wrong with this man's head. I asked our local psychologist to have a look at this man on his own and he confirmed that this man's brain has been cooked or broiled or grilled to well-done."

"Yes?"

"The psychologist is convinced he's not pretending to be dumb or demented or dimwitted. He really is in a sorry state. I'm afraid I gave him an overdose of anesthetics, by accident. I'm not an anethetist and, therefore, I may have overdone it. Or, perhaps, the combination of sleeping gas and anesthetics was too much for him. Before we caught him, he downed half-a-bottle of whiskey and that's also an catastrophic combination with anesthetics. His mind is gone, good-bye, aif Wiedersehen arrividerci. He doesn't know who he is anymre. His memry has been erased. He's worse than a zombie."

"OK, you call yourself a neurologist. You understand how the brain works. How will you be able to kick-start his head again'?"

"Sorry. That's impossible. I know it's a sordid set-back for us. The damage is permanentt. He won't be able to get accused and subjected to a trial. We will get zero info from him regarding Swapo's pitiful plans. Sorry."

"Fuck."

23. OPERATION TEQUILA

The Cape Argus | Tuesday, 3 November 1987

Politics

Pres. Botha Warns Soviet Union, Cuba & Angola

Bill Barlow

Staate President P.W. Botha gave the Soviet Union, Cuba and Angola a stern warning yesterday during a press conference at the Union Buildings in Pretoria.

He emphasized that South Africa was locked in a war against the terrorists of Swapo in the north of South West Africa and the southern parts of Angola for the last twenty years – twenty horrible years for all concerned.

South Africa desires peace, but cannot allow the terrorists to continue with their killings, rape, sabotage, abductions, and the planting of land mines.

The victims of these acts of terrorism are the civilian population of South West Africa and the only organisations that can protect them are the Defence Force and the Police.

State President P W Botha at the news conference yesterday

The South African government has agreed to grant independence to South West Africa, but it is unthinkable that the management of the country's affairs can be placed in the hands of a terrorist organisation that wishess to impose the principles and policies of communism on that country.

The problem is, though, that the Soviet Union has, for many years, provided these terrorists with military equipment and the training of these fighters by Russian and Cuban officers. There are various Cuban military units that protect Swapo actively – and that cannot be tolerated any longer.

On top of everything, the terrorists of Swapo are often housed in bases of the Angolan Army and that often led in the past to clashes between the South African Defence Dorce and Cuban and Angolese units – also in the recent past.

President Botha declared pertinently: "I warn the Soviet Union, Cuba and Angola that my government has no option but to hit back. This aid to Swapo must end immediately and I have given my generals the order to take the necessary steps in this regard if this aid does not stop."

The State President declined to dis-close which "necessary steps" he had in mind – only that the Defence Force will be involved.

Walvis Bay, Thursday, 12 November 1987

Walvis Bay is not a strange place for me because I was stationed here as a junior medical officer a number of years ago. I am now sitting in a place in which I've never been during those years – the conference room at the naval station at the harbor.

There are four men with me here – an officer of the Air Force, namely Captain Fabio Gomes, Lieutenant Mike Meyer of Three Two Battalion, and two naval officers, Commander Fires van Vuuren[62] and Lietenant Commander Jonaththan Jordan. We are being addressed by Colonel Neels Nel.

---

[62] The nickname of "Fires" is derived from the family name of "van Vuuren" because "vuur" means "fire" in Afrikaans and Dutch.

"Gentlemen, thank you for coming – from all around, north and south. Your call-up papers gave you no idea what you can expect, except that you must be ready to stay busy with a secret operation till after New Year's Day. The only one who may perhaps have a faint idea about what is going on, is Captain Gomes. But we will get to that later on.

"Before I proceed any further and give you some details about this top-top secret operation: if anyone of you gents feels like pulling out, he is free to do so now. It won't be held against you. It won't appear on your personnel file. Is there anybody who wants to leave?"

We all remain sitting.

"Right-oh. You all certainly must have seen a story in the press that the SP[63] warned Russia, Cuba, and Angola that we cannot tolerate it any longer that they help Swapo. After that, the SP ordered the chief of the Defence Force to plan a special operation to sink Russian and Cuban ships in the harbor of Luanda to prevent them from downloading supplies for Swapo.

"After that, the chief of the Defence Force ordered the chief of staff: operations to plan such an ops. A team immediately started investigating various possibilities to give effect to the order of the SP. Most of the work was given to me and a team. I was also given overhead command of the operation."

Fires van Vuuren asks: "What is this operation called?"

The colonel: "I don't know where the people at HSO[64] find names for their operations, but the name for this ops is Ops Tequila. Now, Tequila is a type of Mexican liquor and I don't believe you will get a single drop to taste of this stuff during this ops. Sorry. Can't be helped."

---

[63] "SP" – South African military slang for "State President".

[64] "HSO" – the abbreviation for Head of Staff: Operations.

The two men of the Navy sigh.

"Well yes, it's like I said. It was the order of the SP that Russian and Cuban ships in the herbor of Luanda have to be blown up and sunk – just as our recces did in the harbor of Namibe."

I lift my hand: "Colonel, with respect, but what the hell am I doing on this ops? I'm a medical officer. I know I've taken part in a few operationsm but my task was always to look after our men from a medical point of view, such as pasting band-aid on men who are bleeding or to distribute head-ache pills. It was sometimes necessary to administer anesthesia, but unfortunately, I've overdone it recently and I made a zombie out of that particular patient. About the sinking of ships I know sweet-blow-all. I have zero knowledge and zero experience of that type of thing."

Colonel Nel: "Doc, your participation very necessary. You didn't buy thos parabat wings on your shirt at a church bazaar – you worked for those. You have lots of operational experience, as you reminded us. You know about keeping a cool head in difficult situations and you know about shooting instruments and thngs that go 'bang'. You were hand-picked for this ops and you will be in command of one half of this ops – the part that has to draw the attention away from the divers who have to plant mines in the harbor of Luanda."

Me: "Oh."

The colonel: "Yes. You and a team of Three Two Battalion's SP's[65] are going switch off the lights of Luanda over Christmas, while you also entertain the Angolans with a little bit of fireworks. That will provide the opportunity for the divers of Commander van Vuuren to penetrate the harbor of Luanda unseen and to detonate a few outsize crackers beneath all the Russian and Cuban ships there.

---

[65] "SP's" – the abbreciation used in army slang for the Afrikaans expression of "Swart Portugese" (Black Portuguese).

Of course, the divers may not be seen. But to stay invisible, no lights may be burning in the vicinity. You are going to sabotage the power network of Luanda. And at the same time, another Portuese-speaking team of Three Two Battalion under Lieutenant Meyer will provide some loud bangs and lots of sparks and huge smoke clouds so that everybody will look in their direction – and don't notice the divers in the harbor."

Me: "And how must I switch off the lights of Luanda? Apply anesthetics on the manager and technicians of the power station?"

The colonel laughs: "Hell, no. The power station is hundreds of kilometers inside the interior. You are going to sabotage the power lines a few kilometers outside the city. With explosives. And remember – the recces have learnt a few expen-sive lessons. With dangerous operations, like this one, they always take a doctor or a medic along because somebody will get hurt. That's certain. Doc, you are going to play a double role in this adventure – you are going as a trained parabat, but also as the man who must patch up the casualties."

Me: "All right. But – why isn't this job given to the recces? They are, after all, the specialists."

The colonel: "Two good reasons. The reconnaissance commando's are very busy elsewhere at this moment. And we need people who can mingle with the people of Luanda without being noticed. Black Portuguese, SP's of Three Two Battalion, therefore. From their reconnaissance wing. We will help you sometime to get second-hand civvies with which you can disappear in the crowds. Of course, you can't walk around over there in your browns – actually, driving all over the place because you will be provided with wheels."

Me: "Thanks."

Mike Meyer: "There's still lots of time before Christmas."

The Colonel: "That gives us ample time to do some reconnaissance and to perform a throrough cloth repetition or two. The reconnaissance will start tomorrow and that's where Captain Gomes gets involved. Captain, please forgive me for using the word but I'm sure that you've got used to it by now. Gentlemen, Captain Fabio Gomes is a South African Porra and he is able to masquerade as a Brazilian. He spent a year in Rio and he can speak Portuguese like the Brazilians. Am I right, Captain?"

Gomes nods his head.

"OK, Captain Gomes can converse with the Angolans in the Porra language as if he is a Brazilian. Just this afternoon, he's going to take you two footsloggers (and he points at me and Mike Meyer) to Lüderitz. There is a landing strip in the Sperrgebiet[66] where no nosy and inquisitave freaks can watch you. Tomorrow, he will fly you with a freight plane with fake Brazilian registration numbers out over the ocean and then approach Luanda as if he's coming from Brazil. You are going to deliver a beautiful explosive cargo – eighteen crates with hand grenades for FAPLA, die Angolan army. Every crate contains six dozen hand grenades. Payment will be made with a bag full of diamonds. You two footsloggers stay out of sight while the plane is on the ground because you can't speak Portuguese."

Mike Meyer: "Why are we flying along?"

The Colonel: "You must help Captain Gomes to do reconnaissance. His plane is fitted with three secret cameras, all looking in different directions. You are going to take pictures while you are approaching Luanda and again when you lift off again and fly somewhat over the country. You must identify targets that have to be photographed properly."

---

[66] "Sperrgebiet" – the old German name for a restricted area where diamonds were mined in the Namib Desert along the Atlantic coast.

Me: "What type of places must we get pictures of?"

The colonel: "Of course, the harbor and surrounding areas. But we also have to know where the power lines from the power station are somewhere near a major road so that you can cut them during Christmas more easily. I think it will be a good thing if you could fly along the main road into the interior to see where the power lines are near that road or even crossing the road."

Captain Gomes opens his mouth for the first time: "That road is called the Estrada de Catete – that's what my old man told me. He knows Luanda because that's where we lived before the civil war."

Lieutenant Meyer: "Did I hear correctly that we are going to deliver a bunch of crates filled with hand grenades to the Angolans? But that's something they can use against our troops, if I'm not mistaken. How must I understand that?"

The colonel: "No need to be concerned about that. In every crate there will be at least one grenade that is really a booby trap. It will be primed to detonate three days later and that will cause the whole crate to blow up, sky-high, somewhere in an ammo store of the Angolese army. Perhaps that big bang will cause the whole ammo store to blow up and then it will be impossible to determine the cause of that exciting explosion. Then they won't be able to blame Captain Gomes and become angry at him. Of course, they know him under another name."

Fires van Vuuren: "Certainly and completely clever and cunning!"

The colonel: "Thanks."

Me: "Do these Angolans expect in any way a consignment of hand grenades?"

Gomes: "Yes, they do. I spoke to the Angolese military attaché in Brazil two months ago and I promised him that I would be able to get a load of South African hand grenades at a bargain price from the United Arabian Emirates for him. He fell for it like a ton of bricks. That was before anybody was thinking about an ops like this one, but now we can utilize that contact nicely to fit into this ops. The Angolans don't have any money and, therefore, they will pay with a big bag filled with dazzling diamonds. They expect me tomorrow with the goodies."

Fires van Vuuren: "I like that!"

Me: "All right, tomorrow we are going to do some reconnaissance from the air. Is any other reconnaissance planned?"

The colonel: "That's where the efforts of these two nautical men are needed. Commander Van Vuuren is in command of one of our submarines and he will help the divers to reach the harbor of Luanda. Or actually, to get inside. He will be in command of the maritime part of the operation. Commander Jordan will be in command of an innocent-looking fishing trawler while wearing civvie cloting and he will put the two teams of saboteurs with their motor bikes ashore somewhere north of downtown Luanda so that you can fuck up and spoil the Christmas celebrations in Luanda. The aerial photo's of Captain Gomes will show us how the submarine and the fishing trawler must move and maneuver. But both craft will have to do some surveilance from the ocean before any action can take place."

Luanda, Friday, 13 November 1987

It is already rather late during the afternoon while we are getting airborne after taking off from the airport, south of the city center of Luanda. We had a delay because we had to be refueled.

Sergeant Fernandez, the flight engineer of Captain Gomes – both of them in civilian clothes – requests us to come to the flight cabin.

We gain height and Fabio Gomes flies in the direction of the interior of the country, instead of flying over the ocean, ostensibly back to Brazil. He ensures us: "My three cameras are running smoothly. The town of Catete is now below us. It's east of Luanda and we are flying directly above the highway. Do you see over there? There are the power cables for Luanda, which we wanted to find. Very neat! Now we can turn around. We saw what we wanter to see. My cameras as well."

I ask: "Did air traffic control argue with you because you were flying in the wrong direction?"

"Yes, somewhat. But I explained that I wanted to gain height over land before I fly away over the ocean. And they swallowed it."

Later Gomes asks us: "Do you two guys want to see the bright pebbles, these shiny stones?"

"Of course."

We both push our hands into the bag and let the diamonds slide through our fingers.

While we are flying further, Mike Meyer wants to know how many ships did we count in the harbor at Luanda.

Sergeant Fernandez: "I think I could see ten of them. But the photo's will tell us exactly after we've developed the films."

While we are approaching the coast, south of the airport, I notice a big explosion at the airport.

Gomes: "Oops! One of my little hand grenades went off prematurely. Sorry, boys! I had better get away from this place as fast as possible before they chase us with one of their Migs."

Me: "I wonder how much damage those poor Angolans suffered. I think the truck with the crates and a few planes had it."

Mike Meyer: "Very nice!"

I ask much later, while we are turning south behind the horizon: "How are we going to land tonight after dark at Lüderitz?

I haven't noticed any lights alongside the landing strip this morning."

Gomes: "The colonel promised that two trucks will mark both ends of the landing strip with their lights. When I fly over Lüderitz, I must flash my landing lights twice as a sign that we're almost there. We must maintain radio silence."

Me: "You are damn clever for a Porra."

Gomes laughs: "All of us Porras are very clever. That's how we discovered South America and the Cape. I'm also clever enough to know that both of you have hidden two little shining stones each…"

Me: "That's exactly what you and this silly sergeant of yours also did!"

Meyer: "How are you going to explain to the colonel that there are not enough diamnds?"

Gomes: "Easily. It was the Angolese who did us in."

Still later, I say: "Have you noticed that today is Friday the thirteenth?"

Gomes: "Yeeees…. That must be why those hand grenades exploded too soon. It was the unlucky day for those Angolans. After all, they chased us Porras out of Angola when they got independence. This was a little bit of revenge, which they deserve."

Walvis Bay, Sunday, 15 November 1987

The war never stops over weekends and, therefore, the same group as of last Thursday is again assembled on this holy Sunday in the conference room of the Navy station. We all, though, first attended the church parade led by the Navy chaplain.

Colonel Neels Nel laughs while he enters the room: "Oh, yes! You lot ruined a few things in Luanda!"

Captain Gomes: "Colonel, and how do you know that?"

The colonel: “One can sometimes believe Radio Luanda. We have – as you ought to know – a few men at the HQ in Oshakati who monitor the comms of Swapo and FAPLA. They also listen to Radio Luanda.”

Gomes: “And what does Radio Luanda say?”

The colonel: “The Angolese Defefense Force is very, very angry. They are spitting flaming fires, smoldering sulphur, burning oil and glowing embers. They are calling for all the eternal condemnations from heaven and hell upon those who are guilty. They want to know how in hell Jonas Savimbi and his Unita rebels were able to cause such a big explosion at the airport in Luanda. Three airplanes and two trucks were blown into their glory. Three people died and six were injured. Heads will roll of those who were supposedly lax with security at the airport.”

Gomes: “Oh. They don’t suspect me?”

The colonel: “Apparently, it never occurred to them that a Brazilian ally would ever pull that sort of trick on them. And now we scored a bag full of diamonds and the Angolans don’t have any of our hand grenades!”

A pile of photographs is lying on the table – the photo’s taken by Captain Gomes; “Brazilian” aircraft that were taken the day before yesterday while flying over Luanda and were developed yesterday.

Commander van Vuuren is the first one to comment on them: “Gomes, thank you for your beautiful pictures. We can clearly see where the entrance to the bay is and where the quays for the freighters and tankers are. As you can see, here are five freighters, two tankers and two warships. Russian frigates. That’s apart from the fishing trawlers at the fishery wharf. Our divers will have to be downliaded, here, just ourside the entrance to the bay. We will take them in with collapsible Bracuda boats. Fortunately, they have converted torpedoes that can tow them while hanging onto these craft and which will deliver them to the relevant ships so that they need not swim the whole distance."

Jordan: "But look at all these fishing boats in the sea (and he points with his finger to some of the photo's). How will the submarine and the Baracudas stay invisible?"

Van Vuuren: "We have often placed recce's in Angola ashore – even with a number of fishing craft in the vicinity. It's not really a problem."

The colonel: "What type of mines are you going to use?"

Van Vuuren: "Magnetic mines. There are two types. The first type has magnets with which one can attach the thing against a ship's hull. They're called limpit mines. One sets a time mechanism for a certain point in time and then a hole is blown into the hull – more or less on the same priciple as an armor-piercing round. You Pongo's call them HEAT rounds – 'High Explosive, Anti-Tank'. And then we are also going to leave a few magnetic mines of the second type on the sea bed at the entrance to the bay. They register the magnetism of the hulls of the ships passing over them and then they say 'Boom!' Or perhaps 'Bang!' And then it's good-bye to that ship."

The colonel: "And how do you retrieve the divers afterwards?"

Van Vuuren: "The limpit mines have time mechanisms. They will be programmed to denoate the mine six hours later. At that time, the divers were brought back on the Baracudes and will be safe in deep waters on the submarine."

Jordan: "You can only do that if these gents (and he points at me and Mike Meyer) make sure that it is totally dark and that a number of bangs go off at another spot to draw the attention away from the divers in the water."

The colonel: "That goes without saying. Commander (and he looks at Jordan), you are going to download the infantry at this beach, north of the city center and the harbor. Already the previous day. Actually, during the previous night. You are sailing away from here timeously so that you all can do some reconnaissance from the sea on the twenty-third of December – the submarine with her periscope and you with binoculars from the fishing trawler. You must make sure that no warship or patrol boat is lying at anchor in the bay or is sailing along.

"During that evening, you send two scouts to reconnoiter the beach where the infantry has to land later on. They must secure the beach. The moon sets at about half-past-ten and thereafter it will be dark enough. When the two scouts are satisfied that the beach is secured the rest of the saboteurs can join them – together with their motor cycles and everything else they will need.

"The infantry must hide somewhere in these bushes, here (and he points to a spot on a photo) during the rest of the night. During the next day, the twenty-fourth, they must move to their targets to see the lay of the land. Doc, you and four more men must travel through the city onto the main road to take a look at the power cables beyond Catete (and he presses his finger on another photo). The city will be very busy. It's the day before Christmas and you will easily disappear into the crowds. And then you must make sure that the power is cut off and that it becomes beautifully dark.

"And Lieutenant (he looks at Mike Meyer), you team takes a sixty millimeter mortar pipe along on your bikes with a dozen nice mortar bombs. As you can see, directly north of these fuel tanks next to the fishery harbor is an open field. That's where you will park yourselves. As soon as the Doc's team has switched off the city's lights you start throwing your bombs. It will be nice if you can cause a few of these tanks to develop some flames and smoke and go bang, but that's not the real focus of the ops It's only a side show. Your noise will draw all the attention on you lot and then you disappear with your bikes into the dark. You simply move into the city where you will merge with the multitudes of humanity there. And then the crew members of Commander Jordan's trawler will take you off the beach the next night – here at this beach where you landed (and he points to a spot on a photo)."

Meyer: "Brilliant. I like it. We will certainly be no more that a dozen men, the divers included, and we will throw the whole city into a pretty panic and a colossal chaos!"

The colonel: "Don't count your chickens too early. They must hatch first. Anyway, we start assembling our teams tomorrow. The Doc gets four men and you, Lieutenant, get two men. There will, therefore, be eight of you on land. The two of you fly straightaway this afternoon to Buffalo to select your people from the recce wing of Three Two Battalion. And as soon as you have your six helpers, you come back here. Then our training will start. First of all, we must teach you how to drive motor cycles. You must also practice with Commander Jordan's people how to get ashore in the dark and how to be retrieved again, also in the dark. The new crew of the fishing trawler must learn how to handle that boat. Lieutenant, your team will also have to practice witth the patmor, the patrol mortar. Doc, you and your team must sharpen your skills with explosives."

Me: "Colonel, I think we must identify the best spot where we can cut those power lines. What do the pictures tell us?"

We all have a look and I declare: "Colonel, I can count four different lines, each one with half-a-dozen cables. Fortunately, these pictures were taken during the late afternoon and we can clearly see the shadows of the pylons. They are not placed directly next to each other, but are spread out somewhat. We will, though, be able to find them in the dark of the evening of the twenty-forth will that little bit of feeble moonlight.

"I see that these power lines cross the highway here (and I point to a photo). About six hundred meters further on there is a dirt road to the south and I think that's where we will leave the main road to reach the power lines. The Angolams made it easy for us because they cleared the whole stretch under the lines of vegenation. We can work there without being observed from the main road and then we make sure that we are far away when the explosives explode an hour later and make the pylons topple over."

The colonel: "I believe that each pylon has four legs. You will have to pinch off at least two legs of each pylon to make them fall down."

Me: "Of course. I think we must make some of them fall over each other in such a manner that they cause short circuits. Perhaps they will shoot so many sparks to cause a bush fire – some more consternation for the nation over Christmas."

The colonel: "At CSO this date was specifically chosen because the chances are good that the security forces will be too busy kicking Christmas parties and will be too drunk to react rapidly. They may perhaps organize some road blocks, but it will be too late."

Fires van Vuuren: "Beautiful!"

The colonel: "Another last thing. You will all be fitted out with frequency-hopping radio's. The two teams on land will then have comms with the submarine and the fishing trawler. If you two teams on land pick up any troubles or hick-ups, you must contact Commander van Vuuren. He's the senior officer in the ops."

Walvis Bay, Monday, 15 December 1987

The submarine with a four man team of divers left the harbor already during the night and our fishing trawler gets underway at ten o' clock. The team of diver has the code name of X-Ray. Lieutenant Meyer's team is Team Yankee and my group is Team Zulu. Our eight motor cycles and other equipment were loaded onto the boat in a big container to prevent unwelcome eyes from spotting what we are taking along.

All crew members of the trawler are members of the South African Navy, but they look like the crew of any other fishing trawler in their civilian clothes. The Navy rents the vessel from the firm of Strauss & Stein of Walvis Bay for two months and it really looks as if she is just another fishing boat looking for a catch along the coast.

This boat is emeinently suitable for this type of operation. At her stern, there is a slope where nets full of fish are being hauled aboard. The ship carries two inflatable flat-bottomed boats, which may easily be launched through that slope and where they can be pulled back afterwards. These flat-bottomed boats are very suitable to deliver us right onto the beach where we will be able to get onto land with dry feet. We land-rats and the sea dogs practiced these procedures often enough along the coast of the Sperrgebiet and we know exactly what we have to do along the coast north of Luanda.

The owner of the trawler, Mister Stefan Strauss, held an inspection early this morning to make sure that everything is ready before our departure. When I was intruduced to him as Doctor David Scholtz, his eyes grew large: "That name causes a lot of bells to ring somewhere in my mind. Are you perhaps related to that Doctor Dave Scholtz who was a medical officer during the Second World War?"

"Yes, he's my my outoppie. How do you know him?"

"The two of us finished a bottle of vodka in a joint effort towards the end of '44 and talked lots of nonsense. He worked on me twice when he was a medical officer of the Waffen-SS"

"Were you also in the SS?"

"No, I was in the Navy. U-boats and later war trawlers."

The two teams that have to be dumped on land are very proficient with their motor bikes by this time. We recruited six member of the reconnaissance wing of Three Two Battalion who could speak some Afrikaans – apart from Portuguese and other indigenous languages of Angola. Because motor cycles are able to wind rapidly through the traffic, it will be easy to get away from Police vehicles and Army trucks, should they chase us. Each motor bike has a box of steel mounted behind the driver's seat and we store our gear in those – guns, explosives, a mortar pipe, mortar bombs, water and food for two days. The steel chests must also serve as simple pieces of armor, should it happen that the Police or soldiers shoot at us while we're trying to escape.

I packed some first aid stuff, as well as the necessary tools to fix minor break-downs on the bikes, if necessary. I insisted that we be supplied with containers with tear gas. With those, we can retard or even shake off any potential pursuers.

Because all of us will be wearing crash helmets, my and Mike Meyer's white faces won't be visible.

Luanda is more than eleven hundred leagues from Walvis Bay. At a speed of six knots it takes a little more than a week to reach the place.

Luanda, Wednesday, 23 December 1987

When we woke up this morning, shortly after daybreak, we went to the deck and found that we were floating on the sea water outside Luanda. There are three other big fishing trawlers in the vicinity, as well as about two dozen small boats with fishermen. I agree with Jonathan Jordan that we don't really look suspicious – especially because we are sailing under the flag of Tunisia. It would, of course, amount to suicide if we displayed the South African flag.

Through the day I, Mike Meyer, Jonathan Jordan and one of his officers scanned the area with our binoculars. We don't notice any warships or patrol boats.

I ask Jonathan:"What will we do if we are discovered by a Russian frigate or something?"

Jonathan: "Nothing. Absolutely nothing. It won't help to talk to them over the radio because they won't understand plain ole English. But it could perhaps be rather different if we should get involved with some American warships."

"What do you mean?"

"Well, there was this famous South African mariner, Bruce Daling. He was sailing from Hong Kong back to South Africa after competing in a yacht race with his yacht Voortrekker. One morning, when he woke up, he was suddely surrounded by the American Sixth Fleet, the fleet covering the Pacific Ocean."

"What did he do?"

Jonathan laughs: "Talked to the Yanks. One of the American ship signalled to him: 'Please identify yourself.' He replied: 'This is the South African sloop Voortrekker, sailed single-handedly from Hong Kong to South Africa. Won't attack unless provoked.'"

Our submarine must also be somewhere here, but she is invisible, of course. We had, though, a meeting with her two days ago when a sick crew member had to be transferred to my makeshift sick-bay on board where I had to remove an inflamed appendix.

With my binoculars I watch the big fuel tanks at the refinary and I remind Meyer: "You keep your paws off those fuel tanks at the refinery. Our recces revved the place two years ago and security there will certainly be very strict."

He immediately agrees. During our last instructions, this point was stressed.

We also look at the fuel tanks directly next to the harbor. Meyer says: "My fingers are itching to fire a RPG-7 grenade at one of those tanks. That will cause some nice sparks and a blaze on Christmas Eve!"

I agree: "That would be in the place of an illuminated and decorated Christmas tree."

During the day we land rats inspect our gear for the last time and we discuss our procedures for the last time.

When it became quite dark at nine, despite a crescent moon above the western horizon, the first of our flat-bottomed boats is launched. I and Sergeant Felipe da Silva are taken to the beach to the north of Luanda by a seaman. According to our aerial photo's, there are dense bushes just behind the beach. The nearest inhabited area is quite far away.

Just before we reach the beach, the boat suddenly increases speed and we shoot forwards to land on the sand of the beach. I and da Silva jump off and push the boat back into the water. The seaman throws the engine into reverse, turns the boat around and disappears into the darkness.

After the sound of the boat's engine has beome inaudible, I and my mate are still standing motionless to listen whether we can hear any suspicious sounds. We only hear how the waves break against the coast. We move slowly to the edge of the bushes and mark our position by drawing a big cross in the sand with our boots. The sandy strip of the beach is about twenty meters wide. We move in the shadow of he bushes to our left for about fifty meters where we encounter the mouth of a river. We see a number of sciffs and rowing boats where they are moored to the bank of the river, but no human being is visible or audible. We can't even smell any people.

We move back, past the cross in the sand and reach a pile of rocks later – the end of the sandy beach. I get onto my frequency-hopping radio and inform Jordan that the beach is secured and safe. Half-an-hour later, hust when the crescent moon disappears, the two flat-bottomed boats appear at the beach where I and da Silva mark the spot with a small torch. Our motor bikes are carefully offloaded to prevent their engines from getting wet and we help the boats again to get away from the beach and return to the trawler. We all move into the bushes and then erased the wheel tracks of our bikes on the sand with leafy branches.

Although it is clear that there is not a single human being anywhere near us, I talk in a whisper: "I think we are quite safe here. I can't even hear a dog barking. We spend the night here between the bushes, but we will have to draw lots to decide who will stand guard – just in case somebody discovers us."

Two men volunteer to guard us during the first two shifts of ninety minutes each and the lot falls on me to take the last shift just before first light. Mike Meyer has to take the third shift. It's his task to wake me up when it's time for my turn.

Luanda, Thursday, 24 December 1987

My shift as guard ends when first light appears and I wake up the other men as quetly as possible. It was a mild night in die middle of summer, but we are all used to sleepin in our clothes in the open air.

We enjoy breakfast from our ratpacks in silence. We make coffee with smokeless fuel pellets burning under our fire buckets.

Although we can't detect the presence of any other human beings, I address the men while whispering: "It won't work if we start from here as a group of eight bikers. I and my four buddies must depart first because our target is further away than the target that Meyer's group has to attack. The three of you depart thirty minutes later and you go and do some reconnaissance of your target area in daylight. After that, you do some window shopping or drinking coffee somewhere and you wait until the lights of the city are switched off before you attack those storage tanks next to the harbor. Before that, you stay as invisible as possible."

My group members grab their bikes and start up. We wave to the other guys and start to weave through the bushes. Suddenly, Corporal Fernandez starts swearing (in Portuguese) and stops: "That stinking shitty sharp stick punctured that turd of a tyre!"

We kill our engines and we have to help our mate to fix his tyre. We succeed in removing the tyre with great difficulty and to patch the hole from the inside of the tyre with a piece of flat rubber and glue. With great trouble we manage to fit the tyre onto the rim again. We have a single bicycle pump between the lot of us and it takes an hour before the tyre is hard enough.

Our repair work took about two hours. Meyer's team has left in the meantime while we stayed behind. Just as we get started again, a woman comes in our direction to gather firewood. Fortunately, she doesn't pay us any attention and we disappear through the bushes until we reach a dirt road. There are a few shacks with barking dogs, but we get going along the road before any dogs can worry us.

We memorized the route through the ciry on account of the aerial photo's and we progress through the city traffic in two groups of three and two. We strike the main road, the Estrada de Catete, quite easily and proceed in an easterly direction, into the interior. The traffic is rather heavy and it looks as if the whole population of the city is moving around at the same time – going somewhere to celebrate Christmas Eve tonight.

At the outskirts of the town of Catete we leave the road to enjoy lunch under a tree and to empty ur full bladders. After that, we move through Catete and ten kilometers further on we find the power cables that cross the road askew. About six hundred meters further on, we turn off into a narrow road to the right and pass a hamlet with a few shacks. After passing this hamlet, we reach the power lines, about two hyndred meters from the main road. We drive on the open strip between the pylons and observe that there are actually four parallelle lines, each ne with six separate cables. The pylons are spaced abut sixty meters from each other.

After we have brewed some coffee, we decide to move back to Catete. We don't want to be seen lingering under the power lines during daylight. It's about five o' clock when we leave.

We reach the highway again, Sergeant da Silva rides in front and the rest of us follow at a distance. The traffic is quite heavy and we reach the outskirts of Catete. A big truck that overtakes us, swerves out to avoid something big coming from the opposite direction. With that, he forces da Silva from the road.

I see how da Silva gets airborne as his bike strikes a stone and throws him off. The other four of us immediately stop next to him. It's clear that his crash helmet prevented a serious head injury because the helmet is dented. He sits upright and holds his left hand with the other hand.

I immediately dismount to examine him and it's apparent that his left fore-arm is broken. With my hands I direct the thers to pull our biks into the bushes next to the road and I help da Silva to stand up. We join the others in the bushes.

There is no alternative – I must fix a splint onto the man's broken arm. I help him to take his jacket off and I give him an injection for the pain. With my dagger I chop off two straight branches from a tree and strip all the leaves off. While one of the other holds his forearm in position, I place the two sticks on both sides of his arm and fasten the lot with some bandages. This is the best I can do, but he will have to get some plaster for his arm later on.

Da Silva smiles because the pain has lessened and he knows that he's in good hands.

We are stuck with a big mess, a hole full of excrement, to put it mildly. The sergeant ism't able to drive his motor bike any further. It also appears that the bike got hurt, as well. There is a hole it her fuel tank and most of the fuel has already leaked out. It is getting dusk and we are far from our target.

The explosives and detonators in da Silva;s bike are essential for the success of our mission. The steel trunks on the other four bikes are full and it's impossible to place da Silva's supplies in those. It's also impossible for him to get a lift on one our other bikes because the back seats are occupied by the steel boxes. I ask the men whether they think if we can leave da Silva here and collect him later on, while we continue without him.

Not one of them is prepared to leave their sergeant here on his own. What would happen is he were found and got arrested? Such a scenario is totally unacceptable.

Da Silva has a clever plan: "Two of you can stay here with me. The other two go and steal a truck or a van here in Catete with which you can transport me and the wrecked bike."

Me: "Tops. Good plan. Who are going to swipe a truck?"

Two the men are immediately willing and they depart with their bikes to the town center of Catete. In the meantime, the other two of us keep da Silva company.

It's already dark when the two vehicle thieves stop next to us in an ancient Volkswagen Beetle.

Me: "And where are your blooming bikes?"

"There wasn't space in this piece of junk. We must take sombody back to help us to drive the bikes back to this spot."

I sigh: "Take Pestana back with you and then you bring back your bikes while the third man drives this joke of a vehicle. Get going!"

The men stay away for a long time and it's already eleven o' clock when two of them appear with their cycles.

Me: "Where is Pestana? And where is the Beetle?"

Januario: "She suddenly refused to go on. No fuel. Pestana waits for us at the motor car."

I roar: "Donnerwetter! Dammit! Didn't you think of stealing another vehicle? Even if you have to hi-jack one. Get back, you fools!"

The two disappear, looking dejected and I and da Silva make iurselves ready to get some sleep under the bushes.

Catete, Friday, 25 December 1987

It's shortly after midnight and there is still no sign of the three men who had to steal another vehicle and bring the two bikes back. I have no choice but to hop onto my frequency-hopping radio and try to contact the submarine. It doesn't work. I do reach Jordan on the fishing trawler, though, and I tell him that our plan seems to be stalled for the time being. I have to tackle too much misfortune, but perhaps we may still be able to do something.

Jordan: "We can't postpone or cancel this operation at this time. I've already received a message from the submarine that Team X-Ray has been launched and they are supposed to be inside the harbor by this time. They are only waiting that the city lights are switched off before they can venture any nearer to the ships in the harbor."

Me: "This is a hell of a fuck-up. I'm sitting here on my own with a wounded man. Three of my men are gone with threir bikes and there is no way for me to reach the target and complete my work as of now. Perhaps my men will return before daybreak so that we can perhaps try to do something."

Jordan: "It's in your hands. But in the meantime, I will make comms with Walvis and tell them everything."

Me: "Thanks. Over and out."

I reach Meyer on the radio and order him not to throw his bombs prematurely.

The sun is already shing when the three men arrive with a truck with their bikes loaded onto the back of the truck.

Me: "Where the hell have you been staying so long?"

Pestana: "There were road blockades. I think the owner of the Volkswagen has pals in the Police and when he discovered that his car was gone, he hit the alarm bell. And then the Police started looking for the robbers. We had to wait for the road blockades to end before we could return."

I mumble a few unfriendly and inaudible oaths and walk to tne side with my frequency-hopping radio. I manage to make comms with Commander van Vuuren on the submarine. He knows of my problems and I tell him that the long-awaited men joined me only a few minute ago. I have no choice but to wait till tonight to go ahead with my part of the plan.

Van Vuuren: "What the hell will it help if the city's lights go off tonight? My divers are already back on board and we are busy sailing away. Orders from Walvis. There is no way that I can send them back again to complete their work in the harbor."

Me: "What did they achieve, if anything?"

Van Vuuren: "They left four magnetic mines on the sea bed at the entrance to the bay. They couldn't dare to go near any of the ships because the bloody lights never got switched off. They waited a number of hours and then came back so that they could get back on board before daybreak."

Me: "I'm sorry. Those were circumstances over which I had no control."

Van Vuuren: "You and Team Yankee withdraw tonight according to plan, even if you have achieved fuck-all. Perhaps the four magnetic mines on the sea bed will achieve something."

Walvis Bay, Sunday, 3 January 1988

Colonel Nel addresses us again in the conference room at the naval base in Walvis Bay where we gathered for the debriefing. The other attendees are I, Lieutenant Mike Meyer, Commander Fires van Vuuren and Lieutenant-Commander Jonathan Jordan.. Captain Gomes is absent. We are here to do a post mortem regarding Operation Tequila.

The colonel: "Do you gentlemen realize what a hellish, blasted, bastardly, bloody, fucking mess this whole ops amounted to? Do you know what was the end-result of all our piss-filled planning and crappy exercises?"

We stare at him in silence.

The colonel: "The only people who did any constructive work were the divers of Team X-Ray who left four magnetic mines at the entrance to the bay. One of those mines blew up a freighter yesterday. Do you perhaps think that was a success?"

Fires: "It depends on what type of ship it was, I suppose."

The colonel: "Exactky. Do you perhaps think that it was a Cuban ship? Or a Russian ship? The simple and straight answer is: negative! It was a ship that loaded a cargo of timber and diamnds in the harbor of Luanda and was leaving again."

He stays silent for a few seconds while the sparks shoot from his angry eyes: "It was a blooming Israeli ship on her way to Haifa! And now she lies with a big hole in her hull in the water. And the worst part is that the Israeli government is extremely angry, hell-out angry. They know it wasn't Unita, but us."

24. OPERATION VODKA

Oshakati, Friday, 27 May 1988

We have a hectic time at the sick-bay in Oshakati and even I, as a neurologist, must often help at Casualties. Our Defence Force has a few thousand troops inside Angola and it seems as if a stalemate situation has developed there. Our men don't succeed in driving the Cubans, Angolams, and the fighters of Swapo from their positions. And, in the meantime, helicopters land every so often and deliver wounded men and then we have to get them ready to be taken by airplanes to one of our three military hospitals in South Africa.

Directly after my arrival at the sick-bay at seven o' clock this morning, I am summoned to the conference room at our HQ complex. When I arrive, I find Colonel Viljoen there. He tasked me last year to abduct an important leader of Swapo from Angola. He is the senior staff officer: operations here in Sector One Zero's HQ. There is also another acquaintance, Captain Fabio Gomes of the Air Force. I am introduced to Lieutenant Mark Stephens of Four Four Parachute Brigade's Pathfinder unit.

The colonel: "Doc, allow me come to the point immediately. We need you urgently at short notice. Operation Vodka must have its kick-off tomorrow. A team of three pathfinders must do reconaissance at a target in Angola and – if possible – help a company of parabats to land at the right spot. We have learnt that a doctor or a medic is essential for this type of reconaissance because it often happens that somebody gets hurt. The doctor who was supposed to go along pulled out yesterday suddenly to attend to the funeral of his father."

I interrupt the colonel: "Colonel, it is so that I was trained as a parabat, but I know that the pathfinders have received very specilized training, which I haven't had."

The colonel: "Doc, you are the only available useful midical person whom we can use at short notice. You have lots of operational experience. I have read your report on Ops Tequila of last December. It wasn't your fault that you couldn't reach your objective, but if it wasn't for you, one of our men would have fallen into enemy hands with a broken arm – and that is not something we relish. I believe you have the necessary knowledge and skills to be able to help us. Are you able to get your kit together so that you can do an ops for us, together with this lieunentant and another man? If we can't get you, we will perhaps be compelled to cancel the whole operation – even if a company parabats trained for it a whole fortnight. What do you say?"

Me: "Colonel, it seems as if I don't really have a choice. My wife, who is also a medical practitioner, thinks by this time that I am somewhat cuckoo, or suffer from shell-shock or a stroke or some sort of brain damage, but I do feel okay, nevertheless. Okay. I am going along."

The colonel: "Bakgat.[67] Then we can start to tell you what will be going on with Ops Vodka. Sorry, but we won't be rading a Russian bottle store. In short: it means that a company parabats must go and attack an air base at Huambo in Angola. Your team of three scouts must go and see the previous night whether such an operation is in any way practicable and viable and attainable."

Me: "And if it is viable, must I and my team mates stay behind to help with the shooting?"

The colonel: "It will be necessary."

Me: "Then I must go to the shooting range directly after this after I have drawn all the necessary fire arms to go and practice. I haven't handled a fire arm for quite a while."

---

[67] "Bakgat": an unranslateable Afrikaans expression that means more or less something like OK.

The colonel: "That has already been organized. We hoped that we can rely on you. But allow me to tell you, first of all, how it came about that we had to plan this ops. Do you see these aerial photo's of the air base at Huambo (and he points to a pile of photo's on the table)? They were taken about six weeks ago by Captain Gomes. This, is, therefore, outdated info, old news. We must know what is going on there at this moment and that is where you and this lieutenant get involved. "

Me:"How dd Captain Gomes succeed in taking these photo's?"

The colonel points with his index finger at the captain who immediately responds: "Doc, you surely know that I've made clandestine contact with the Angolans as if I were a Brazilian. With my airplane with a Brazilian registration number – but which actually belongs to our Air Force. I am, after all, a South African Porra and Portuguese is my mother tongue and, therefore, I can converse with the lot in Angola in this language. You were with me last December when I delivered a load of jinxed hand grenades in Luanda – in exchange for a bag full of diamonds. I'm sure you can remember that?"

Me: "How can I ever forget it? I also remember how that load of hand grenades said 'boom' shortly after we had taken off again." And on my own I also remember how I secretly swiped two of those diamonds for my dear German wife. I still have to get to a jeweller to have two nice earrings made with those diamonds.

Gomes: "Well, yes, the Angolans thought that it was the Unita rebels of Savimbi who sabotaged those hand grenades. Their military attache in Brazil contacted me again and placed another order for hand grenades. I got the assignment hand grenades from

Krygkor[68] and I fly with that to Huambo – as if I came from Brazil with the load. The Angolams were afraid that another accident could happen if I flew it to Luanda and they requested me to deliver it at Huambo instead."

Me: "And that was when your plane with her secret cameras took these pictures?"

Gomes: "Exactly. You Boer boys are almost as clever as us Porras by figuring that out."

Me: "And a few hand grenades were jinxed with the result that they blow up the whole lot, sky high, three days later?"

The colonel: "That's right. We heard via a spy of Unita that there was a hell of an explotion in the vicinity of Huambo, but we don't know if we can believe it. Unita often provides us with inaccurate info."

The colonel continues: "Anyway, we are very grateful for these photo's. But they're old news. Come and have a look. Here is the long runway, as well as a shorter runway. To the south east of this building complex there are a few parking spots for Cuban Migs. They stand at a distance from each other and all of have earth works arount them to protect them against possible schrapnel. We can count six Migs here. The other two were probably in the aur at that moment. To the north east of the building complex there are six parking slots for attack helicopters – Mil Mi-24's. That's easily the ugliest thing that flies, but also one of the deadliest. Armed with a twelve comma seven millimeters Gatling machine gun under her nose, which she can swing in all directions. She also carries bombs or missiles and can accommodate eight troops. Here are three of the six on their parking spots and the other three were probably at that moment busy elsewhere."

[68] Krygkor: the state-owned armaments manufacturer.

Me: "I think I've treated a few of our troops who have been wounded by that ugly thing."

The colonel: "It's very necessary that we take out this base. It won't do to send our bombers over there. Unfortintely, our Air Force is not what it used to be. Too few pilots. Too few servicable fighter aircraft. We can't risk our few remaining aircraft by sending them on a mission over there. The place is full of anti-aircraft artillery, as you can see. Here and here (and he presses his finger on a few spots on a photo).

"But we must prevent these ugly egg beaters from shooting at our troops any longer. The Cuban pilots are much, much better than the Angolans. When the Angolese tried to throw bombs on our troops, they always missed by many hundreds of meters. Often many kilometers. That doesn't happen with these Cubans."

Me: "The wounded troops with whom I often worked, tell me that the Cuban Air Force very often hit our Ratels, Buffells, Casspirs and Samils. And then our men get all sorts of sore places."

The colonel: "You realize, therefore, that we have to act fast."

Mark Stephens: "Doc, thanks that we can rely on you. We fly tomorrow afternon just after sunset and an Oryx will download us a number of kilometers from Huambo. Together with our three bikes. I understand you know something about motor bikes, or that is what the colonel told me."

Me: "Yes, last Christmas I and three men of the recce wing of Three Two Battalion travelled on bikes through Luanda and we almost had some sports."

Mark: "Then you are just the right man to take along. I requested that one of the recces of Three Two accompanies us because we need somebody who can speak Portuguese. It is necessary that we get to know each other just this afternoon."

The colonel: "You take the same bikes that you used in Luanda last December. Armed with RPG-7 missiles to shoot out the airplanes and kelihopters, should it get to that point. Also R-4 automatic rifles and a few hand grenades for self-Defence."

"Of course, I take my first aid bag along and I would like to have a few cannisters of tear smoke."

Mark: "Tear smoke?"

Me: "It may help a lot if the Cubans and Angolans should chase us. They won't be able to shoot at us if their eyes are full of tears."

Mark: "Oh! I like that!"

The colonel: "A last point. It is necessary that this ops takes place at this point in time. The moon is almost full and our parabats will need the moonlight to see what they are doing. That is to say, if you let us know that such an ops is possible and won't amount to a suicide mission."

Me: "Colonel, please inform the sick-bay that I have been posted to the parabats."

Huambo, Saturday, 28 May 1988

It was a pleasant surprise when Sergeant Felipe da Silva of Three Two Battalion joined us yesterday.The first thing he did was to punch me in my ribs with his left fist: "Doc, as you can see, you fixed this broken arm of mine very nicely."

And now I, Mark Stephens. and da Silva are riding into the ciry of Huambo after an Oryx helicopter dropped us three with our biks six or seven kilometers outside the city in the bushes in the dark. The pilot flew in low so as not to be detected by radar at the air base. The arrangement is that the helicopter is to pick us up again tomorrow before daybreak at the same spot if it proves to be necessary to extract us again – that is, if the operation cannot go ahead. It is planned that he gets refuelled in southern Angola, the area controlled by the Unita rebels. Huambo is about seven hundred kilometers from the northern border of South West and the Oryx would not have been able to make the whole trip to Huambo and back on one tank of fuel. It would, as well, been too dangerous to await our return at the spot where we landed.

During the limited time at our disposal we memorized the position of the air base to the south east of the town on account of the aerial photo's and an outdated road map.

On the aerial photo's of Captain Gomes we could clearly see watch towers all along the perimeter fence of the air field. We have to answer the question: are they manned during the night? What type of weapons do the guards have? We must also find out how the illumination everywhere on this base is. Are there search lights?

We find the air field easily. It's not easy to miss such a big piece of real estate. According to the aerial photo;s, there is a road more or less right outside the fence of the base on all sides. We decide to ride along the western fence of the base and then take the road on its northern side. After that, we swing around the most easterly point of the longest runway to see what is going on there. We end our survey off with a ride through an inhabied area with some traffic on the southern side of the base.

After having seen what we wanted to see, we return to the road on which we entered the city. Just outside the town, we stop to discuss what we have seen.

Mark Stephens gives his opinion first: "Men, that place is being guarded jolly well. There are two men in every guard tower with a LMG."

Sergeant Da Silva: "I also wouldn't like our men to be shot to shreds by machine guns."

Me: “There are hopelessly too much illumination. The only spot where helicopters with parabats can land, is at the south eastern point, at the end of the long runway – far away from the building complex. But I’m also sure that the runway has lights that can be switched on when an aircraft has to land at night. That will cause our troops to be sitting ducks if those lights are switched on when they are flown in.”

Mark: “I could see the tail fins of a few Migs, but they are well protected by earth wotks. We will only be able to shoot them out if we are able to get near to them – which will not be easy or simple or doable. I vote that we send a signal that this ops is still-born.”

Me: “I had a good look. There is nowhere a place where we can enter the base unseen so that we can prepare a landing spot for the men or signal them where to land. The fence is too strong and solid and there are too many lights and watch towers.”

Da Silva: “Yes. Those Cubans are very security conscious. We will see our own arses if we try to take this base out.”

Me: “Or just to penetrate the place.”

Mark: “If the parabats landed outside the base and throw mortar bombs over the fence, it might just work.”

Me: “I didn’t notice any places where a whole flight of helicopters could land, except on the air base itself. And if our parabats took up positions outside the fence they would still be targets for those men in the towers with their machine guns. All those lights on the towers will shine directly into their eyes and blind tjem so that they won’t be able to aim their mortar pipes accurately.

Mark: “Yes, that makes sense. There’s one positive point to report, thogh, but it won’t help this ops. I’m sure you noticed that one of the sheds had it roof blown off. That must be the result of those jinxed hand grenades that blew up.”

Me: "I would like to knw what was in that shed and got damaged."

Mark: "I guess there must have been some important equipment. Perhaps spare parts for the aircraft. But it won't work to go back and try to find out."

We ride to the spot where we must meet the helicopter again and we wait for midnight. Mark Stephens takes his radio from his motor bike's luggage bin. He succeeds in making comms with a relay station in the area of Unita. This relay station must then inform the signals room at Oshakati of our message. Mark says short and sweet: "Mike Sierra One here. Abort. Repeat: abort. Over and out." The voice on the other side merely says: "Roger."

He immediately switches the radio off because we don't want to give our prsence away.

Southern Angola, Sunday, 29 May 1988

The three of us feel rather downhearted where we are sitting again in the Oryx. It is clear that our men won't be able to spoil and smash and ravage and ruin the Angolan and Cuban air base. The sun has risen in the meantime while we are flying south. We fly a few meters above the tree tops to avoid detection by enemy radar.

Suddenly, Captain Monty McGregor, the pilot, calls over the intercom: "Boys, hold on tight! We can expect some sports!"

And with that, ge pulls the chopper steeply up into the air.

I look through the open hatch to see what is going on. Two extremely ugly Cuban helicopters approach us from eleven o' clock.

Monty calls: "Our only chance is to gain altitude rapidly. Those Mils seem to be heavily loaded and they cannot ascend as fast as we can. We can also fly higher than them."

The first Cuban helcopter swings her machine gun under her nose in our direction and it seems certain that she wants to shoot in our direction. Monty is, forunately, an experienced pilot and he succeeds in staying out of range of the machine gun with its four barrels.

Mark suddenly fumbles in the bagage bin of his bike that is secured against the back side of the cabin and he takes his RPG-7 out. He calmly takes place on the floor of our helicopter with his feet hanging outside and shoots the missile in the direction of the Cuban.

The rocket flies away with a roar and a rumble and zaps the front end of the Cuban a second later. The missile grenade, which is designed to penetrate armored steel, explodes against the wind shield of the pilot's cabin and shoots a thick stream of fire into the cabin's interior. The Mil immediately tumbles down, out of control. The poor pilot must have been grilled or fried in an instant.

Monty calls over the intercom: "Keep that up, boys! Well done!"

The second helicopter seems to be a bit more intelligent and does not attack us from the side. Instead, she slides to a position below us, apparently with the goal of shooting at us from that position.

Suddenly, I get a bright brain wave. I release Mark's bike where she is fastened and push her towards the open door. Mark gets up and helps me. It's easy to push the bike out and she falls down – and the rotating blades of the helicopter below us are shattered into small pieces as the heavy metal contraption strikes them.

Mark exclaims: "Another one bites the dust! She's making a nose dive! Doc, that was beautiful. You acted rapidly! And correctly. You saved the day."

Sergeant da Silva shakes my hand.

Five minutes later, Monty announces over the intercom: "I don't have enough juice for us to reach Ondongwa. These sports emptied my tank rather rapidly. We fly to Unita."

Mark remarks towards me: "Doc, all three of us need a big mouth full of medicine, right at this very moment. Klipdrif.[69] Five minutes ago, I still had a half jack of the stuff, but now it's gone."

Me: "And what happened to it?"

Mark: "It was in the lugage bin of that damn bike that you threw out a short while ago!"

Oshakati, Monday, 30 May 1988

Colonel Viljoen enters the conference room where I and Mark Stephens are waiting for a debriefing session with him.

"Men, this is really a big fuck-up. Operation Vodka is very dead. All our preparations were in vain! A waste of time!"

Me: "Colonel, not quite in vain. After all, we got two kills."

Mark: "And we could report that those hand grenades blew off the roof of a shed."

---

[69] Klipdrif: a well-known and popular brand of brandy in South Africa.

The colonel: "And in the process the two of you did a naughty thing for which you may be court martialled."

Me and Mark say simultaneously: "Yes? Why?"

The colonel: "Destruction of military equipment. Thanks to you, a valuable motor bike has been fucked up. At present, it lies in the Angolan bush as a piece of scrap metal. Written off. A valuable radio got lost at the same time. Perhaps a member of Swapo will pick it up and listen to ur comms. But I also think that I will recommend both of you for a medal. Also the pilot of your chopper. There are now two Cuban gunships less to hit our boys."

Me: "How about downing a glass of Vodka because of all this?"

The colonel: "Doc, I think you are the only medical officer in our whole Defence Force who can boast that he downed a Russian-built helicopter during an aerial dogfight. That's a nice example of unconventional warfare. I will join you this afternoon after work for a tot of vodka."

25. OPERATION TRANSPLANT

Voortrekkerhoogte, Wednesday, 4 January 1989

It's lunch time at 1 Military Hospital at Voortrekkerhoogte[70] and I sit in the cafeteria with a light lunch on the table in front of me. This is my second day at One Mil since being redeployed from Oshakati. Suddenly, I feel a hand on myshoulder and I look up.

Me: "Louis Lancaster! Is this really you?"

Louis: "Hi, Doc. Yes, this is the same me. Actually, I should stop calling you 'Doc' because we are now colleagues."

I get up and I shake the hand of my former medic: "I see two pips on your shoulders and I notice you are a medical officer now."

Louis: "Just so, Doc, just so. I was your medic exactly nine years ago. Lots of things happened in this time. After my national service, I went to study and now I am a GP[71]."

Me: "And how did you get into the Permanent Force?"

Louis: "Doc, that's a long story. I want to tell all of it to you when we have enough time. But I must run. My patients are waiting. Anyway, congrats with your promotion. I see you are a major now. Better pay, I believe?"

Voortrekkerhoogte, Friday, 13 January 1989

My whole family – my lovely wife, Hannelore, a general practitioner, and our kids, Dave Junior and little Heini – arrive at

[70] "Voortrekkerhoogte" is the old name of a suburb of Pretoria where military personnel are based, where various military units have their headquarters, where the Army College is housed , and where 1 Military Hospital is situated. Its original name was Roberts Heights and it is presently called Thabo Tshwane.

[71] "GP" – general practitioner.

Louis Lancaster's home in Voortrekkerhoogte. He invited us for dinner at his place, which we find to be very thoughtful because we are still busy arranging our new home in Voortrekkerhoogte since our arrival from Ovamboland, ten days ago. Things still look chaotic and we are not yet in a position to receive guests.

Louis meets as at his front door and invites us in. "Please meet my dear mom. She is Sylvia. Before her marriage, she wasy Sylvia Smithson. Mom, this is the good doctor about whom I told you – Doc David Scholtz. He's a wonderful man and we became pals on the Border."

Hannelore and I shake the hands of Missus Lancaster. It is immediately noticable that she suffers from dementia because she almost doesn't react when her son talks to her. In truth, he even had to take her hand so that we could shake it.

Louis: "My dish is in the oven. You are getting 'land mine chicken'[72] in a pie. It will be ready in half-an-hour. And then we can have dinner."

Hannelore: "Can I help with something?"

Louis: "No, ma'am. Not necessary. Or must I also call you 'Doc' , the same as your husband? He told me a lot abut you when we worked together on the Border, including that you are a German from South West and that you are a wonderful Gee Pee."

Hannelore: "Louis, we are now colleagues because I'm also a Gee Pee. Call me Hannelore. And my husband is Dave."

Louis: "Nice to meet you, Hannelore. Thanks that you want to help but I am a competent houseman. As you can see it's only me and my mom in this house and I prepare the meals. You will get chicken pie, baked potatoes and green salad. A glass of wine?"

Hannelore: "Rather with the meal, thank you."

---

[72] "Land mine chicken" – Army slang for chicken chopped into small bits.

Louis: "Okay. And how do you find life here in civilazation?"

Hannelore: "It's quite an adjustment. We are being transplanted from one world to another. Fortunately, it does seem as if the war in Suth West is drawing to a close. All fighting must stop in April. Over there, in Oshakati, we had little space to move around. When you wanted to leave the base it had to be as part of a convoy. Here, we can move around as we like and it feels almost strange.

Me: "But here we are also in a war situation. Our Defence Force is fighting against the ANC. In South West, the war was limited to Ovamboland and the southern parts of Angola. In this war, we are fighting an invisible enemy in every city, town, and village. Nobody knows how long we will be able to carry on with that."

Louis: "Yip, that's another type of war. I also had to adapt to this type of war. For me it also was a transplant from academia into a harsh reality."

Me: "Louis, please tell me, how did it happen that you became a medical officer and we became colleagues?"

Louis: "Doc – hmm, hmm, Dave – I told you the ther day, it's really a long story. I wish to tell it to you and that's why I invited you. We have enough time to chat now."

Me: "I've seen you for the last time in 1980 before I went to specialize as a neurologist. You were one of my medics during Ops Sceptic when we invaded Angola."

Louis: "Yes, I remember that ops very well. We sat around for long periods of time while we were very busy doing nothing. You will remember, I joined the Army for an extra year of national service so that I wouldn't be called up for camps later on. And it also helped me to make some dough to pay for my studies."

Me: "I remember that you used that time to swot up my manual on anatomy."

Louis: "Yes. I had enough time because we sat around while waiting for nothing to happen. It was a waste of time for our unit, but I made good use of the time to brush up my knowledge of anatomy."

He tells that he was fortunate to get admitted to the Faculty of Medicine of the University of Cape Town. He believes that his service as a medical orderly during the war helped in that regard. Because his mom lived in the southern suburbs of Cape Town he had no problem with lodgings.

His mother, who was still working at that time, could pay for a part of his study fees. He augmented his finances by working as a waiter during the vacations and some week-ends. During the summer vacation, he used the time to summarize the manuals for the next year and sold these summaries to his fellow-students. In addition, he offered classes in needle work to his fellow-students so that they could apply these skills during operations and while stitching open wounds – just as he was able to apply the skills he was taught by his mother when he served as a medical orderly.

Because he had already completed his national service, his application to become a member of the Permanent Force was rapidly approved. Then he had to be trained as an officer of the Medical Service, together with other prospective medical officers.

"That was actually a joke. I had to do basics all over again as an ordinary private, although I was a lance dorporal in the past. That training took place at Klipdrif, the base near Potchefstroom where I as earlier trained to become a medic. And then the whole group of us was transferred to Voortrekkerhoogte. They wanted to find out whether we were officer material and for that, we had to complete some psychological questionnaires. I knew that something of the sort was due. In our group there were two clinical psychologists and they told us to mess up this testing business because it was actually meant for young national servicemen directly out of school. We were, though, men who had degrees in medicine, dentistry, and psychology."

Hannelore: "And did you really mess up your psycholo-gical tests?"

"Yesk we did. We all agreed that we would complete these questionnaires as if we were homosexuals. Afterwards the psychologists who scored our questionnaires were extremely angry because we actually sabotaged their work. They wanted to use the data taken from our questionnaires to refine these questionnaires and to write an article about it."

Me: "And then all their data were useless, of course?"

Louis chuckles: "That's right!"

He also tells that he completed his house doctor's year and training as medical officer two years ago. After being a candidate officer for a year, he was promoted to the rank of lieutenant last year.

During the meal he helps his mother to eat. She often drops some food onto the apron he has dressed her with.

After we have finished with the meal and we have complimented him with his cullinary skills, he excuses himself: "Please give me a few minutes. I must help Ma to get into bed. Only a few minutes."

The conversation continues after his return.

Louis: "And now my Ma stays with me here. She can't work anymore. She retired at the age of sixty-five just when I became a member of the Pee Eff.[73]"

Hannelore: "And now you look after your mother because she looked after you, all those years?"

---

[73] "Pee Eff" – the abbreviation PF stands for Permanent Force (of the Defence Force), consisting of people who follow a military career.

Louis: "Exactly. And Dave, now I want to tell you: You were my inspiration to become a good doctor."

Me: "How's that?"

Louis: "Because you treated me decently as a human being. With respect. With real interest. Especially when my twin brother Lance died. I'm sure you can remember, I brought him to you when he was accidently shot. But it was too late. He died while being transported by a chopper. And then it was you who comforted me and saw to it that Lance's body was treated with respect. You did your utmost to make things as easy as possible for me. Because you are a quack, you could book me off for a month with special compassionate leave so that I could attend to my brother's funeral and help my poor mom."

Me: "I only did what any decent doctor would have done in those circumstances."

Louis: "No, you did more. You went the extra mile. Lance wasn't just another casualty. I wasn't just a troop who became bossies. You were a real father figure."

Me: "That was just my duty."

Louis: "And while I was busy with my extra year, I was very grateful to participate in Ops Sceptic as your medic. You spent real time with me, explaining things about anatomy that I didn't understand. I saw that you loved your work – and that's the sort of quack I also want to be."

Me: "My pa was a wonderful doctor and I only tried to follow his example."

Louis: "You were almost the father I never knew. And, therefore, I want to follow your example."

Hannelore: "Louis, thank you very much for that wonderful compliment you gave my husband. That's also how I got to know him – somebody who just doesn't treat an illness, but also has an interest in the ill patient. That's why he became a neurologist."

Louis: "Dave, it's wonderful that you are a neurologist. I want to tap your brains. I'm sure you saw that my mom isn't quite all right. Even I can see it's serious dementia. Do you agree?"

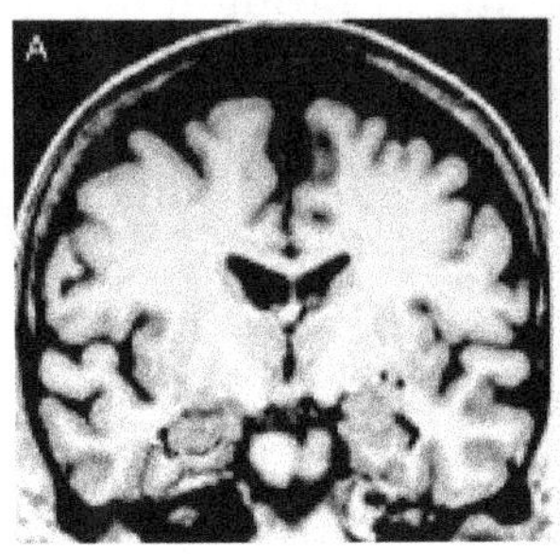

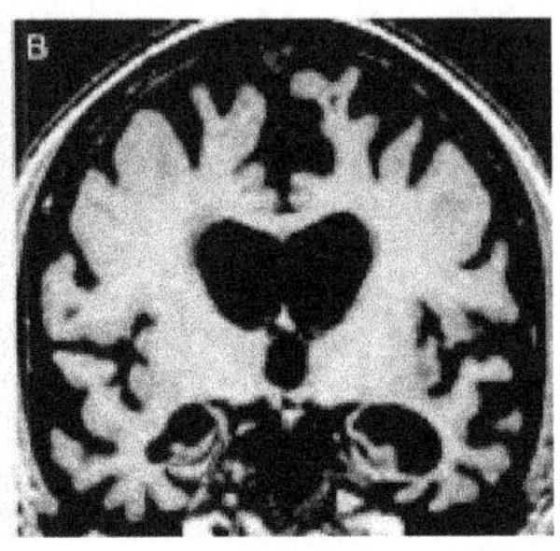

Me: "It seems that way. She never spoke a single word the whole time – not even when I greeted her when we arrived. She was able to eat by herself, although with your help, but that was more or less all of it. Perhaps you must bring her so that we can do a brain scan of her at One Mil. I am rather certain that it will show that her brain has shrunk considerably and that the ventricles in her brain grew in sizet."

Louis: "Do you think it's Alzheimer's?"

Me: "You ought to know that we can only diagnose Alzheimer's with certainty with an autopsy. But it's not impossible. More or less one half of the people with dementia can be diagnosed with Alzheimer's."

Louis: "Dave, is there anything you can do for my ma? I'm the only relative she has. She is also my only family and I'm the only person who can look after her. She helped me when I studied and I cannot allow her to become neglected."

Hannelore: "Louis, that's wonderful of you. But, in the meantime, life goes on and you're staying behind. It's only you and your mother. I'm sure that you need a good girlfriend with whom you want to spend the rest of your life and that you want a family of your own."

Louis: "Actually, you are right. There is a nice nurse here in One Mil whom I would like to date, but I can't. There's no time. She always smiles when she sees me."

Me: "Who looks after your mother when you are working?"

Louis: "There is a black woman, a trained carer. She looks after my mom and she also does the washing and other chores."

Hannelore: "Does your mother know what's going on around her?"

Louis: "Not really. It doesn't seem as if she registers anything. She only breathes and stares into nothingness."

Hannelore: "It will become too much for you to keep on caring for your mother. Have you ever thought about placing her in a nursing home? She won't miss you when she's there because it seems as if she doesn't recognize you anymore."

Louis: "I won't have the heart to do that."

Me: "If you want to enhance your mom's welfare, then that is something you must think about. In such a place she will get specialized care. You asked me whether I can do anything for her as a neurologist. The answer is, unfortunately, 'No'. The deterioration can, unfortunately, not be reversed. There is no known treatment for her condition as yet. I'm sorry."

Louis: "It will break my heart to let her go."

Hannelore: "And that will break the heart of that cute nurse if you don't ask her for a date! You will have to choose!"

Louis gets up to brew some coffie and when he returns, Hannelore asks: "If I've heard correctly, you mentinoed that your mom's maiden name was Smithson?"

Louis: "That's right."

Hannekoire: "Is she perhaps distantly related to the actress Harriet Smithson?"

Louis: "My great-great-grandpa had an elder sister with that name – a long, long time ago."

Hannelore: "Was she perhaps the Harriet Smithson who was married to Hector Berlioz?"

Louis: "Who the heck is this Hector, aaah, Somebody?"

Hannelore: "Hector Berlioz was a famous French composer of the nineteenth century. He wrote a whole symphony to put into sound his obsession with this actress, Harriet."

Louis: "My grandpa told me that his grandpa often mentioned that 'fucking Frenchman' and that 'friggin' Frog' who messed up his sister's life. I suppose he couldn't remember this Frenchman's name, but it must have been the same guy."

Me: "Well, I never!"

Louis: "What you are telling me there, Hannelore, makes me think. I don't want the reputation as the guy who broke a lovely girl's heart. Perhaps I ought to date that nice nurse."

26. OPERATION DIAGNOSIS

Voortrekkerhoogte, Wednesday, 18 January 1989

Hannelore, my lovely wife – who joined a private practice with four other general practitioners since we arrived in Pretoria a fortnight ago – phnes me at my consulting rooms at 1 Military Hospital: "It's necessary that you listen to the news on the radio. Something happened that will interest you as a neurologist. One of my patients told me a few minutes ago."

"What's going on?"

"The State President had a stroke this morning. His office announced that he was admitted to Two Mil in Cape Town, that his condition is stable and that he's fully conscious. Minister Chris Heunis is the acting State President now."

"Thanks, a lot. That's certainly very interesting. It's twelve-thirty now. I will switch on my radio as son as it's lunch time."

Voortrekkerhoogte, Friday, 20 January 1989

The telephone in my consulting room rings at four o' clock, just as I am getting ready to go home. If it had rung two minutes later, I would have been gone for the start of my weekend. I feel like ignoring the ringing phone, but I, nevertheless, pick it up due to military discipline kicking in. I silently decide that this discipline on my part must have a neurological explanation.

After I have mentioned my name, a voice on the other side says: "Major Scholtz, this is Captain Dirk van Deventer of the office of the Surgeon General. You are requested to appear exactly at five at the main entrance of One Mil. A staff vehicle will pick you up to take you to Blenny."

"Right. Will do."

"Thank you. Good-bye."

I am totally blown over. Blenny is the nickname of the Defence Force's operational headquarters in Pretoria. I have never been there, but I was told by my dad that it consists of a series of subterranean bunkers that can withstand an atomic bomb. What on earth does the SG want to do with me? Is there any connection with the stroke the State President has suffered? I phone Hannelore and tell her that I will be working late tonight and that I don't know at what time I will get home.

Exactly at five, I stand ready with my brief case in my hand at the main entrance of the hospital. A Mercedes-Benz with a R registration number appraoches me and the driver, a staff sergeant, asks me whether I am Major Scholtz. I nod my head and think that the man must be blind or blocvk-headed or something because my rank is clearly visible on mt shoulders and a name tag is fastened to my shirt. I wonder whether there is a neurlogical explanation for this block-headedness. I move over to the other side to take a seat next to the driver.

When we reach Blenny, all I can see is a low building on street level. Uniformed personnel enter and exit the place. The staff sergeant parks the fancy limousine at a spot reserved for generals. He locks my brief case into the car's boot and takes me inside. He tells me: "They don't allow people with briefcases to enter, unless you have an office inside here. And then they scan the insides of the briefcase with X-rays to see whether there are any forbidden items inside, such as a bread knive or a bottle of brandy or a bomb."

I move through an X-ray machine that registers my office keys in my pocket. The staff sergeant accompanies me to a row of lifts and we descend into the bowels of Mother Earth. On a certain level we get out and a sign announces that we have arrived at CSI. I know that as the abbreviation for Chief of Staff: Intelligence. It is certainly the office of a big shot that I am visiting. What the blazes does he want from me, a mere major? Am I unknowingly in possession of state secrets that they want to press or squeeze out of me?

I am taken to a conference room. At the door, I immediately freeze and my right arm automatically swings up in a salute, as if in an instinctive reaction. At the head of the table, I notice General Jannie Geldenhuys, the new chief of the Defence Force – also known as CSADF. I also see Lieutenant General Niel Knobel, the Surgeon General, and Vice Admiral Dries Putter, the CSI.

General Jannie Geldenhuys

The CSADF says, while I am still feeling dizzy (quite a normal neurological reaction in these circumstances): "Major, Doctor, thank you for coming. Take a seat. We are waiting for a few visitors who will arive presently. Niel, will you please do the explaining?"

This is the first time in my life that I meet any generals or admirals face to fce, although I've seen some at a distance, such as at a parade. The highest ranking officer with whom I've rubbed shoulders, is a brigadier – including my outoppie who is a retired brigadier.

I take a seat opposite the SG who starts to explain: "Dave, we need your expert knowledge. As a neurologist."

He slides a big envelope over the table towards me: "Please have a look at these and tell us what you see. We are waiting for a few cabinet ministers and it's necessary to hear what you find."

I open the envelope and take out three sheets that look like X ray scans, but are actually MRI[74] brain scans. The first sheet contains scans of the head of somebody on a horizontal level. The second sheet contains a series of sagittal cuts – scans taken from the side and the third sheet contains coronal views, taken from the front.

Me: "Thanks. I need an illuminated screen to study these properly."

Genral Knobel: "I have ordered one. There on the table in the corner."

This is what I expected: a record of the State President's head after he has suffered a stroke. Hell! Suddenly, I have serous confidential stuff in my hands – the state of health of our SP, the head of state! What must I do with these records? I almost breathe out a big sigh, but I check myself in time. After all, the SP is just another human being with a brain and I am expected to say something about his head and what is inside.

Me: "General, how did you obtain these records?"

Knobel: "They were taken two days ago, at Two Mil. When I heard of the stroke of the SP, I directly ordered that copies of his scans had to be sent to my office. We can't expect any old technician or radiologist to give us an expert interpretation or analysis. There are state secrets contained in those scans and you are requested to find them and explain them to us."

"General, you ought to know that these brain scans won't tell us nothing about all the secret information stored in this particular brain (and I point to the sheets). I'm sure that the State President has knowledge of many state secrets. Nobody is, though, able to dig any state secrets out of these scans."

---

[74] "MRI" – magnetic resonance imaging.

Lieutenant General Niel Knobel

"No, my friend, that's not what I mean with state secrets. The state of health of our State President is a state secret at this very moment and you must inform us about that."

Me: "Okay, I understand. And, must I now have a look at these state secrets? Isn't there a more competent neurologist at Two Mil who could have done this?"

Knobel: "Two Mil's neurologist is away on leave. You are the best we have. You will also find in that envelope a short report by the pathologist or radiologist that states that the stroke occurred in the patient's left prefrontal lobe. Full stop. Nothing more. You must now explain to us how serious this state of affairs is. What is your diagnosis? What is the prognosis? What type of influence will this stroke have on the State President's behavior? Will he be able to continue with his work? We gathered here beause the minister of Defence has ordered this meeting, after consulting with the acting State President. They are expected shortly and they will want to hear your expert opinion."

I switch the illuminated screen on and I place the sheets on top of that, one after the other. I study each cut in silence. There are about twenty cuts in the first sheet, taken from the top, down to the bottom of the brain. The other two sheets contain about the same number of cuts. These views from three different angles provide a good idea of the state of the brain in three dimensions.

After ten minutes, the door of the conference room opens again and four ministers come marching in: Minister Chris Heunis, acting SP, General Magnus Malan, former CSADF and minister of Defence, Minister Pik Botha, minister of foreign affairs, and Minister FW de Klerk, minister of education. All the members of the SADF stand at attention in the presence of these important visitors.

Jannie Geldenhuys starts: "Gentlemen, thank you that you sacrifice your time to attend this meeting. Because the health of the SP is the responsibility of the Medical Service of the Defence Force and he was taken to Two Military Hospital after having suffered a stroke, we must now discuus this unusual situation and decide what has to be done in this regard."

He looks at Magnus Malan: "May I assume that this meeting is highly confidential?"

Magnus Malan: "Of course."

Geldenhuys: "Gentlemen, may I assume that you know General Knobel, the Surgeon General, and admiral Putter, Xhief of Staff: Intelligence?"

All the ministers nod in the affirmative.

Geldernhuys continues: "May I also introduce to you the chief neurologist of One Mil, Major David Scholtz. He will provide us with some guidance about what is going on inside the head of the SP."

He looks at Magnus Malan: You must have known his father, Brigadier David Scholtz. He was the acting 2IC to the SG at some stage."

Magnus Malan: "I remember him. He removed my appendix when I was still a young lieutenant. Okay, Major, what can you tell us?"

Before I start speaking, I decide that it wn't do to be intimidated by all these big shots. I am the expert on the brain and they just have to accept what I tell them. Only the SG, who is a nedical practitioner, will know something about what I will tell these gentlemen.

Me: "Gentlemen, Generals, Admiral, thank you for this opportunity. It's a great responsibility. Anyway, all of us know that Mister PW Botha had a so-called mild stroke, the day before yesterday. I am afraid that it wasn't as mild as the media tell us. It's clear that an artery in his left prefrntal lobe got blocked and that inerrupted the supply of oxygen-rich blood to this part of the brain. The left prefrontal lobe is situated just above the left eye. A part of this lobe got damaged, due to a lack of blood and oxygen. I'm afraid, the damage is permanent. A few million brain cells had it.

"If the stroke had occurred in other spots in the brain, it could have caused other types of problems. If it had, for instance, occurred in the occipital lobe at the back of the head (and I point with my right index finger at the back of my own head), his sight would have been affected. That's the place in the brain where signals from the eyes are being processed and transformed into contents of the conscious mind.

"If the stroke had happened in his temporal lobes, for instance, his speech and long-term memory would have been affected. That's the part of the brain next to the temples and the ears (and I point with my left index finger at the spot, as if these gentlemen have to be reminded where their ears are).

"If the parietal lobes were damaged – that's more or less in the middle of the brain, on top (and I tap with a few fingers on the top of my skull) – some parts of his body could have been paralyzed. That part of the brain controls body movements.

"The stroke also didn't affect the innermost parts of the brain. That's the so-called limbic system. That's where your emtions and instincts are at home. Also your short-term memory.

"But now, the stroke happened in the prefrontal lobe, on the left side (and I stroke my forehead above the left eye). That's where your thought processes, your capacity for judgment, your self-control and your voluntary decisions take place. The left side is especially attuned to logical thinking. We may expect that Mister Botha's judgment will be compromized. He may, perhaps, make irrational and irresponsible decisions. Because his self-control may be lessened, he may become very aggressive. After all – with respect – he is known as the 'Great Crocodile', always ready to bite somebody. This inclination to lose his temper can become worse."

I stay silent and my audience show the shock in their eyes and expressions.

Chris Heunis ventures the first word after ten seconds: "Major, Doctor, is it your expert opinion that the State President is not able to stay on in his position? During my career as a lawyer, it happened more that once that I had to sub poena experts to defend their reports in court. Are you willing to put all this that you explained to us in a report in the form of an affidavit? Wil you be able to withstand aggressive cross questioning and to stick to your point of view?"

Me: "Sir, I don't want to jeapordize my professional reputation by submitting a superficial report. That which I've told you is certainly my professional finding and I will be willing to defend it in court, should it be necessary. I am convinced that the SP is not fit to continue in his position."

FW de Klerk: "Major, I don't think it's really necessary to go to court. That is certainly the very last resort or course of action to take. If necessary, we can use your report – together with an independent second opinion – as the basis for a court order declaring the SP unfit for his job on medical grounds and that he has to be removed from office. But, as I said, that's the very last avenue we can pursue. I believe we will have to convince him to relinquish his post voluntary. That's the most preferred way out of this dilemma and constitutiona crisis."

Magnus Malan: "And who will convince him of that?"

Pik Botha: "I propose that the four us, senior members of the cabinet, visit him on Monday afternoon in hosputal and inform him about our concerns. I'm sure we will be able to convince him."

Magnus Malan: "That sounds acceptable."

Chris Heunis: "As acting State President,I will do the talking and you must support me."

FW de Klerk: "He wiil have to resign both as State President and as leader of the party. Who will we support as his successor in the caucus?"

Chris Heunis: "FW, you are the most suitable man for that. You are the party leader for Transvaal. Since the time of Advocate Strijdom, the leaders of Transvaal were always chosen as prime ministers or executive State Presidents. That is, after all, where most support for the party is to be found. Therefore, keep yourself ready. We will call a caucus meeting next week if Mister Botha resigns. I will propose your candidacy."

Pik Botha: "And I will second that."

Jannie Geldenhuys: "Gentlemen, it seems as if we have reached consensus about the road ahead. Is there something that anybody wants to add? Any questions? Major?"

All those present shake their heads and all stand up, ready to depart.

After the departue of the four ministers, General Knobel asks that the military personnel stay behind: "Colleagues, as I know the SP, these ministers won't be able to convince him. While I listened to the sermon by this major, I concluded that the block-headed PW

Botha will only becme more stubborn after this stroke. Major, do you agree?"

Me: "Yes, General, I think so."

Knobel: "I propose that you keep yourself ready so that both of us can fly to Cape Town next week, or even later, so that we can talk to the SP himself. As medical specialists. He has always respected me as SG since his days as minister of Defence. He will also listen to you as a neurologist. We wear our step-outs so that he can see our medal ribbons. I know that you have rendered sterling, serious, and solid serice on the Border and that will certainly impress him. Right?"

"Right, General."

Knobel: "Jannie, if you approve, I will discuss this plan with General Malan and Minister Heunis."

Geldenhuys: "Go ahead."

Cape Town, Friday, 27 January 1989

Two downhearted men in uniform are waiting at the Cape Town International Airport to board the airplane to Johannesburg.

When I and General Knobel flew to Cape Town this morning, he was reasonably optimistic that our mission would be successful, in spite of the fact that four senior ministers were unable to achieve anything with the State President last Monday. I wasn't so hopeful, considering the lesion I saw on the scans of the State President's head.

During the flight to Cape Town, we were chatting gaily where we were siitting in business class. The SG wanted to hear everything about my exploits during the Border War – including the failures.

Mister PW Botha was willing to receive us at Groote Schuur, his official residence, where he was convalescing. He listened attentively to my explanations, which I illustrated with some drawings.

After that, General Knobel played the trump card: "Mister President, it will certainly be to your advantage if you retire with grace at this time. You had a long and distinguished career as politician and statesman. However, the time has arrived that you deserve a rest. I am sure that a wonderful career as senior statesman is awaiting you. You wil often be consulted and you will still be respected as a leading figure. It will be in your own interest. If you continue with this stressful and very responsible position as State President, your health will certainly be broken, finally broken and cracked. I doubt that you will wish that for yourself."

PW Botha held up his hand to silence Knobel, looked him straight in the eyes, and after a a few moments of uncomfortable silence, replied: "Niel, I've always respected you. You are an excellent medical practitioner. You were even professor at a medical faculty. But I can't agree with you. Just as I can't agree with those four wise guys who call themselves ministers and who visited me the other day.

"They tried to tell me that I'm not able to do my work anymore. I think they were rather arrogant to preach to me. Perhaps I should shuffle my cabinet again to give them a fright. I may have had a mild stroke, but my movements and my thoughts were not affected. My mind is totally clear and compos mentis. As soon as I feel better, I wil go back to my office. Thank you for coming. Goodbye."

And with that, he leaves his seat and that is the sigh that we also have to get up and leave. He waves at us as we drive away in the staff car of Two Mil that picked us up at the airport.

When we are at last seated in the plane, the SG asks me: "What now? What do you think?"

"We can't do anything more. Perhaps those ministers must try again. Perhaps they may get through to him in the end. But in the meantime, we may expect some funny things from the man. He isn't able to think clearly anymore. Perhaps an application in a court case may be the only way forward. But then the possibility also exists that our visit may pay off in the end. It is possible that our visit will make him think about his own future."

Voortrekkerhoogte, Thursday, 2 February 1989

The telephone in my consulting room rings. It's General Knobel, the SG: "Dave, I have news. Interesting news."

"Yes, General?"

"Man, the parliamentary caucus of the National Party held a meeting this morning in preparation of the opening of Parliament tomorrow after the recess. Minister Heunis was supposed to deliver the opening address as acting State President. Ten minutes before the start of the meeting, a messenger delivered a letter from PW Botha to the chairman of the caucus."

"Hmm. Does he resign?"

"Yes, and no. He resigns as party leader, but stays on as SP. He is ready to deliver the state of the nation address, he says."

"That's jolly interesting."

"And irratinal. The man doesn't seem to realize that his authority as State President depends upon his position as leader of the governing party. If he is no longerleader of the party, the members of his cabinet can challenge and obstruct him, left, right, and center. The ministers may even insult him."

"I don't think he will last very long.If his ministers make his life difficult, he will be forced to resign some or other time. And he will go as an embittered, embarassed, unpolular, and unemployable old man."

"Your explanation of the state of his brain cells must have made some sort of an impact. Our visit wasn't a waste of time, But there's more news. The caucus chose a new leader of the party, immediately after PW Botha's resignation as party leader has been noted. It's FW de Klerk. He won with a slim majority against Barend du Plessis. Du Plessis was PW Botha's favorite, but he didn't make it. That amounts to aslap in the face for PW Botha. And FW will succeed him as SP one of these days."

"General, thank you for this news."

"I simply had to tell you. You were, after all, closely involved with the whole episode and your talk with PW Botha may just have tipped the scale."

Later, during the afternoon, I receive a signal that the Commendation Medal for Meritotious Service of the CSADF is to be awarded to me on the recommendation of the SG.

27. EXERCISE POST-MORTEM

Gordon's Bay, Friday, 10 November 1989

The tears are rolling over my father's cheeks. "At last! That scandalous wall is being demolished! That's something about which I have prayed for years."

We are visiting my aged parents in Gordon's Bay after we have made a hasty visit to Namibia so that Hannelore could cast her vote in the first democratic election in the country of her birth.

My dad is a retired brigadier and military medical officer. His career as medical officer started in 1939 with the German Waffen-SS after he had qualified as a specialist surgeon in Berlin. He had a choice: either participation in the war on the German side, or a cot in a concentration camp as a citizen of a country at war with Germany. After the war, amnesty was granted to him and he joined the Union Defence Force of South Africa. Nobody can blame my father for still feeling loyal towards Germany.

I agree wholheartedly: "It's clear that the days of communism are numbered. The Soviet Union has lost its grip on eastern Europa and I'm sure that nothing can prevent the reunification of Germany."

My dad: "That blasted wall divided Berlin into two parts, with the result that the part of the city where I lived, disappeared behind the Iron Curtain. The building in which we rented an apartment doesn't exist anymore because an American bomb destroyed it during 1944."

Hannelore, my German wife, is standing with us on the veranda of my parents' home and she also looks at False Bay. She takes my dad's hand in her hand and comforts him: "Vati, was für einen Tag! Wir Deutsche in Südwest sind alle sehr, sehr glücklich und froh, obwohl wir natürlich erstens Südwester sind. Aber wir sind jedoch noch immer verbunden an den Leuten in dem alten Heimat! Wir freuen uns auch heute!"

"Genau, meine Tochter, genau. Danke, daβ du verstehst."[75]

We stay silent for a few minutes while my emotional father dries his eyes and cheeks and blows his running nose.

I can understand that my father, who is seventy-seven years old, is very emotional today – especially because I and my family are visiting my parents for a fortnight. Because he lived and worked in a German environment for many years he regards himself as almost a German. And now it came to pass that my Hannelore is more or less the splitting image of his first wife, Josephine. She died when that American bomb flattened their apartment block in 1944. That explains why she occupies such a special place in his heart and I believe that he is secretly in love with her, although he naturally loves my mother dearly. He always behaved himself very correctly towards Hannelore.

My dad breaks the silence: "And to think that South West started to hold free and fair elections two days before the Berlin Wall fell. Swapo managed to win the elections, but not with a great majority. They won't have enough votes in their parliamment to mess with their democratic constitution. Even they must realize that communism must be something of the past."

Hannelore: "Exactly. Many people think that we lost the war against Swapo. But that is not true in all respects. It cannot be denied that Swapo will form the government now, but the plans of their big shots to turn South West into a communist dictatorship are now

---

[75] "Vati, what a day today! We Germans in South West are all very, very happy and glad, although we are, in the first place, people of South West. But we are also connected to the people of the old Fatherland! All of us are celebrating today!"

"Exactly, my daughter, exactly. Thank you that you understand."

impossible with this democratic constitution that has to be drawn up after this and which cannot be finalized without the consent of the other parties."

Me: "And Swapo can't rely on any help from the Soviet Union anymore. The Soviet Union, which lies belly up at the moment, is tired of supporting the war in Angola and South West and became unwilling to donate shiploads full of expensive equipments to Swapo. Swapo's leaders are now angry at Moscow for abandoning them and their enthusiasm for communism has waned."

My dad: "While the Americans and the international community is overseeing the process."

Me: "It would perhaps have been better if our boys could have broken the back of Swapo completely, but it is questionable whether they would ever have been able to do it. The help that Swapo received from Russia and Cuba kept them going, even if we gave them big hidings and caused severe losses. Unfortunately, we didn't have the resources, the money and the manpower to achieve a knock-out blow."

My dad: "We can go onto our knees every day and say thanks that the evil Russian empire is disintegrating. I spent almost six years of my life in uniform to battle the Russians. My service in our Defence Force was, in a certain sense, a continuation of that. I am proud of my son who did his thing during the war in South West."

Hannelore: "The war, therefore, wasn't a waste of time and manpower – even if so many people didn't make it. South West can now look forward to peace and prosperity and pleasant times – the same as the East Germans who can hope for a better future without the Wall. If our men – and women – didn't build a bulwark against the forces of communism, a huge deluge of misery would have flowed over South West – just as East Germans had to suffer under a communist dictatorship."

28. OPERATION INTIMIDATION

Gordon's Bay, Sunday, 12 November 1989

My uncle Willie, my father's twin brother, and his family are visiting us today in Gordon's Bay. Uncle Willie is just as glad as my dad that the Berlin Wall is being demolished. He studied together with my dad in Berlin before the war – not in medicine, but in nuclear physics. He was a professor in pgysics at the University of Stellenbosch before his retirement.

We are watching False Bay after lunch where we are sitting on the veranda in front of the house.

My Pa: "I wish the world was as tranquil as that sea water down there. It does seem as if Europe is quiet after the fall of the Berlin Wall. South West is peaceful because they are to gain independence one of these days and our troops will return home. FW de Klerk became State President, but it doesn't seem as if he is taking the struggle against the ANC seriously enough."

Uncle Willie: "You may perhaps be correct regarding FW. But we may be thankful that we have been able, after all, to negotiate an honorable and profitable peace accord regarding South West. It almost happened that the Cuban troops of Fidel Castro invaded South West and created chaos and calamities."

Me: "I've heard that he assembled forty thousand troops in southern Angola. We were able to gather a number of Citizen Force men – about ten thousand of them – and that lot were suddenly named Ten Division."

Hannelore: "My dad's people were very concerned that our troops wouldm't have been able to stop the Cuban gangs. And then suddenly, they were willing to go home and say 'good-bye'."

Unvle Willie: "Do you know it came that they were suddenly willing to retreat and accept a peace accord?"

Hannelore: "PW Botha warned them a while ago that there would be trouble if a single Angolan or Cuban soldier stepped with the toe of his boot over the border. He would regard that as a declaration of war and South West would be defended to the last man."

Uncle Willie: "That's only part of the strory. Not all of it. My brother, do you think I may tell them the whole story? The true story?"

My dad: "Ah, yes. Do it. It's now more than forty years after we have escaped out of the grip of the Nazis in South America. You do the talking and I will add, where necessary."

Hannelore, my mom, Uncle Willie's wife Aunt Soetlief[76] (we always address her on this nickname) and I all shift to the edges of our chairs to listen better. Our ears are wide open. I suspect that something big is coming.

Uncle Willie: "I'm sure that your dad told you a few things about his role during the Second World War. He was a SS soldier and a medical officer. He fought on the German side against the Russians, as well as a bit against the Americans. After the war he managed to hide in Argentina because he was afraid that he could be punished in South Africa as a traitor or a war criminal."

My Pa: "That's actually besides the point. The important fact is actually what *you* did during the war and after the war."

Uncle Willie: "Yes, of course. You all know that I studied nuclear physics in Germany before the war. Something you certainly don't know is that I and a number of German scientists did research to develop an atom bomb for Germany. All sorts of circumstances slowed us down and we were not ready to test our first bomb before the end of the war."

---

[76] "Soetlief" – this nickname may, perhaps, be translated as "Sweetie Pie". Soetlief was a character in one of author C J Langengoven' stories.

My dad: "It would have created a big mess if you had thrown an atom bomb on London, as you had planned."

Uncle Willie: "That never happened, though. But a bunch of Nazis managed right at the end of the war to settle in Argentina and continue their work. Something the world did not know, was that Adolf Hitler didn't commit suicide as everybody believed. He escaped in a submarine together with his wife and also settled in Argentina. And there he was your father's patient."

My father: "Yes, I and my dear wife Rebecca – who was my nurse at that stage – operated on this man. I visited his secret hide-out on three occasions."

My Ma: "You will never believe all the naughty tricks your dad played on this poor ex-Führer. It almost happened that I laid a complaint with the Argentinian Medical Council."

Uncle Willie: "And I visited his place twice. There, we made plans to detonate atom bombs in America, England and Russia and thereby start the Third World War so that Hitler and the Nazis could regain power in Germany and dominate the rest of the world."

My mouth hangs open: "Did you manage to build your atom bombs as you planned?"

My dad: "I was present when they tested their first model somewhere in the Atlantic Ocean. But all sorts of things happened thereafter, which caused the whole project to flounder. Fortunately, the world was saved from a Third World War with nuclear devices. That would only have caused colossal calamities and casualties."

Unvle Willie: "And then the National Party won the elections in forty-eight and I and my brother could get amnesty from the new government. Doctor DF Malan, the prime minister, organized a job for me at the University of Stellenbosch and my brother was appointed as a military medical specialist."

My eyes are wide open: "And then?"

Uncle Willie: “And then I and a number of other men started building atom bombs for Sout Africa during the sixties. The government was thankful to have somebody like me who has worked on atom bombs in the past. In the end, we assembled six devices after we have tested the prototype somewhere deep in the Indian Ocean. That was in September, seventy-nine.The Americans think they observed the explosion with a satellite, but they were never sure.”

Me: “And we planned to drop one of those bombs on the forty thousand Cubans, should they ever invade South West?”

Uncle Willie: “Almost something like that. We would never have dared to throw atom bombs all over the place, but Fidel Castro and his generals didn’t know that. Our ambassador in Uruguay – who is, incidently remotely related to us and the son of a distant cousin whom we met on the boat to Europa in 1933. Anyway, thisambassador cornered the Cuban ambassador during some or other party or reception. He pretended to be drunk and started boasting about South Africa's nuclear arsenal. We purportedly had the plan to blow Luanda or Havanna from the face of the earth if the Cubans didn't behave themselves. The Cuban ambassador swallowed this story, of course, and reported it to Castro the same night."

Me: "And then they were sudden;ly ready to take part in peace talks?"

My Pa: "Exactly. And now you know."

Hannelore: "And now the Cubans don't threaten us in South West anymre. Uncle Willie, you were able to intimidate them effectively. By bluffing them."

Uncle Willie laughs: "That's right."

My Pa: "I'm going to fetch us a few Windhoek lagers from the fridge so that we can drink real German South West beer. Brewed according to the German 'Reinheitsgebot' of fifteen hundred and something. On our South African atom bombs!"

29. EXERCISE CENTENARARY

Vortrekkerhoogte, Wednesday, 27 May 1992

While we are preparing supper together in our kitchen, Hannelore tells me about her day: "I had the most remarkable patient of my whole career today."

Me: "What made him so special? Does he have four arms and three heads like a Hindu deity? Or is he the first known case in medical history with Brazilian Toad Fever?"

"Stop being so silly. Get serious. This was truly a very, very remarkable patient in all respects."

"Okay, tell me."

"Okay. This outoppie came to me for a general check-up. He told me that he didn't really need it, but his wife, who brought him, insisted that I give him a through go-over. She explained that they are planning a huge family feast next Sunday and that she wanted to make sure that her husband was in a good shape."

"There's nothing remarkable about giving a patient a good check-up. I've done it dozens of times, if not hundreds of times."

"But not when the patient is a few days short of one hundred years of age. He insisted that he is fighting fit and highly healthy and functionng at full revolutions. In the end, I had to agree with him. He seems to have the most remarkable constitution. I could tell his wife, who is ten years younger than him, that her husband may still outlive her."

"Well, that is truly remarkable."

"That's not all. This old-timer spoke German with me. He says his father was a German Jew and he grew up here in Pretoria, speaking German and Afrikaans. His dad used to be a tailor and he inherited the business. He expanded it to a thriving clothing factory and he still manages it. He has, though, the help of his son."

"That must be the Jew, Mister Davidsohn.[77] The Defence Force has a contract with him to provide us with socks and underwear for our troops."

"That's just him. He gave me permission to tell you that he is my patient, otherwise I would have kept his indentity private. He specifically came to me because he has more trust in German-speaking pill pushers. He needs a certificte from me declaring him to be healthy and fit, with all his faculties functioning and his organs operational. I had to attach the results of all his blood tests and heart tests onto this report, because he wants to show it to his two daughters and sons-in-law when they come for the family feast. They are all retired medical practitioners in Germany and they want to put him into an old-age home, which he finds totally unnecessary and unacceptable."

"I would like to do a brain scan on this outoppie."

"I suspect you won't fimnd any symptoms of Alzheimer's or something of the sort. But let me tell you the best part. He told me that I am the second doctor with the surname of Scholtz to work on him."

"The other Doctor Scholtz can't be me. I've never seen the old guy. And I only treat military people – and he's a civvie."

"He's not really a civvie. He assured me that he was a German general during the Second World War."

"Jeez! But he's a Jew! How's that possible?"

"He said that he had kept this a secret for many years, but it doesn't matter if the truth comes out at this stage when he reaches a full century. Anyway, I told him that my father-in-law is a retired specialist surgeon and hs name is David Scholtz Senior."

"How did he react to that?"

---

[77] See the novel FIVE WARS, FIVE NAMES.

"He became very excited. He asked me whether my dad-in-law was a German 'Oberarzt' during the war. I said that he was actually a 'Stabsarzt' and he said that your dad treated him twice. The first time was in Norway where his appendix was slaughtered out and the second time was when he was wounded on the Russian front. He was only a colonel at the time and only became a major general after he had joined the Afrikakorps under Rommel."

"And he's a Jew? Unbelievable. How did he managed that?"

"There was no time for him to tell his whole story, but he wanted to know what happened to your father. When I told him that your father is due to visit us next week, he insisted to have a meeting with him. He even said that he will have a second birthday party to which we all will be invited. He asked your dad's phone number to invite him personally."

"I must say – this is certainly the most remarkable patient you can ever imagine. Hell! A Jewish Nazi general…"

"I don't think he was ever a Nazi. Impossible. Remember, he is a Jew. He was only an officer in the German Army. Your dad was also an officer in the Waffen-SS, but he was never a Nazi!"

Pretoria, Friday, 5 June 1992

A group of Germans and South Africans are babbling along in German in the Davidsohn residence. The company includes four South Africans who fought on the German side during the Second World War – the centenanrarian Herr David Davidsohn, my father, retired Brigadier Karl Krause, and Herr Stefan Strauss of Walvis Bay.

Our host, the birthday boy, welcomes everybody with a formal speech after all those who were invited, had taken a seat and had been given something to drink.

"Meine Damen und Herren, thank you for giving me so much joy to have you all here today. I'm exactly one hundred years and five days old today and that calls for celebrations. There was a family feast last Sunday, but I believe in stretching out a birthday party over several days – and that's why we are all here today.

"It's impossible to tell you all that happened to me during the past century and five days. I experienced a lot, including five wars. As a boy, I knew President Paul Kruger, the last president of the Transvaal Republic. I also did my little bit during the Boer War when I was a boy and that inspired me to follow a military career during the first half of my life.

"I think all of you have met my Irish wife, Harriet. If she didn't insist on taking me for a medical examination a few days ago, this party would never have happened. I saw the charming Doctor Hannelore Scholtz and I was pleasantly surprised to learn that she is the daughter-in-law of Doctor David Scholtz, whom I last saw more than fifty years ago on the Russian front.

"Doctor Hannelore Scholtz told me that she's a German from South West Africa. I also lived in that country a number of years, before settling in Germany.

"You must have met my twin daughters, Gudrun and Gertrud. They are both retired medical practitioners. They got married to two doctors and they chose to stay in post-war Germany afer I had decided to return to Pretoria where I grew up and help my father with his business.

"There is my son, Sepp. He also has a military background. During the war, he was a 'Korvettenkapitän'[78] and in charge of a flotilla fast torpedo boats of the Kriegsmarine[79]. He is now my assistant in our business, although he's already in his seventies.

---

[78] "Korvettenkapitän" – lieutenant commander.

[79] "Kriegsmarine" – German war-time Navy.

"I'm glad to see Doctor David Scholtz Senior here, together with his wife, Rebecca. I met him in Norway during 1941 when he removed my rotten appendix. I was an 'Oberst'[80] in the German Army at that time and I used the false name of Thomas Freiherr[81] von Traubenstein. It's a long story how I got that name and noble title. I've written a book about that and I may present you with copies, should you be interested.

"Anyway, Dave Scholtz unmasked me as a Jew when he treated me. Fortunately, he never reported me for being a fake with a forged birth certificate. Ha-ha, that could have created a big mess and even a snotty scandal if my true identity came out at that time. But, as a good doctor, he kept my secret hidden."

"And now Dave is a retired brigadier. In Germany, he would have been a 'Generalarzt'.

"And there is also retired Brigadier Karl Krause. He was Major Krause of the Luftwaffe[82]. I never met him during the war, but his charming German wife, Sonja, who was a spy in the Abwehr and the Sicherheitsdienst of the SS, gave me some secret jobs to perform. I also met Sonja's brother, also of the Luftwaffe, who flew me to Sicily in 1941.

"Ah, and there is Doctor Hannelore Scholtz. She gave me a medical report, which I could present to my daughters and sons-in-law to convince them that I am still alive and all there. I refuse to become a prisoner in a facility for octogenarians with Alzheimer's or Parkinson's and that certificate proves that I'm still too young for such an institution. She confirmed that I have a remarkable constitution. Dave Scholtz will also confirm that, although he hasn't seen me in fifty years.

---

[80] "Oberst" – a German colonel.

[81] "Freiherr" – a German baron.

[82] "Luftwaffe" – the German Air Force.

"I want to welcome Korvettenkapitän Stefan Strauss and his Norwegian wife, Hilde. I have fond memories of him as a little boy when I worked with his father in Walvis Bay, during and after the First World War. When I phoned Dave Scholtz the other day, he mentioned that he and Stefan also became friends before the war. Stefan joined the German Navy before the war and served on U-boats and other craft. He lives in Walvis Bay, but promised to come to Pretoria specifically for this occasion when I phoned him.

"There is another reason to celebrate today – apart from my birthday. Exactly fifty years ago, on 5 June 1942, I was at Erwin Rommel's side when he gave the British Army, together with the South Africans and the New Zealanders, a big hiding at the Battle of Gazala. This was followed up with the capture of Tobruk a fortnight later."

Retired Brigadier Krause interrupts him: "And I was shot down over Tobruk at that time. I was a POW for a few days until Rommel's boys liberated me. Everybody thought that I was killed at that stage and a death certificate was issued. I still have it. But I also want to celebrate something else from fifty years ago I was promoted to the rank of 'Hauptmann' on 1 June 1942 and I was also decorated with the German Cross in Gold on that same day."

David continues: "Well, well. Something else to celebrate, then. I was also deemed to be dead after I had escaped from a POW camp in Wales and fled to Ireland in 1944. There I became Johannes Jansen, a Dutchman with a forged passport to prove it. And when I married Harriet, I got married as David Davidson, without the 'h'. For a brief period I was also Brigadier Summersby, an British officer, with papers and a uniform to back it up. That's how I managed to liberate my two sons-in-law from Russian POW camps after the war.

"But, enough about myself. I'm glad to have all of you here. Enjoy yourselves, please."

After this speech, people start mingling and after a short while, the men and the women divide into two groups – as always happens at a party. After all, women are not interested in the same things as men.

The birthday boy addresses me: "So, you are also a medical officer? Your dad told me that you have the rank of commandant, which is the equivalent of a lieutenant colonel?"

"That's right."

"And you also have gained lots of combat experience during the Border War?"

"That is so."

"So, you helped to chase the Russians out of Angola?"

"I did my little bit."

Brigadier Krause: "He's a hero. He also chased all the Russian ghosts out of my mind with his knowledge of the human brain."

Me: "But Herr Strauss also helped us against the Russians."

"How?"

"We used a fishing trawler of his to reach Luanda in order to do some sabotage there."

David Davidsohn: "Goodness! Stefan, I worked with your father who also had some trawlers in Walvis Bay. He helped me and my team in 1915 to get behind the South African lines and sow some chaos and confusion."

Stefan Strauss: "I remember. I followed in his footsteps to help to drive the forces of evil away. That's why I gave one of my trawlers to transport Dave Junior and his team to Luanda to blow up Russian ships transporting ammo and guns for Swapo."

My dad: "Talking of the Russians: the Soviet Union, against which we all fought, fell apart during Christmas, last year. Halleluyah! That evil empire caused much misery in this world. These Russians also helped to train the fighters of Swapo and the ANC."

David Davidsohn: "You mention the ANC. Those thugs, those terrorists, will certainly take over the government of this country when a new constitution comes into effect. Not only their fighters were trained by the Russians. Their leaders were also indoctrinated by the ideology of communism in Moscow.

"The American government declared this lot a terriorist organization, together with their leader, Nelson Mandela. Margaret Thatcher of Britain agreed. I predict that they will make a mess of governing this country.

"I was trained and deployed as an intelligence officer in the Wehrmacht. I still have the habit of finding out as much as I can about the enemy."

Karl Krause: "You are totally correct about the ANC."[83]

David Davidsohn: "The ANC is one big corrupt criminal syndicate or conglomorate. They proved that during the time they were still operating from Zambia and Tanzania. They are ensuring a victory in future elections but intimidating and even killing potential

[83] The American Department of Defence removed Mandela's name from their list of terrorist leaders only in 2008, nine years after he had retired as State President of South Africa and five years before his death.

opponents. They mislead innocent black people by threatenung them with violence if they vore for any other party than the ANC."

Me: "But each vote is supposed to be secret."

David Davisohn: "But the unsophisticated black people are convinced that the ANC will know who voted against them. That's a trick they were taught in Soviet Russia and in Vietnam."

My dad: "Yes. I think you hit the nail squarely on its round head. And talking about the Russians: although the Soviet Union broke up into a number of bits and pieces, the biggest part, the Russian Federation, inherited the Red Army with all its armaments, including an arsenal of atom bombs. I have witnessed the destructive power of an atom bomb when the Nazis in Argentina tested one in the Atlantic Ocean in forty-eight. We'll never know when they will start a nuclear war if they feel threatened."

Me: "I predict that we can still expect lots of trouble from the Russians. We kept them from our doorstep with the Border War, but they will be back and cause lots of mischief and misery in the world. Mark my words."

My dad: "I was involved with the battles against the Russians in Finland and the Austrian Alps, from mid 1941 till the end of the war in 1945. It must be granted: the Russians produced wonderful authors, poets, composers, and other artists. But the greatest majority of them are uncivilized, uneducated, uncouth, and cruel barbarians. When they invaded the eastern parts of Germany and Austria in 1945, they raped, murdered, looted, and destroyed – far worse than the ugliest Nazi attrocities. I agree, even if the Soviet Union has broken up, the time will come when the Russians will start with their criminal behavior all over again. They will do their best to avenge the humiliation after losing the Cold War."

Karl Krause: "And South Africa will have an ANC government, consisting of friends of those Russians. Let's hope they get the message that communism and socialism have failed totally and cannot work."

Stefan Strauss: "That also goes for the Swapo government in Namibia. Some of then are very proud of the fact that they have visited Russia during the time of the Border War. Fortunately, we got a democrattic constitution, which will prevent the horrors of communism."

Florian Fischer, the husband of one of David Davidsohn's daughter, opens his mouth for the first time: "I can only be very grateful that my father-in-law rescued me from a Russian POW camp. We've heard from so many of our friends and colleagues that your chances of survival in a Russian camp were slim. Most men who managed to get home again, were totally broken – mehtally and physically. The Russians are really barbarians who are addicted to vodka. I got to know them."

Karl Krause: "I and my wife have often agreed that the Allies had made the biggest mistake imaginable by helping the Ivans during the war with equipment and other supplies. Stalin was just as guilty as Hitler by attacking Poland in 1939 from the east – and then the Allies made friends with these barbaric hordes from Siberia and attacked us, the Germans, who were fellow Europeans. The West discovered their mistake too late and the Cold War was the result. But wait, the Russians won't lie down and forget. I'm sure they will want to take revenge for their defeat during the Cold War when America and the West wrecked theur economy and helped countries like Poland, East Germany, and Hungary to slip out of their grip."

David Davidsohn: "Hear! Hear! Well spoken. I think it's time for the dinner. Harriet has given me a sign. Let's proceed to the dining room. For 'Nachtisch'[84] there will be a big Black Forest Tart with one hundred little candles. I intend blowing them all out with one big breath! Watch me."

After dinner, we watched the remarkable lungs of David Davidsohn who blew out all the candles with one breath,

---

[84] "Nachtisch" – pudding.

Stefan Strauss takes the word: "I propose that we form a club consisting of all of us who participated on the German side during the Second World War. Herr Generalmajor Thomas von Traubenstein, alias Herr David Davidsohn, must be the president of the club."

All thos present call out in unison: "Hurrah!"

I ask: "How will we name this club?"

Stefan: "What about The Lucky Survivors?"

Pretoria, Saturday, 20June 1992

Rabbi Schlomo Schlesinger looks uncomfortable where he takes the word in the funeral parlor of Doves & Co in Pretoria. I and Hannelore, together with the other members of the club of Survivors, are attending the funeral service for the late David Davidsohn, alias Thomas von Traubnestein, alias Johannes Jansen, alias Stephen Summersby, and alias David Davidson, who died in a tragic traffic accident three days ago.

"Dear Friends, I have never been in such a difficult situation as today. I have been placed in a very uncomfortable position to officiate at a funeral of an old friend and to discover that a Protestant reverend and a Catholic priest have also been tasked by the family to do their bit during this service. Out of respect for the wishes of my old friend, David Davidsohn, I complied, albeit with misgivings.

"I was severly saddened by the news of the passing of one of the respected members of our Hebrew congregation. Not one of us ever suspected that he was also a member of the Dutch Reformed Church, the church of his late mother, as well as a member of the Catholic Church for the sake of his Irish wife. That is a totally unique state of affairs and I don't know of any other person who accomplished something like this.

"Joseph, the son of the deceased, told me only yesterday that his father was in possession of ancient documentation that proves his ancestry from biblical times. Their family name, Davidsohn, was meant to convey the fact that they are descended from King David, the Israelite king, who made Jerusalem his capital. Our Hebrew congregation had the unique distinction of having had such an illutrious member – without realizing it.

"Fortunately, we also have as a member Joseph Davidsohn, with the same ancestry. I suspect that he is also a member of the other two religious groups, just as his late father.

"After I have completed our traditional Jewish rites at a funeral, I will make way for the other two clergymen to do their bits."

Hannelore whispers in my left ear: "He was definitely and certainly and surely the most remarkable patient I ever had. Member of three opposing religious movements at the same time… Hell! Or rather, good heavens!"

Me: "He must have been one of the the last generals of the German Wehrmacht to leave this earth. Really remarkable."

30. OPERATION MARATHON

Cape Town, Saturday, 2 April 1994

My newest patient in Number Two Military Hospital in Cape Town receives a visit from me today: "Ah, Chaplain Wagner! It's you and me again! Do you still remember me from One Mil?"

"Are you that Doctor Scholtz who treated me last time?"

"That's me. I'm, mot a major anymore. I was promoted to commandant. I follow in the footsteps of my father. He was chief surgeon and commander of this hospital before it was modernized. And now, you are again my patient! I've brought all my old files from One Mil along and I had another look at yours just now."

"Doc, what are you going yo do to me this time?"

"Perhaps an operation. For that, a colleague of mine will take care, a neurosurgeon."

"You said 'perhaps'."

"I don't know yet what we will have to do. I want to discuss your case with colleagues elsewhere. And while you are lying here and getting a rest, I want to talk to your wife and ask her a few questions about your health."

The wife of the patient, who sits next to his bed, replies: "Doctor, at your service."

"I want to talk to you somewhere else. We don't want to tire your husband. He must rest."

"Thanks."

Some time later, I, my neurosurgeon colleague, and the patient's family are gathered at his bedside. Missus Wagner takes the word while she points at my colleague: "Chris, this is Doctor Louis Lancaster, the neurosurgeon. He and Doctor Scholtz both think that it's necessary to operate on you, but you have to give your permission for that, naturally. I think you must go ahead with it."

Doctor Lancaster takes over: "Doctor Wagner, a lesion in the left temporal lobe of your brain has been discovered earlier. We saw it again this morning on your scans. Doctor Scholtz informs me that he can remember that he prescribed anticolvulsants way back at One Mil. It's clear that they didn't work and that's why you had an ugly fit today. Because the medication didn't help, we will have to operate."

"Exactly what will that entail?"

"We will have to open the skull and remove the affected part very carefully. Here is a drawing to show you where the center for your epilepsy is situated. Do you see the part at which the arrow is pointing – the colored part? That's where we will have to remove a small part of the brain. The rest of the brain stays intact. The temporal lobe contains, inter alia, your long-term memory. Because the area occupied by that lesion isn't working normally, the removal thereof won't affect your memory significantly. It will, though, prevent an accident such as the one that occurred this morning.

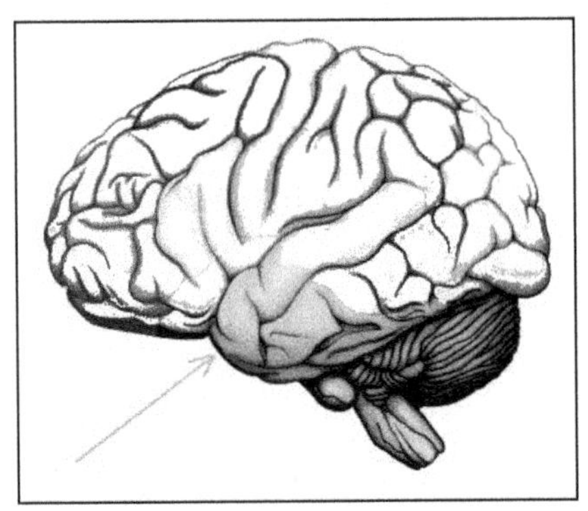

"One of the wonderful attributes of the brain is its plasticity. That means that it can make adaptations. If some part doesn't worl properly, other parts take over and that will certainly also be the case with you."

"What are the chances of success?"

"Oh, about seventy, eighty percent. There isn't really a risk, except there's a slight chance that the epileptifc fits may return."

I add: "Doctor Lancaster has already performed many such operations. He knows what he does and you are safe in his hands.

The operation can take place rightaway, this afternoon. We regard it as an emergency."

Missus Wagner holds a piece of papier in front of her husband's eyes: "Here is the permission form and I think you must sign it. I have already completed all the other particulars. Of course, you have the right to refuse, but I really want you to get better. It was a nightmare experience when you fell down there in Kalk Bay this morning and hit your head against the edge of the sidewalk. I don't want to see that ever again in my life."

"All right, hand me a pen."

Cape Town, Monday 4 April 1994

During the late afternoon, I pay my patient, Doctor Chris Wagner, a visit, two days after his operation: "Doctor, Reverend, Chaplain, Padre, or however you are to be addressed, the time has come that I must explain to you exactly what was going on with you."

"If I remember correctly, you told me it was epilepsy of the left temporal lobe."

"That's right. That part of your brain sent abnormal electrical impulses through the rest of your brain and that's why you have lost consciousness during the Two Oceans Marathon[85] on Saturday morning and also had some extraordinary experiences."

"I've always thought that epilepsy means that you get convulsions, that you get foam around your mouth and that you stay lights-out for a long period of time."

"That's major epilepsy – the worst form of it. Fortunately, you got a lighter variation. And then also a special type. It is known

---

[85] The Two Oceans Marathon is an annual event over the Easter Weekend in Cape Town. It starts in Claremont and follows a beautiful scenic route over Fish Hoek and Hout Bay, back to Claremont for a distance of 56 kilometers. Number 2 Military hospital is situated in Wynberg, along the route (see map on page 7).

as the Geschwind syndrome. Norman Geschwind, who died a few years ago, was a very well-known Anerican neurologist and much of the knowledge we currently have about the brain is the result of his investigations. Geschwind syndrome is a special type of temporal lobe epilepsy, in particular of the left temporal lobe. That's the part of your brain just behind the left eye."

"What makes it so special?"

"It is characterized by a number of extraordinary symptoms – apart from the lesion in your brain, of course. The first symptom is an extraordibary interest in philosophy and religion. Many religious leaders through the ages are suspected of having suffered from it. Possibly the apostle Paul and the prophet of the Muslims, Mohammed"

"Of course, I have an intense interest in religion and theology. That's why I've obtained my doctor's degree in New Testament studies."

"When did you decide to enter the service of the church?"

"That was when I was srill a school kid."

"Your mother told me last time when you lay in One Mil that you had a nasty fall as a school boy and you hit your head against a rock. Your father had to rush you to a doctor."

"Yes, I was about fifteen at that stage."

"It is highly probable that the brain lesion was caused by that fall."

"I can believe that. I hit my head very hard and my brain could have suffered something from that."

"The brain scans show that you had a slight skull fracture long ago, at your left temple. That must have been caused by that fall. The fracture healed all by it self, without anybody being aware of it at that time. That fracture and the lesion lay next to each other and I'm sure the fracture caused the lesion in the brain."

"That's interesting."

"Did you decide to enter the ministry before this fall, or only afterwards?"

"Now that you mention that, it was during my last year at school that I started to hear the voice of the Lord, calling me to enter his service. That was after that fall."

"How did you hear his voice?"

"It was audible and clear. Some times, He called my name and at other times he gavce me some or other message."

"Was that while you were sleeping, or otherwise?"

"No, I fell from time to time into a light trance when I sat completely still and was staring into the void – that's what my friends and my wife told met – and that was when the Voice spoke to me. Sometimes I fell over if I was on my feet, just as on Saturday during the marathon when I had this fall in Kalk Bay."

"And this Voice – as you call it – urged you to study theology?"

"Correct."

"Will you believe me if I tell you that that Voice was the result of the lesion on your left temporal lobe that also caused your epilepsy?"

"If you say so."

"And will you accept it if I tell you that that Voice was nothing but a hallucination?"

"Perhaps I must."

"Did you ever get funny smells when you fell into that trance?"

"Yes! Often."

"That's also part of this Geschwind syndrome. That is regarded as olfactory hallucinations."

"I always wondered where those smells came from. I concluded that must be how heaven smells."

"Was it a pleasant or unpleasant odor?"

"Certainly pleasant. Initially, I couldm't identify it, but later I thought that it must be some or other sort of perfume or ncense."

"Did you ever see an apparition while being addressed by the Voice?"

"Yes, usually. It was always a nebulous apparition, such as a person who is transparent with the light from behind shining right through him."

"Another hallucination – a visual hallucination."

"That sounds acceptable."

"Your wife explained that you sometimes get very emotionally upset. You may even start crying when hearing beautiful music."

"That's right."

"And you easily lose your temper."

"Somewhat. Sometimes rather severely."

"Would you describe yourself as a very orderly and disciplined person?"

"I and my wife are both very neat. I believe my self-discipline is the result of my military background. But it may also be the result of this syndrome you mentioned."

"You also love speaking and writing?"

"It was always the most pleasant part of my work to prepare and deliver sermons. I also wrote a good number of articles for a theological journal."

"That also fits in with the Geschwind syndrome. Were you very active regarding your sex life?"

"Rather, yes, I and my first girlfriend at university often jumped into bed. Fortunately, the professors at the theological seminary never knew about it, otherwise I would have been kicked out in disgrace for committing an unforgivable sin, namely sex out of marriage. Fortunately, my wife has a warm nature and we often make love."

"That's another symptom of the Geschwind syndrome."

"Thanks. Are there other symptoms that I am supposed to display?"

"That's the lot. And now I want to venture a forecast: your intense interest in theology and religion will propably deminish after this operation, or even disappear totally. We must wait and see."

"I think you're right. I tried to have conversations regarding spiritual matters with these men in this ward with me, as I usually do when I'm in contact with some troops of the Citizen Force unit of which I am the part-time chaplain or with members of my congregation. I just could not bring myself so far to talk to them about their relatinship with God. It is as if it doesn't really matter to me anymore whether or not they have a good relationship with God."

"How do you feel about returning to your congregation and continue your work, also as a part-time Army chaplain?"

"Now that you ask: not really. If I think back about the work that I did in the past, I can hardly picture myself continuing with that. While I was lying in intensive care after the op, I thought a lot about my life and whether I did the right thing to become a minister of religion."

"What do you mean?"

"Were all my sermons to my congregation and to the troops on the Border perhaps nothing but wishful thinking and superstition? Dit it have any value when I explained the Bible to them? Wasn't it just a waste of time? Doc, what will I do if I can't and don't want to continue with my work in the church because I've lost all interest in it?"

"Are you old enouth to retire?"

"I am almost fifty-six, I may retire honorably at fifty-five."

"And if I and Doctor Lancaster both write medical reports in which both of us recommend that you retire due to medical reasons – will that work?"

"Yes, certainly. If I retire on medical grounds and I'm not able to continue with my work, I may retire with full pension."

"All right, we can certify that you won't be able to continue with your work on account of neurological reasons. But you are too young to become a pensioner and sit on your veranda the whole day while watching the people passing along on the sidewalk. Are you able to pursue any other career?"

"Yes, thanks be to God! Ah! – and there I use this expression again, just out of sheer habit – and I don't know whether I have to thank God or whomever else. But, nevertheless, I have a law degree as well and I am also admitted as a lawyer. That's besides the fact that I am also an ordained minister of religion. I'm surely not too old to start a new career in this direction. It was always my dad's wish that I become a student of the law. He was a lawyer himself."

"Excellent. Do something to realize this opportunity."

"Yes, I think I will."

"Wonderful."

"What did you do with that little bit of my brain that you slaughtered out?"

"Why?"

"It's my property. You didn't have my permission just to throw it away. I want it back."

"I will have to talk to Doctor Lancaster about that. But I have a strong suspicion that it has been destroyed soon after the operation."

"Sis, man."

"But why do you want it back?"

"To remind me that that little piece of brain material made me believe that a Voice from heaven spoke to me every time I fell into a trance."

"Sorry."

"It can certainly not be made undone. But something else: when can I be discharged?"

"We will have to see. Perhaps on Thursday or Friday. We must keep you under observation for a few days to see whether any complications occur. But then you may not drive back to Transvaal after your discharge. I'm giving you, in any case, two more weeks of sick leave. Do you have a place to stay over here in the Cape in the meantime?"

"My beach house in Gordon's Bay."

"That's all right. Just before you drive back, you have to return to me and Doctor Lancaster for a final consultation. Ask the nurse to organize the appointments."

"My wife can easily take my pulse and my fever and phone it through to you."

"I want to do that myself. Personally. And we must make sure that the Voice – as you call it – doesn't return."

"I doubt that. And if he does return, then you must kick it under its butt for my sake."

I can only laugh.

"And there's yet something else. I can't see anything of my top story in the mirror because it is bandaged like an Egyptian mummy, but I assume that you have shaved this side of my head (and he points at the left side) quite bald and left the rest of my hair as it was. Must I proceed through life from here on with a bald patch on my head?"

I laugh again: "You will have to ask your wife to shave off all your hair when you get to your beach house. Then you will lok the same from all sides. That will also remind you that the Voice has gone AWOL."

Gordon's Bay, Saturday 9 April 1994

Because I was on call last weekend, I have this weekend off. I and my family are now visiting my parents in Gordon's Bay. My fatyher is a retired military medical practitioner with the rank of brigadier.

While we are sitting on the veranda and watching the water of False Bay, my father looks in the direction of his neighbor and waves at him where he is also sitting on his veranda.

My father: “Have you met my neighbor? He is also a military person.”

Me: “No, not yet. Every time when I come here, that house is locked up.”

My Pa: “That’s my neighbor’s holiday home and he is seldom here. Come with me and then I can introduce you to him.”

We walk to the fence and my dad calls out: “My good neighbor, good afternoon! I want to introduce you to my son.”

The man gets up and approaches us. His head is shaven bald and there is a wound on his left temple that has been fixed with stitches.

The neighbor: “Doc! This is a coincidence! Never knew you were my neighbr’s son. I must have guessed that because both of you have the family name of Scholtz and both are military medical doctors."

Me: "Hi, Padre! And I never knew you were my dad's neighbor!"

My dad: "Oh, you know each other?"

Neighbor: "Yea, Brigadier. Your son has worked on me at Two Mil and this operation wound (and he points at his head) is due to his efficient efforts. He insisted on it. He also had a look at me a few years ag at One Mil."

My father: "Why don't you come over to drink something? Then we can swop yarns about our days in the Defence Force."

The neighbor, Chaplain, Padre, Reverend, or Doctor Christiaan Wagner, walks over and we sit down on the veranda again.

Pa explains to me: "This padre's wife inheritied this beach house from her father. His late father-in-law was a big shot in the Navy."

Pa looks at the neighbor: "Padre, I can see a big operation wound on your head. What happened? Did this son of mine transplanted a new brain into your skull? Has he made sure that it wasn't a female brain?"

Christiaan smiles broadly: "No, Brigadier, that didn't happen. Your son discovered a lesion on my left temporal lobe. That caused me to to get epileptic fits. I took part in the Two Oceans Marathon here in the Cape last Saturday. I suddenly got an attack and landed with my head against the sidewalk's edge. I was immediately lights-out. Because I took part as a member of an Army team – I'm a part-time chaplain at the headquarters of an infantry brigade of the Citizen Force in Transvaal — I was taken by a military ambulance to Two Mil. And there this good Doctor Scholtz and a colleague serviced this thinking machine in my head."

Pa: "And now you see each other again! Did the operation help in any way?"

Christiaan: “I believe so. That little part of my cerebral organ that was removed caused me to lose my faith. When I return to the Transvaal one of these days, I’m going to see to it that I leave the service of the church with early retirement and a pension. Unfortunately, that will also mean that I will have to say good-bye to the Army because I won’t be able to remain a chaplain any longer – not that I want to be one any more.”

Pa: “Lost your faith? And you are a reverend, a padre?”

Christiaan: “I am officially still a minister, but I cartainly don’t feel like one anymore. In spite of the fact that I have a doctor’s degree in theology. After my retirement, I’m going to practice as a lawyer. I was already admitted as one and I want to come and join the Cape Bar.”

Me: “May I call you Christiaan? You certainly don’t like the title of ‘Reverend’ anymore?”

Christiaan: “Please, just plain and simple Chris.”

Me: “Right. You tell us that you have lost your faith on account of an operation. My faith slowly disappeared as a result of my medical studies – especially the discipline of neurology. I know how the brain works and I can’t see how an immortal soul can be hiding somewhere inside. On the day you breathe your last breath, everything disintegrates. Your memories and your personality disappears for ever. Your soul, your personality, your self-consciousness, is simply a collection of programs with which the noodles within your skull operate.”

Chris: “Programs?”

Me: “Yes, just as in a computer. You have programs in your brain for speaking Afrikaans, for speaking English, for writing, for driving a motor vehicle, for reading, for eating with a knife and fork, and so forth. There are programs that got fixed in your gray matter through repetition, practice, through training. All that, taken together, is simply your soul, your psyche. There is nothing that remains after you become ready for your funeral and there is nothing that gets transferred into an afterlife. There is nowhere place in the whole universe for a heaven filled with little angels and other spirits or souls."

Chris: "I also have a program for speaking German."

Pa: "And both of you have programs for speaking nonsense. I firmly believe that something of you survives death But I'm not going to fight with you over that. And besides: I can also speak German well. I got my medical training in Berlin before the war."

Chris: "I also visited Berlin, but I obtained my doctorate in Tübingen."

Pa: "Ever seen East Berlin before the wall was demolished?"

Chris: "Oh, yes. I was also elsewhere in eastern Germany. It made me realize that communism is evil, wrong, bad. and horrible. I am proud of the fact that I fought against it my whole adult life – from the pulpit, during meetings, on the Border and at the home front."

Me: "I also did that. And now we are due to get a gevornment of the African National Congress as soon as the coming elections have been held."

Pa: "There are surely a bunch of commies within the ANC, but I don't believe that all of them are like taht."

Chris: "You are advized to read their so-called Freedom Manifesto. It's a pure communist document. They demand in this document the nationalization of all banks and the mines, amongst others. At our headquarters, I attended an information session every Friday morning – especially regarding activities in the black townships. I am holding my breath. The ANC strengthterned its position in the black communities by means of intimidation, arson, and the murder of litteraly thousands of adversaries – just as the communists achieved power in Russia, eastern Europe, China, Cuba and Vietnam. Fortunately, we held out long enugh till the Berlin wall came tumbling down and we got a very acceptable new constitution. Fortunately, communism fell out of favor. But I have my doubts that the ANC has received that news. They will, in addition, be just as corrupt as the commies in Russia. They will plunder the riches of the country and make themselves guilty of gross maladministration.

"And the worst of it all: some short-sighted churches don't see the danger. There are even well-known ecclesiatical figures who regard the ANC as a blessing from above and they sing its praise. I believe that will make the churches less and less relevant. I am thankful that I can get rid of my ties to the fosilized structures of the church."

Pa: "It's clear that you are still able to think clearly and rationally, even if a part of your brain has been scratched out. Let us hope that our courts will uphold the good principles of our new constitution."

Me: "I also wonder what will become of me as a medical officer in the Defence Force. Will it be held against me that I served during the Border War? Will it count against me that I am white? Is there a future for my children under an ANC government?"

Pa: "Hmmm. That's a good point."

Chris: "Fortunately, our new constitution guarantees freedom of speech. We will just have to continue exposing the sins and crimes of the ANC to the whole world. The world must know about that."

Me: "The churches will only have a future if they help in that regard. But, will they have the courage for that?"

Chris: "That's to be doubted. There are already a number of praise singers for the ANC in the leadership of various churches - also a number of teachers at the theological seminary in Stellenbosch. The same applies to a number of universities. Fortunately, my brain works now properly for the first time – thanks to you Doc (and he nods with his head in my direction). And I will devout the rest of my life as a lawyer to promote justice and righteousness – even if I regard Christianity as obsolete, just as the system of apartheid that was simply based on injustice and repression."

Me: "Our rigid application of apartheid certainly helped the ANC to gain so much support – and some stupid churches actually helped the ANC when they tried to justify apartheid from the Bible. I agree that it won't work to exchange one system based on injustice with another, which is also based on injustice and corruption. The alternative to apartheid is not communism. Apartheid was definitely wrong and bad and we had to abolish it. But it won't work to put communism or socialism in its place. I regard myself as a rationalist – somebody who relies on common sense and scientific facts."

Chris: "I think I like such an approach. And, may I add, that apartheid was perhaps entrenched in a number of laws by the National Party government after they got a majority in Parliament in 1948, but they simply continued with a system and traditions inherited from the hypecritical British administration of South Africa since the nineteenth century."

Pa: "I agree with you regarding the British who practised apartheid long before it was made into law, but I also want to differ from you regarding the church. The church played an important role in my life and I'm very thankful for that. Have I told you who my best friend during the war was? It was the chaplain of our regiment, a Romish priest. I often wonder what happened to this good man. Have I told you that I was sought by the British after the end of the war because I was a member of the Waffen-SS – even if I was merely a medical officer? I hid in an Austrian covent during that time and I was even a novice monk. And it was an ex-reverend, Prime Minister Doctor Daniel Malan, who granted me amnesty in 1948 for my so-called war crimes. I will always feel grateful towards the church."

My pa get up and asks: "Who wants a beer?"

Chris: "Doc, it it okay if I drink a beer after my op?"

Me: "You will be disappointed if you think that a beer will bring back that mysterious Voice into your head. But I, as your doctor, hereby give you permission. You may swallow a beer."

After my dad returned with three cold bottles and three glasses, he asks: "We more or less agreed what are the things against we fought in our wars – the war on the Border against Swapo and the war here at home against the ANC. But what were the things we wanted to improve and promote by fighting? Do we have any clarity about that?"

Chris: "Until last week, I tought that I was fighting to preserve our Christian civilization. Since the beans inside my skull were reorganized throughly during a big operation, I'm not so sure whether that was a praiseworthy goal to pursue during our wars."

Pa: "For me the preservation of our Christian civilization was always important – also during the Second World War. It was unthinkable that the godless communism could achieve victory anywhere. And since the fall of the Berlin Wall, everybody agrees that the time of communism has passed."

Me: "I can summarize in a few words what are the things I fought for, even if I wasn't always on the front line, but somewhere at the back in an armored ambulance, a sick-bay or a military hospital. I wanted to defend the following things: freedom, prosperity, peace, progress, joy, and justice."

Chris: "That sounds very acceptable to me. I also fought for justice and, therefore, I was against Swapo and the ANC, against communism, but also against apartheid."

Pa: "All thos things that you have mentioned, all boil down to good old-time Christian values. That's what I always wanted to help along."

Me: "I think we will have to continue the fight to preserve these values. That's something on which we agree. Here in South Africa, we will have to watch the ANC closely. In South West – nowadays Namibia – my in-laws will have to do the same regarding the Swapo government. Some day, we will be able to explain to ur grandchildren why we fought these wars, namely to promote freedom, peace, propserity and all the other good things. We needn't be ashamed about our war service."

Pa: "Amen."

Chris: "Halleluyah."

31. OPERATION KORSAKOFF

Cape Town, Tuesday, 27 March 2012

There are still four working days left before I retire with pension at the end of this month. I turned sixty and I won't be allowed to serve any longer as a professional soldier in the Permanent Force.

At this moment, I am the second-in-command of 2 Military Hospital in Wynberg, Cape Town, as well as head of the neurology department, with the rank of colonel. I have reconciled myself long ago with the idea that I won't be able to progress any further than the rank of colonel because I don't jave the right skin color.

It is also held against me that I served in the old SADF and I am regarded as somebody who helped to maintain the evil system of apartheid. I find the present system simply a continuation of apartheid because white peole have to face discrimination under the ANC government. Blacks get all the important positions.

Anyway, it is my plan to take a holiday of four months. During the first two weeks, I will only take a period of rest in my late father's holiday home in Gordon's Bay. After that, I and Hannelore will go and visit her brother Helmut on the family farm in southern Namibia. We plan to travel through Namibia because we want to go and look at all the places where we stayed during the Border War. My holiday will be concluded with a visit of six weeks to Germany and Austria. We want to see the places where my ancestors lived, where my father studied and fought, where my uncle worked on the German atom bomb and the place where Hannelore's family came from.

It isn't our plan to sit around and play with our toes after both of u us have retired. I have already agreed with a practice in Windhoek that I join them as a neurologist. Hannelore will work at a state hospital as a general medical practitioner. At sixty, I certainly don't feel like a pensioner and I want to continue working until I fall over, some or ther time.

A short parade will be held on Friday where I will hand my position over to my successor and where the unit will take its farewell of me. But, in the meantime, I still work today, tomorrow and the day after tomorrow.

Shortly after I got settled in my consulting room this morning, I am suddenly confronted with one of the most difficult and delicate cases in my whole career due to the political implications of it. Commander Enoch Kekana of the naval base at Simonstown is brought to me by a medic, together with a note from a general practitioner of the sick-bay at Simnstown. The comander is in his working uniform with a white shirt and three golden stripes on each shoulder, white trousers and a cap with golden leaves on its vizor. The note reas as follows:

27/03/2012

Dear colleague,
Please take Comdr Enoch Kekana under your care. He is CO of one of our minehunters. He is the nephew of the Chief of the Navy.
My provisional diagnosis is Korsakoff Syndrome.
Please write a report with recommendations for the SSO: Personell of the Naval Base Simonstown, Rear Adm (J G) John Molewa.
Yours truly,
[Illegible signature]

Korsakoff syndrome of all things! And the damned man is the captain of a war ship. He must surely have gotten this position because uncle is the chief of the Navy.

Commander Kekana sits on a chai opposite me with an empty stare in his eyes, as if he doesn't really see me.

I don't have a choice. I have to examine the man throughly and then write a report. First of all, I must have a chat with this man and hear from him why he needs my attention – that is, if he is able to answer my questions. If he really suffers from Korsakoff syndrome, as my colleague at the sick-bay suspects, he has serious amnesia due to chronic alcoholism. People with this syndrome often have the most fantastic stories to tell, simply because they cannot remember what happened to them.

Nevertheless, I try to coverse with the man. He is, though, able to tell me his name, rank and service number. I ask him about his position in the Navy and he tells me that he is the captain of a war ship – one of those at the naval base. "Itsha mine hunder."

A mune hunter of the South African Navy

And how long is he already captain of he ship? He can't remember clerly, but it must already be a number of years.

I ask him what today's date is and he answers that it was New Year's Day a short while ago and, therefore, it must be some time during January. "Perhapsh itsh de tenth teday."

Which day of the week are we having? I ask him. He reckons it must be Sunday because he isn't working today and nhe also went to church this morning.

Where was he trained as naval officer?

"Shomewhere in Ruzzia. Eye can't remember de name off de place eddymore. Eye forget how te pronounsh eet. Eet may alsho had bin in Tanzaniya, perhapsh. Eye forget. Eet wash sho long agow."

Did he play any role in MK, the armed wing of the ANC? Yes, it was his job to shoot the shit out of us Boers. It's actually strange that I am still alive, because he shot a big bunch of captains, commandants, colonels, commodores, and corporals.

Wht did he use? Artillery, machine guns, and hand grenades. Also flame throwers and rockets. Sometimes he used mortars, land mines and pistols. Never knives or swords or axes because didn't get trained to use them.

Why did he get into the sick-bay at Simonstown? He seems to think that it was the medic on his ship who took him there.

"What was the reason for your admittance at the sick-bay?"

'Eye can't really shay. But eet waz perhapsh becoz eye throo up. Perhapsh shee shicknesh."

"What is the matter with you?"

"Abshoiludely nothing, exshept that eye ahm ecshtreemly thirshdy. Can you perhapsh give mee someding te drink? How aboud a beer?"

I test the man's reflexes. They are rotten. I inspect his eyes. They are blood-shot. His throat is sore – surely because of daily bouts of nausea when he has been drinking too much. His breath smells of alcohol, even if it's still early in the morning. I draw some blood and I ask my nurse to take it to Pathology where it has to be tested on an urgent basis for Vitamin B, iron, zinc, calcium, magesium and alcohol. The report has to be faxed to me immediately.

I phone for a porter and give him the order to take the commander to Radiology, together with a note in which I request that the man's head be scanned. I also phone the colleague at Radiology urgently and ask that a fMRI scan be done on Commander Kekana's head.

While the commander is still away, I take a few other cases.. The results of the blood tests come through. The level of the man's Vitamin B1 is dangerously low and his blood also contains very little of the other minerals, which is an indication of acute malnutrition. This low level of B1 confirms my colleague's suspicion of Korsakoff syndrome. Alcohol was, in addition, found in his blood, an indication that he was drinking heavily during the past twenty-four hours.

Two hours after the commander went to Radiology, he is sitting opposite me again. I study his brain scans, which I download from the hospital's system onto my computer. His brain has shrunk a lot and his ventricles, the hollow spaces filled with fluid, are as big as those of an octogenarian, even if he is is only forty years old. I inspect especially his thalamus – the brain's "switchboard" – and it is clear that it has sustained much damage. His hipocampus, which deals with the short-term memory, is very attrophied. The tempral lobes, where most of the long-term memory is processed, look like pieces of seaweed that dried out in the sun. The frontal lobes, where most of the thought processes take place, are heavily shriveled like old lettuce leaves.

I ask him whether he would like to be booked off for a few days. He can't see the need for that, but I decide that it will be a good thing if he could stay in hopspital for a few days to receive some treatment. It will help him to get rid of his nausea and he agrees unenthusiastically.

There is no doubt – this man has serious brain damage and the diagnosis is certainly Korsakoff syndrome. According to the ICD-10 of the World Health Organization, the International Classification of Diseases, tenth edition, the technical term for his condition as follows: "F10.6 – Mental and behavioural disorder due to use of alcohol, amnesic syndrome".

I arrange a bed for the man in the hospital and I write a prescription for Vitamin B-comlex injections, three times per day, plus a multi-vitamin together with each meal. I will visit him in his ward later during the day.

Cape Town, Wednesday, 28 March 2012

During the early morning, I arrive again at the commander's bed. It's empty. According to the head nurse, he discharged himself during the night. He complained that he couldn't stay in that bed any longer because it was filled with bugs and insects. They crawled over his body and made him itch.

I look at the bed and, of course, there are no bugs and insects. I conclude that the man got extremely thirsty, apart from his hallucinations, and escaped to get to his supply of alcohol in his ship's cabin. His withdrawal symptoms must have become unbearable because he hasn't tasted alcohol for some time.

In my consulting room, I write a report and recommend that the man be declared unfit for his position due to an advanced case of Korsakoff syndrome with hallucinations and that he be discharged and take early retirement from the National Defence Force with pension. He is simply not able to command a naval vessel. A court order has to be obtained to commit him to a rehabilitation center.

I call on my friend and colleague, Lieutenant Colonel (Doctor) Louis Lancaster, who can see me immediately. I ask him as a neurosurgeon to look at the results of the blood tests and brain scans and to send his conclusions to me in writing. The report of Louis arrives an hour later and he diagnoses severe brain damage, most likely Korsakoff syndrome on account of extreme alcohol consumption.

The two reports are being sent to the SSO: Pers[86] of the Navy in Simonstown and I am thankful to be rid of this matter. The day after tomorrow is my last day here when I say good-bye to Two Mil and then Kekana with his political ties are no longer my problem.

Gordon's Bay, Saturday, 14 April 2012

Louis Lancaster and his family visit us today in Gordon's Bay before we tackle the long road to Namibia on Monday. We were working together since the eighties during the Border War and we don't want these ties of friendship to get severed.

While I am barbecueing two big chunks of snoek, a big fish, on the coals, Louis asks me: "Do you remember that naval commander you sent to Pathology the other day to get a brain scan?"

"Do you mean Kekana? That's the guy who's a nephew of the chief of the Navy, right?"

"That's just him. The submissions of the two of us were handled by the SSO: Pers and he provisinally places the guy on pension on medical grounds. But he also sends his decision through to the chief of the Navy for final approval and clearance."

"And what did the admiral do?"

"He reverses the decision to pension the guy off. He reinstates his nephew as captain of his ship."

'What else can you expect from an admiral who knows bugger-all about maritime warfare and administration? He was merely trained as a terririst in Soviet Russia and he only got his

[86] Senior Staff Officer: Personnel

present job for being a loyal supporter of our not so honorable State President."

"Talking of that State President. People predict that he will be thrown out on his ear for being inept, unrelaible, corrupt, and dishonest. He will eventually be caught out, even if it takes time. Fortunately, our courts haven't been hi-jacked and hacked ... yet."

"The whole ANC government is one big crimnal syndicate. People will get tired of their hollow promises and vote them out of power, some or other time."

"That is, if they don't cheat and rig the elections as has been done elsewhere in Africa. Anyway, this alcoholic nephew of the admiral gets his job back. And then one big blasted blooming bugger-up is the result."

"Yes?"

"This pal of ours was again under the influence two nights ago and in the middle of the night he gives the command that his boat must leave the harbor – without authorisation, of course. By hook or by crook they exit the harbor safely and that's just where the purple paw-paw strikes the fucking fan and that messes up the whole nutty navy yard. He thinks that he can navigate and steer the ship better than anybody else and he rams a sordid sailing craft at anchor just outside the harbor."

"Goodness!"

"But that's not all. After the yacht has sunk, he orders reverse at full revolutions and he rams the boat's bloody back end, the stern, against the harbor wall and the rocks piled up against it. The propellor and the propshaft are gonners and there's a huge hole in the hull. The cursed craft sinks slowly. All hands abandon ship. One mine hunter written off. Permanently. Only part of the superstructure is visible above the waves."

GLOSSARY

Many German and Afrikaans expressions and military slang were used in this book. They were explained in the footnotes, but they are also listed here for the benefit of the reader who is not familiar with South Africa.

German Words and Expressions

Artzt – medical practitioner.
Ärtztin – a female medical practitioner.
Fräulein – Miss.
Freiherr – baron.
Kneipe – saloon
Korvettenkapitän – lieutenant commander.
Kriegsmarine – the German Navy during the Second World War.
Luftwaffe – German Air Force.
Mannschaft – team.
Nachtisch – pudding.
Oberleutnant – lieutenant.
Oberst – colonel.
Schutztruppe – Protection Troops, the German Forces protecting South West Africa before the First World War.
Sicherheitsdienst – German for Security Service, the intelligence branch of the SS.
Sperrgebiet – the old German name for a restricted area where diamonds were mined in the Namib Desert along the Atlantic coast.
Waffen-SS – German for Armed SS. The SS or Schutzstaffel (Protection n Squadron) was initially Hitler's bodyguard but developed into the political police of the Nazi Party. A number of SS divisions fought alongside the regular Army divisions and these were known as the Waffen-SS.

Afrikaans Words and Expressions and South African Army slang

Bakgat: an unranslateable Afrikaans expression that means more or less something like OK.

Bivvy – Army slang for a bivouac shelter, which may be used as a rain coat.

Blood box – SADF slang for a field ambulance.

Boer – this word literarily means "farmer", but it is often used for an Afrikaans-speaking person.

Bossies – Army slang for shell-shock or post-traumatic stress disorder, acquired during the Bush War in Namibia.

Browns – Army slang for battle dress.

Bundu bashing – Army slang for bashing with military vehicles through dense vegetation and bushes.

Clicks – Army slang for kilometers.

Comms – communications (usually by radio).

De Put – this name can be translated as The Well. There wasn't actually a well at that spot, only a bore hole with a diesel pump to provide water for the military base and the nearby village.

Flossie – Army slang for the Hercules C-130 transport plane.

G1K1 – the military classification for healthy and fit troops – perfect cannon fodder. The classification of G2K1 was used for men who wore spectacles, but wereotherwise healthy and fit. Somebody with a G2K2 classification or lower had some ailments or other disabilities. G5/GP: The SADF considered these men as ready for the graveyard and of no use and they were discharged on medical grounds.

HSO – the abbreviation for Head of Staff: Operations.

Klipdrif – a well-known and popular brand of brandy in South Africa.

Klipkop – Afrikaans for stone head It may be applied to a stubborn person, but also to a stony hill.

Koevoet" – the Afrikaans word for a crow bar. This was the name of a special Police unit that hunted terrorists and often went too far in their treatment of the local population. The members of this unit were popularly called the equivalent of crow bars.
Land mine chicke – Army slang for chicken chopped into small bits.
LMG – light machine gun.
Maties – the nickname for students of the University of Stellenbosch and for the University itself as well.
Meat Pies – Army slang for Military Policemen or MP's.
Noddy Car" – nickname for the Eland Armored Car, an adaptation of a French Panhard armored car, usually armed with a 90 mm gun.
Ondangs – the popular nane for Ondangwa in Ovamboland where the largest air base in the Operational Area was situated.
Ops Room" – short for operations room, the headquarters of the base.
Outoppie" – Army slang for father or any older man.
Padre – the official form of address of a chaplain in the SADF.
Papa Foxie – Army slang for "Papa Foxtrot", the radio alphabet for
Patat – literally, a sweet potota. It is used as a nickname in this case.
Pee Ef – the abbreviation PF stands for Permanent Force (of the Defence Force).
P F – the abbreciation for Permanent Force.
Ratpack – boxes containing rations for at least one day.
Recces – the nickname given to members of the Reconnaissance commando's, the special forces of the SADF.
Romeo Mike – the abbreviation RM stands for the Afrikaans expression "Reaksiemag" (Reaction Force or Reaction Team).
Rooikop – the Afrikaans name for a red volcanic ourcrop in the desert east of Walvis Bay. The military base at its foot is called after this hill.
RSM – regimnental sargeant major.

Slapgat – an Afrikaans expression that can't be translated directly; it means something like lazy or loafing.

Snotklap – an Afrikaans expression: to slap someone across the face so that some snot will fly in all directions.

SP – military slang for "State President".

SP's – the abbreciation used in army slang for the Afrikaans expression of "Swart Portugese" (Black Portuguese).

Swaps – Army slang for members of Swapo's armed wing.

Waterkloof – the Air Force base north of Pretoria.

Witkop – an Afrikaans nickname for somebody with white or blonde hair and it may be translated with "Blondie" or "Whitey".

RANK STRUCTURE OF THE SOUTH AFRICAN DEFENCE FORCE, 1961–1994

SA Army SA Air Force SA Medical Service SA Navy

Non-Commissioned Officers

Lance Corporal	Lance Corporal	Lance Corporal	Able Seaman
Corporal/ Bombardier	Corporal	Corporal	Leading Seaman
Sergeant	Sergeant	Sergeant	Petty Officer

Staff Sergeant

Flight Sergeant

Staff Sergeant

Chief Petty Officer

Warrant Officers

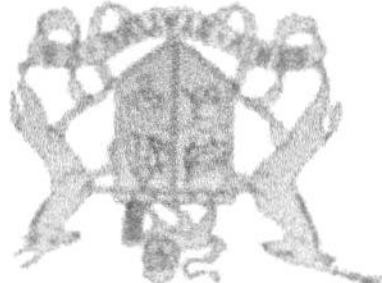

Warrant Officer - WO2

Warrant Officer - WO1

Officers

Candidate Officer

Candidate Officer

Candidate Officer

Midshipman

2nd Lieutenant

2nd Lieutenant

2nd Lieutenant

Ensign

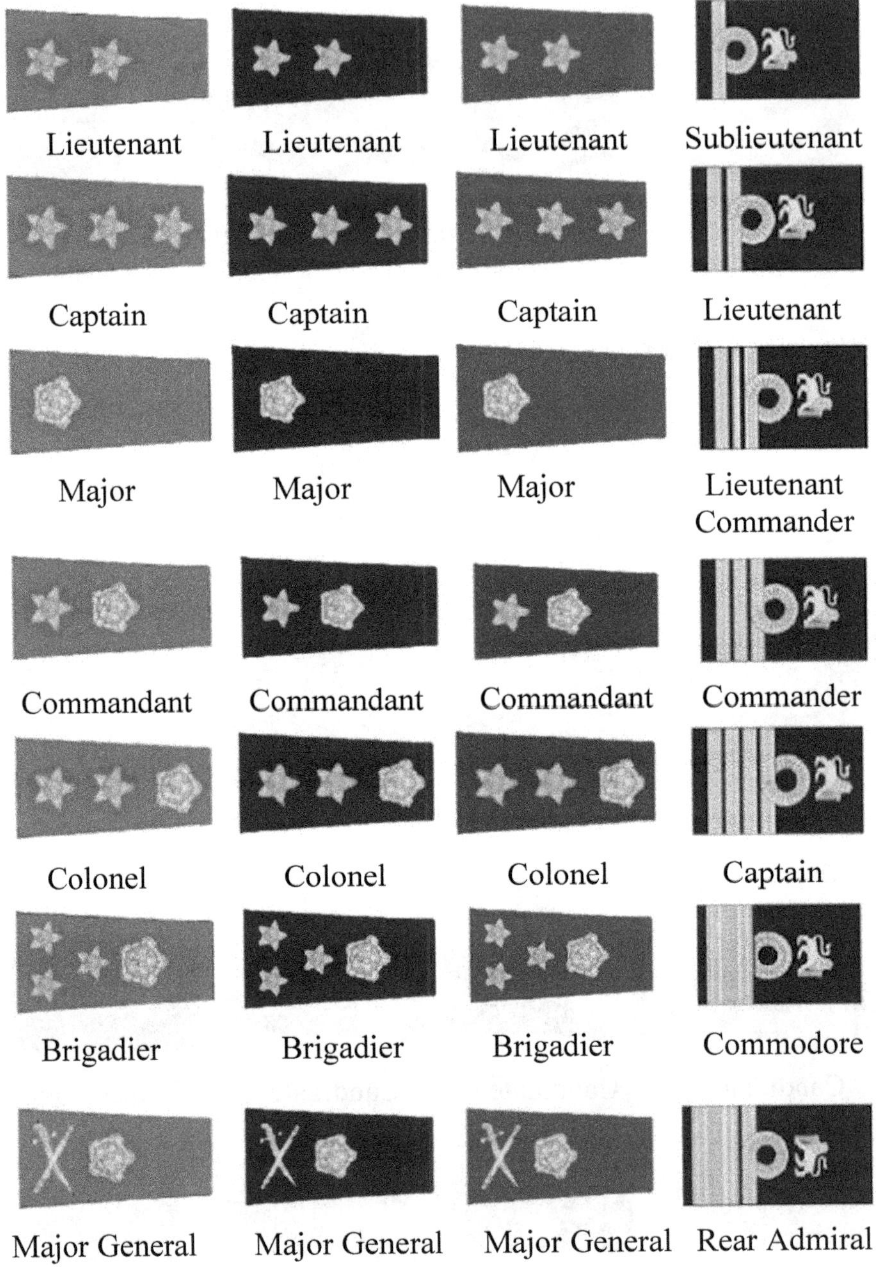
Lieutenant
Lieutenant
Lieutenant
Sublieutenant
Captain
Captain
Captain
Lieutenant
Major
Major
Major
Lieutenant Commander
Commandant
Commandant
Commandant
Commander
Colonel
Colonel
Colonel
Captain
Brigadier
Brigadier
Brigadier
Commodore
Major General
Major General
Major General
Rear Admiral

Lieutenant Genral

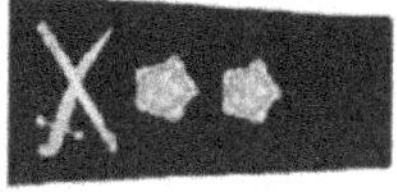

Lieutenant General

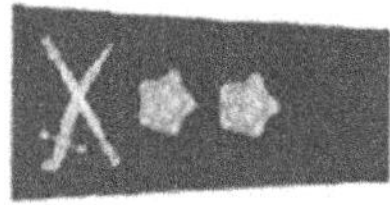

Lieutenant General

Vice Admiral

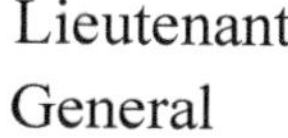

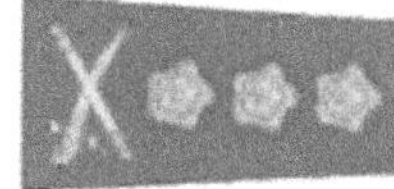

General

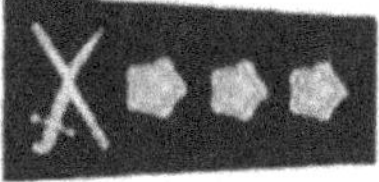

General

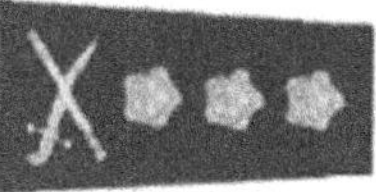

General

Admiral

LIST OF ILLUSTRATIONS

Pier at Swakopmund
https://www.namibia-accommodation.com/listing/the-swakopmund-jetty-16-2018-9e

4. **Operation Reindeer**
Parachute troops
https://www.facebook.com/photo.php?fbid=322877210716650 1&set=g.765952213562161&type=1&theater&ifg=1

5. **Operation Honeymoon**
Buffel Armored and Mine-Resistant Troop Carrier
https://www.keymilitary.com/article/show-stopper

6. **Operation Oxygen**
Samil-20 Truck
https://www.samiltrucks.co.za/trucks/samil-20/

Etale Base
https://www.pinterest.co.uk/pin/834995587144172446/?amp_client_id=CLIENT_ID(_)&mweb_unauth_id={{default.session}}&simplified=true

Aerial photograph of the sick-bay (aka 10 Field Hospital) at Oshakati
https://www.academia.edu/81030772/SADF_Border_Base_Layouts

7. **Operation Land Mine**
Concor Base
http://www.warinangola.com/Default.aspx?tabid=1585&Parameter=7067

Land Munes
https://www.sjhprojects.com/landmines-all-you-never-wanted-to-know

https://yandex.by/images/search?nomisspell=1&lr=102985&text=pakistan%20army%20casspir&source=related-query-serp&redircnt=1676060644.1&pos=16&img_url=http%3A%2F%2Fi.pinimg.com%2Foriginals%2F5b%2Ffa%2F3a%2F5bfa3acc9f85b6d1c4a49048cece0609.jpg&rpt=simage

17. **Operation Tequila**
State President PW Botha
https://www.southafrica.to/history/Apartheid/PW_Botha/PW_Botha.php

Fishing Trawler
https://www.bizcommunity.com/Article/196/520/137595.html

South African Submarine, Emily Hobhouse
https://en.wikipedia.org/wiki/SAS_Umkhonto

18. **Operation Vodka**
Two Russian Attack Helicopters
https://en.wikipedia.org/wiki/Mil_Mi-24#/media/File:Afghan_Air_Corps_Mi-helicopters.jpg

19. **Operation Grafting**
Two Brain Scans
https://www.radiologyinfo.org/en/gallery/index.cfm?image=1051

20. **Operation Diagnosis**
General Jannie Geldenhuys
https://en.wikipedia.org/wiki/Johannes_Geldenhuys

Lieutenant General Niel Knobel
https://en.wikipedia.org/wiki/Daniel_Knobel

State President PW Botha
https://mg.co.za/article/2012-11-09-00-pw-bothas-secret-stroke-blocked-path-of-reform/

Last Page

Casspir mine-protected armored infantry vehicle
https://www.sa-soldier.com/data/07-SADF-equipment/

Cap Badge on Head Gear of the SA Medical Service
https://www.bidorbuy.co.za/item/107833607/South_African_Medical_Services_Cap_Collar_Mess_Dress_From_1983_Set.html

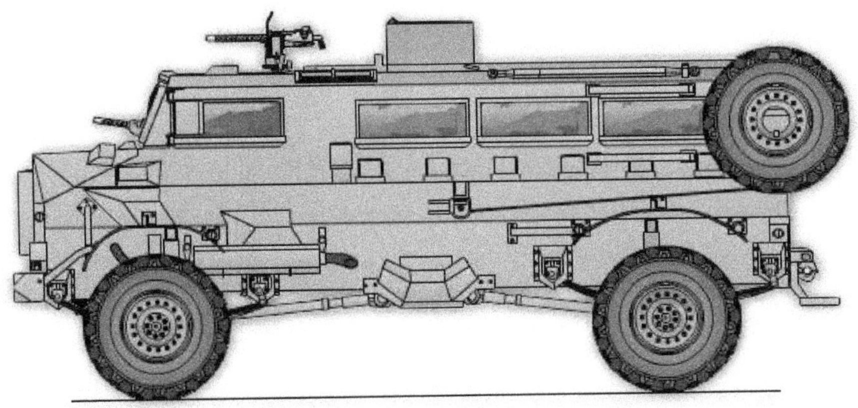

www.ingramcontent.com/pod-product-compliance
Lightning Source LLC
Chambersburg PA
CBHW070638310726
48982CB00001B/317

9781666781410